THE HITTITE WARRIOR

Second Edition

THE HITTITE WARRIOR

DELBERT TEACHOUT

TATE PUBLISHING
AND ENTERPRISES, LLC

Published by Tate Publishing & Enterprises, LLC
127 E. Trade Center Terrace | Mustang, Oklahoma 73064 USA
1.888.361.9473 | www.tatepublishing.com

Tate Publishing is committed to excellence in the publishing industry. The company reflects the philosophy established by the founders, based on Psalm 68:11,
"The Lord gave the word and great was the company of those who published it."

Published in the United States of America

ISBN: 978-1-63122-314-3
1. Fiction / Christian / Historical
2. Fiction / Christian / Suspense
14.04.29

PART ONE

CHAPTER 1

Silently, like a mountain lion prowling for its next meal, Hektor lead three hundred Achaean soldiers from the military garrison in Ankara, through the coal black night. His silhouette like a shadow on an invisible screen was hidden, absorbed by the thick blackness. His destination: Hatusha, once the capital city of a strong empire, now a small town in central Anatolia. Brought down by strong invaders from the west -- Achaean invaders, it continued to survive as an agricultural village. Hatred drove him. Revenge led him. Someone from Hatusha had ambushed a squad from the garrison killing ten men and wounding two others who escaped to report to the commander. Now they would be redeemed. But not as an eye for an eye -- there would be a hundred dead Hittites, as they were called, for every dead soldier. The Hittites, not having a military and lacking any military training, would not fight back.

Hektor seethed. No one can kill an Achaean soldier and live to tell about it.

He vowed to his gods that he would be first to avenge his lost comrades. His soul could not rest until they had been avenged, so he believed. These Hittites had caused problems long enough, a constant source of trouble, they kept talking about the day when they ruled the world before the Achaeans arrived, and someday they would be free again. Did they think they could defeat the mighty Achaeans? Tonight it would end. They will know their place beyond any doubt when tonight is over. Blackness as thick as pitch absorbed his image on the rocky trail and matched the hatred in his heart. He had served his five years in Ankara, an honorable tour of duty, receiving two promotions for bravery, and was scheduled to return to Troy, then to his home in Achaea next week--retiring after thirty years of service. But he was chosen for one more special assignment. Anger engulfed him. Why him? Why now? The Hittites would surely pay for this.

Nothing stirred: no sounds of crickets, frogs, owls, or any nocturnal animals. The squad of death moved through the night, drawing ever closer to their target. The only sound was the steady gait of the horses, trained for military duty, as they moved over the gravel. Even the moon and stars hid behind thick, low clouds, as if they did not want to witness this massacre, like turtles afraid to come out of their shells. Even the air was still. Seemingly, Nature held its breath in horror, afraid to observe the fate of Hatusha, capital of the once mighty Hittite Empire.

Hektor, leaning forward and squinting, peering into the darkness, seeing nothing past the head of his horse, cursed under his breath, how far to town? It must be near. Let's get this over and go home. It seems there would be a torch lit in one of the Hittite homes. If there was, Hektor could not see it. He grasped the hilt on his sword fastened securely on his belt. He anticipated his kill, knowing that his brothers would be avenged tonight. And he would be the first to draw Hittite blood.

Hektor knew that inside the twenty foot rock walls of Hatusha, families slept in stone houses. He had been inside the walls many times to do business. But tonight he had a different kind of business. He also knew most of the Hittites lived in homes outside the walls where their wood frames and mud walls offered little protection. Last to move to Hatusha and forced to build outside of the walls, they would be first to die. Then he would go inside the walls to kill the rest of them. He thought that no one would be expecting them. He sneered. They will be surprised.

Suddenly he heard frightened horses whinnying and snorting, breaking the silence, sounding the alarm. His adrenaline erupted. Startled at first, he turned toward the sound and saw a man dash from his home towards the horses, carrying a torch apparently to see what was happening. Hektor moved in among the horses. As he raised his sword high over his head he could see the man's wife in his peripheral vision, watching and waiting at the door. Without a sound a swift and mighty blow came from the darkness. The man cried out, dropped his torch, and tumbled to the ground like a pine cone falling from a tall tree. Hektor heard the woman scream. More like an agonizing groan, "No!" loud enough to warn the neighbors.

He cursed again. Now to get her.

Ravia, fearing for her life, terrified beyond wildest imagination, fought the instinct to run to her husband, lift his head and hold him in her arms. She could hear her husband's killer breathing and smell his body odor. He was coming towards her. Slamming and bolting the heavy door her instinct changed from running to her husband to saving her family. Fear flowed down her back to her arms and legs, paralyzing, horrifying fear as Hektor began trying to break through the solid wood door with his strong sword. The door would hold only a minute. She had to move quickly. She grabbed her sleeping son by his shoulders and shook him. Her tongue stuck to the roof of her mouth as she tried to shout.

"Uriah, up. Get. . . "

"What?" Uriah jerked to a sitting position on his bed.

"Someone just killed Dad," she half cried, half screamed.

"Who?" he asked as the pounding and shouting at the door continued.

Ravia could see the look of fear and anger on her son's face as if panic and anger baptized him when he seemed to realize what was happening. Why is he asking questions? He needs to get up, now!

"Annitis?" he asked, with the high pitched tenseness of fear in his voice while jumping to his feet.

"Here," Annitis told him. "They killed dad. We are next" as she threw on her clothing.

Uriah shook his head, swallowed hard and fought back tears as he pulled a shirt over his head. "Dad dead? How?" Fear, grief, and disbelief stabbed his heart, stopped his breathing, confused his mind, and froze his actions.

"It is true. We leave now." Annitis said.

The pounding on the door continued as Uriah yelled, "You, what do you want?" as he pulled on his boots.

"I am from the Ankara garrison. Open up. I want to talk."

Ravia shook her head and whispered, "No do not. He just killed your dad. Now wants to kill us. Move faster Uriah. We have to run!"

Uriah pulled his shirt over his head and tied up his woven kilt with trembling hands. Ravia could not believe what she was hearing. She recalled the garrison consisted of five thousand Achaean soldiers deployed from Greece. Hittites hated their occupation and had fought two unsuccessful wars for their independence. Even though she hated their occupation of her country, they were regular customers purchasing honey from Uriah, buying horses from her husband, and wool from her.

"Someone ambushed an Achaean patrol. We found a ring with the inscription for Hatusha," Hektor said as he continued smashing the door with his sword and calling for help, his anger increasing with every strike to the door.

Uriah saw Ravia grab an extra tunic. He motioned towards the back door with a quick nod of his head. Looking at his right hand, where the ring used to be, he remembered selling it to some Assyrians last week who said they wanted a souvenir. It must have been his ring they found. Uriah had sold the ring, a simple thing with the head of bull inscribed on it, representing one of Hatusha's gods, to buy a new horse for his father. Now his father had been killed and who knows how many more will die tonight. Horror induced nausea overcame him. What had he done? He thought of surrendering. Then he changed his mind. If he surrendered he would die for sure and there would be no guarantee of the safety of the rest of the town.

Uriah saw his mother and sister jump when the soldier broke through the door. Panic pulsed through his veins. He had gotten his father killed; his mother and sister's lives were threatened. He could not let them be killed too. Looking around for something to defend himself, he saw on the table the dagger his father had recently given him for his sixteenth birthday. Snatching it up, he plunged his dagger deep into the Achaean's chest. Uriah felt Hector's knees go weak and begin to buckle. He saw his look of surprise, and then saw his eyes grow large in horror and panic, and grow cold from death. He released his tears for the loss of his father, tears for the fear in his mother and sister, tears for his own fear.

He feared because he knew his simple and peaceful life of keeping bees and selling honey would never be the same. He angered because he had no choice except to run. He had no other options. This moment would change his life forever. There will be more soldiers soon. His heart screamed. His veins throbbed. His head ached. Someone else was always directing his life. It was happening again. He would have to stay and fight, or flee. Either way he could lose everything. Someone else seemed to always be in charge of what he did with his life. But this time he knew he deserved it. Why had he sold that ring? Where were the Hittite gods?

Uriah remembered the dagger in his hand, a half cubit of forged iron with an ivory handle carved with eagle designs, bought by his father from some Achaeans who came to buy horses, a talisman he used to kill an Achaean. Ironic. He pushed the man out the door with his right foot as he retrieved his dagger. Hektor fell to the ground, dead.

"That is from father, you pig."

He had never killed before. Fear, human odor, and the sight of blood caused his stomach to erupt all over the dead man.

"Idiot! Now more men will be killed!" Annitis chastised.

"We will be next if we do not run!" Ravia shouted.

"Come." Uriah knew they needed the horses but he also knew they could be killed trying to get them. He also knew of a rally point the people of Hatusha would use to hide but decided against going there -- too much risk of being found. The Achaeans knew where it was and would figure out where everyone went. Instead, they would have to leave on foot and use the concealment of the darkness to escape.

"May the gods give us favor," Annitis gasped as Uriah whispered, "Let's get out of here!"

"Ahead of you," Ravia replied, her voice constrained with fear but relieved they were escaping.

Panic led him and fear chased him out the unguarded back door. He knew if they were caught, they were dead. Their house like others outside the wall protecting Hatusha was timber framed with mud brick walls plastered with clay. The doors had been solid wood and built with strong locks. Most homes had only one door but Uriah's father built this one with a back door looking toward the Halys River "just in case". Running toward the river that flowed through the ravine, past the bee hives, down the steep bank in the rear of their property, slipping on the dew, stumbling over rocks, Uriah led as the trio ran through the darkness. Low branches on the fig trees swatted them, caught on their clothing as if trying to hold them back and scratched their faces, but they dared not cry out. They raised their forearms up to protect their faces and kept running.

His father had often talked of how this ravine would lead them to safety someday if any enemy attacked and they had to get away. But like other things planned for "just in case", Uriah did not think they would ever have to use it. As they passed the fig trees he knew they were near the river. Hearing shouts of the men who found the dead soldier, Uriah thought they were going to be caught and wondered why his gods had failed him. Again! The sound of the voices behind them caused them to run faster.

He did not believe in the gods and only thought of them when they failed him. He believed that the best way to live was to be morally perfect through virtuous living. Obedience to the Law of Nature was the path to virtue. As long as he obeyed the Law of Nature things would be well for him. But why this?

As they splashed into the river and began running down-stream, Uriah knew the sound of the water splashing noisily over rocks and gravel as it raced downstream would mask any noise they made. He heard the Achaeans hollering. It seemed that someone had tripped over a bee hive and was feeling sorry for it. He looked back to see if they were followed. He saw no one. The water was cold but near the shore it was shallow and swift. The autumn rains had not started. Which god should he thank for summer? Uriah knew that a god had created everything, leaving the world in the hands of the Laws of Nature, and not interfering in daily events, controlling only the movement of the sun, moon, and stars. As long as men lived by the Law, everything would be alright. Did not the Law of Nature say to never trust a stranger? How could he forget? Why did he trust that Assyrian?

The night was so dark Annitis and Ravia had to hold on to each other's hands to keep from being separated and falling over the rocks in the river. Uriah asked himself, so this is what fear tastes like? Sour. Bitter, Rancid. He could not see danger if it was right in front of him. He wondered how this night would change his life. Something always seemed to dictate what he did. Realizing he still had the dagger in his hand, he rinsed the blood in the river and put in his belt.

Uriah thought as he waded, most days go by, one like the other, with nothing significant happening. But sometimes when you least expect it the day presents situations that change lives forever. Had he begun one of those days? A seemingly insignificant event at the time, like selling a ring to strangers, had made significant changes in his life. Are the gods punishing him for disobeying the Law of Nature? Can obeying the Law of Nature reverse this situation? What do the gods expect from him? Is there a plan for his life? Or is life an endless sequence of seemingly insignificant events randomly blended together? Maybe life was like this river, different, every day. He wished he knew.

CHAPTER 2

Ravia convulsed in fear and grief, her daughter walking beside her, arm around her shoulders, as life like she knew it had ended. The people of Hatusha kept fig and olive orchards, grape vines, cattle, horses, and sheep. She worked as a weaver of wool for fabric for women's clothing. Her husband had kept sheep and horses. Ravia thought of her children. Annitis, two years older than Uriah and very attractive with her coal black hair, almond colored eyes, high cheek bones, and sleek features, worked in the vineyard. She always wore ankle length woven skirts and pull-over sweaters that came to her chin. Knee high boots protected her feet. Uriah loved his bees. What would happen to them?

It took years for her family to build up a swarm of bees, fruit producing fig trees, customers for the wool, and the horses they sold. She worried what would happen next. What were they to do now? How could they start over? Where would they start over?

Ravia remembered the stories, passed on orally through the generations, of how 3000 years ago their ancestors had faced a major crisis. Unlike tonight, instead of fleeing man back then they were trying to outrun the Great Mother Goddess. She was responsible for the earthquake that caused the land bridge between Black Sea Lake and the Aegean Sea to collapse. Water rose one-third cubit a day for two years until it had risen sixty fathoms to form the Black Sea. A small fresh-water lake became part of a great salt-water sea. All the towns around the lake were flooded, hundreds of people died, and thousands were uprooted. Some of the inhabitants of the region fled as far as Crete. Some fled to the Caucasus Mountains.

Ancestors of Hatusha fled south to escape the rising water and settled in the high plateau region where Hatusha was built. Hatusha had united the surrounding towns to form the Hittite Empire, for hundreds of years one of the strongest empires to ever exist. Their military invented the chariot and the sickle shaped swords which brought fear and fame from their enemies. Then two hundred years ago the Achaeans attacked Hatusha, after they gained control of Troy. Hittites have lived in subjugation ever since. She wondered if there was someone who could set them free. She prayed to her gods for a deliverer.

Annitis looked back and shrieked, “Look, mom, they are burning our house!”

“Wonder of wonders,” said Uriah.

“May the gods give us favor!” said Annitis.

“Gods? I wonder whether there really are a thousand gods in heaven. Is there even a heaven? If so, how is this happening to us? Cannot at least one of the gods protect us? Keep those men from finding us.” asked Uriah.

Ravia remembered she had worshipped Cybele her entire life but had never seen anything come from it. Maybe Uriah was right. Maybe there is no god except Nature. Are not Cybele and Nature the same god?

Pondering the question for a moment she reasoned logic would say there must be one god who could help them. She shook her head. No god was protecting them now. In fact, she never saw any of their gods do anything for anyone. What a waste of time to serve gods that do nothing! But what would the gods do if she did not worship them? How bad would that be?

"Come on. Keep going." Ravia groaned slipping and nearly falling into the river, scratching her ankle on a sharp rock, her heart beating so loud she thought it could be heard back in the town. She never knew such fear. No matter how fast she tried to move, her legs seemed to be standing still as if made of clay. She looked back. Nothing seemed to be moving behind them, but it was so dark she could not be sure.

"Where are we going?" Uriah asked after they traveled far enough from town that he felt safe to talk.

"Follow the river. We can get to Yozgat. We can rest briefly."

"What then?" he asked.

"We can stay with Uncle Sisera. A large Hittite community lives in his town of Tarsus. Maybe we will live with them -- unless our gods have other plans."

"May the gods give us favor," said Annitis.

Rage. Uriah hated the gods. If they were real, how could this be happening? He hated the Achaeans. He hated them for killing his father. He hated them because his mother lost her home. He hated running away from them. He hated the Assyrians. He hated himself for selling them his ring. Suddenly an unseen essence overcame him, like a divine presence, angel or god, he was not sure. Maybe it was only his conscience. Uriah began tingling down his back, his head felt like a hot towel had been wrapped around it, and his breathing nearly stopped as his heart felt large and warm, almost too large for his chest. Then he understood that what he felt was not hatred but love. Love for his family. Love for his town. Love for his neighbors. This situation was his fault. He asked the essence in his heart what he was supposed to do. He stopped moving. He received his answer.

"What is it?" asked Ravia.

"I have to go back!" he said.

"May the gods give us favor" breathed Annitis turning towards Uriah so fast she bumped into her mother and knocked her off balance and into the river.

"What? You cannot go back? They would kill you!" warned Ravia as she landed in the water and tried to keep her voice low so would not be heard.

Uriah stood speechless. The Law of Nature said that if a man brings trouble to his neighbors he must help them out of those troubles. But he also knew he must stay with his mother and sister. What should he do?

Uriah said, "South of Hatusha at the gorge called Yazilikaya, by the grove of olive trees men are hiding. You know the place. It's where we have altars to our supposed gods. Our neighbors may be there, praying, seeking help from those gods. It is our designated rally point for times like this."

"The only gods we know," said Annitis.

"The men may all be dead," said Ravia.

"They may not be dead – we are not. The Achaeans will not find us but they will find them. They know about the gorge. It will not take the Achaeans long to figure out where everyone went. They are like sheep in a sheepfold ready to be slaughtered -- they are our neighbors. I must go back and help them defend our town."

"What do you have to go back for?" asked Ravia.

"It is my fault. It was my ring. I have to go," Uriah said.

"Your ring? How? You did not kill ten Achaean soldiers, did you?" asked Ravia, not believing her son.

"I sold it to some Assyrians."

"You did what?"

"I was trying to raise money to buy father another horse for breeding. Thought it might improve his herd. Make him some more money. It was a beautiful horse. Made a good deal. Was supposed to get it tomorrow."

Ravia said, "What were you thinking? Now you have gotten your father killed and your town destroyed! We are running for our lives. How could you do this?"

"I was trying to help. I did not think. How did I know? They did not tell me they were going to attack the Achaeans and leave the ring behind to blame us," said Uriah.

"How come did you not think?" asked Annitis.

Uriah replied, "When a heart is full of love it does not think. It acts. I just wanted to help father."

Ravia asked, "What about us? If you go back to die, do you expect us to go with you?"

"No. I am not going back to die. But if I do not go back, what kind of man will I be? Keep on going. You can get to Yozgat by sun-up. Just follow the river. You will be okay. No one is following us. I have to go back. I promise I will come and get you and bring you back home. I am not going back to die but to live."

"What do you know about fighting? How do you dare go back?" asked Ravia.

"Courage is like a well. Sometimes it is full, sometimes it is empty. My well has been empty. But now it has been filled. It is my fault we were attacked. I must go back. I have to help. It is my duty. It is the Law of Nature. I have no choice."

Ravia said, "It is your duty to protect your mother too, who will . . ."

Uriah said, "When you get to Tarsus, tell Uncle Sisera what is happening. He may want to come and help. If he does not, he can protect you."

"But you are not yet twenty, not old enough to join the army if we had one. How will you help?" Annitis asked

"I am sixteen. I am now a man. Believe me Annitis the Achaeans will not destroy our town while I am alive. My age is not the issue. The issue is my heart. My heart is ready. I will come to get you in a few weeks. You will see. Just stay in Tarsus until I get there. If I am not there in four weeks, well . . ."

"May the gods give you favor," Ravia said as she embraced and kissed her son. Tears on her cheeks revealed the pain in her heart. She gave him a wedge of cheese "just in case" then she turned and continued following the river. As she left Uriah heard her sobbing to Annitis," I lost a husband and a son tonight. Do not leave me."

"I lost a father and a brother. I will not leave you mother."

Uriah stood motionless for several minutes, a sense of awe in his heart, his emotions on alert, not believing what he had said. He never believed in the gods. Yet, now he was afraid to not believe. He had no choice but to believe in something: gods, or the Law of Nature? Himself?

Something had overcome him. The wall at Yazilikaya had many carvings of men and gods no one has seen or can remember -- legends of legends. People will believe anything these days, but not him, not now.

Maybe he was being delusional. His house had just been burned, he just killed someone, his father was dead, and he was running for his life. Maybe the stress was too much. Maybe the men will not be there. Maybe they will not follow him. Maybe the Achaeans will kill him. Maybe he should try to catch up with his mother and sister. He looked but they were gone.

Then he asked himself, why could I not be the commander, or better than that, the king, like Suppiluliuma II who reigned only two hundred years ago before the Sea People, the Achaeans invaded?

One day Suppiluliuma II, the mightiest Hittite king, and Ramses II, Pharaoh of Egypt ruled the world. For six hundred years Hittites ruled the North while Egypt ruled the South. Now Anatolia consisted of many independent city states including Hatusha, each trying to prevent the Achaeans in the west and the Assyrians in the east, from taking over their land. Maybe someday there will be another king in Hatusha. Why could it not be him?

Uriah did not know what the future would be. He was struggling with the present while thinking about the past. Becoming a victim of events that were out of his control, he knew he had to trust something. He never trusted the Hittite gods. Maybe he should start trusting in himself. He felt the dagger in his belt. Which way to that gorge?

CHAPTER 3

Uriah looked around, he saw no one. He listened, but he heard no one. His mother and sister had vanished in the darkness. Then he thought about his neighbors destined to be killed because of him. He said aloud, "Great idea, me, a bee keeper, help them?" The hair on his neck and arm stood up. He quivered, but he was not cold. He perspired, but he was not hot. He wondered what happened to the fear he felt. It was gone. No. It was still there, but different. It was not fear for himself, but fear for his neighbors. Would the gods come to help him?

He moved through the darkness, fear filling him, love leading him, like an animal protecting its young. His neighbors will be killed because of him. He had to hurry. Perspiration ran down his face and chest drenching his clothing. Pulling cloth loose from his body where it was sticking, he thought about going back to the river and on to Yozgat. His old self argued with him. Forget the Law of Nature and run to Yozgat with his family.

Then he thought of his neighbors. Are they still alive? He held the hilt of the dagger in his hand. He never owned a dagger before but somehow it seemed to give him courage and energy, as if it had magical powers. Soon he found the grove of olive trees and sure enough, in the center, near the well, he heard men huddled together encouraging each other. He listened. Their words sounded brave but their voices revealed their fear. Then he recognized a voice.

"Tokat. Tokat, can you hear me?" he called to them.

"Is that you, Uriah?"

"Yes. I am alone. Can I join you?"

"Come in."

Uriah entered the grove and approached about a hundred men--most too frightened to talk. They cowered back as he approached. Several women and children had joined them. Everyone was too afraid to say or do anything. No one seemed to be in charge.

Uriah told them, "We cannot stay here. They will find us and kill us. After they burn the town they will come here. They know about this place. We have to defend ourselves."

"How are we supposed to fight three hundred trained soldiers?" asked one man

"We are not soldiers. What could we do?" asked another.

Uriah said, "We either risk dying by fighting tonight or risk dying by staying here in hiding. Either way your women and children would be homeless."

After a vigorous discussion they chose to fight. He wanted to know who had weapons. As it turned out twenty men had their hunting bows, five had slings and there were about fifty men with swords or daggers made from the iron mines near Hatusha. Some men had nothing.

"Listen I have a plan. . ." Uriah began. ". . . divide into three groups. One group only slings, one group bows. Swords and daggers in the third group. Are you with me so far?"

"Okay. What is next?"

Uriah felt courage that exceeded his experience. His well was full. He was a humble bee keeper, how is it he felt like a warrior? He remembered two fundamental Hittite military doctrines from the history of the Hittites. First, never underestimate your enemy. Second, make your enemy underestimate you through any means, including lies, and deception. He would not underestimate them but use deception to make them underestimate the Hittites.

"We'll go back to Hatusha. Hide in the vineyard at the edge of town just outside the King's Gate."

When they arrived at the vineyard Uriah sent the men with bows into concealment. "Go out about half a furlong from the gate. Swords and daggers stay here. When I signal, you five men with slings will run through the King's Gate to within a stone's throw from some Achaean soldiers. Sling your rocks at them, and then run back to the vineyard. They will think you are alone and chase you. Run back as fast as you can."

"That sounds simple, but scary," one of them said.

"Right. It is scary. But you can do it. Second group, when the Achaeans come through the gate they will be only two or three abreast. You will have to fight only the soldiers coming through the gates. Fire your arrows at them: volley after volley, three men per volley. Continue until you are out of arrows. Do not shoot at someone who has already been shot. Save your arrows. Make every shot a fatal shot."

"Sounds good," someone said.

"Before long there will be a pile of bodies at the gate that they will have to move to get through. They will be vulnerable. When you are out of arrows then the swords and daggers will attack. Those with no weapons will take a dead Achaeans' weapons and use it to help kill the remaining soldiers. We will outnumber them because only three at a time can go through the gate. We will crush them like these grapes in a winepress. This will be no battle of fleas. But we will have the advantage. They do not expect us to fight. Remember it is our one hundred against their three at a time. Any questions?"

One man asked, "Remember Midas the Phrygian? He tried to sack this town three hundred years ago. But we defeated him. When we fought as one, we won. You think we can do it again, Uriah?"

"Not only do I think so, I know we will do it again. We must be brave. We must win."

There were no more questions. Every man took his position. Fear turned into excitement like the first time they ever hunted deer or held a girl's hand. As the sun rose over the horizon and there was enough light to see, the entire Achaean patrol appeared inside the wall about two furlongs from the King's Gate and seemed to moving toward them, towards the gorge. Uriah could hear the commander shouting at the soldiers for not finding and killing more people.

Uriah observed that most of the homes outside of town had been burned or razed but it appeared they were still looking for more men. Excitement turned to anger, and then anger turned to rage. He said, "If there is a god, give us favor now."

At Uriah's hand signal the men with bows got into position. Then the men with slings ran through the gate and into the opening. They threw their rocks striking a few Achaeans who cursed and began chasing them as expected. They had taken the bait. When the soldiers came through the gate, the first volley of arrows fired, then the second, then the third. Achaean soldiers began falling, dying three at a time, arrows entering their chests and protruding from their backs, never to rise again. The Achaeans kept coming. The first volley fired, then the second, then the third. Achaean soldiers, bunching up at the gate as each volley fired again, their lieutenants ordering them to attack, were being killed as easy as swatting flies. Uriah ordered the sword group and those with no weapons into the battle to butcher the rest of the Achaeans. Blood made it difficult to stand. Men slid on the mud, the blood and the body parts.

Unexpectedly, scores of other men from Hatusha with a loud shout joined the battle from out of their hiding in the temple to Cybele inside the walls of Hatusha. They attacked from behind, trapping the Achaeans. Soon it was over. The men spread out and searched the town. All three hundred Achaeans had been killed. None from Hatusha died in the battle but fifty men were found dead, killed in or near their homes. The men began to shout, "Uriah! Uriah! Uriah! The Achaeans came to kill us, but Uriah came to save us. Long live Uriah the Hittite."

Uriah realized that a few hours ago he was a bee keeper -- now he is a hero. He wondered what would happen next. He wondered if Nature or some other deity had something else planned for him. It seemed that the gods had given him favor. Maybe Annitis was right and there was a god somewhere. Then he remembered Annitis' words, "Now there will be more men killed!"

Uriah raised his hands, a sad look on his face, his lips quivering, to signal the men to stop cheering. When it was quiet, he began speaking. "Men, tonight, well, it was, what can I say? It was a night of nights. You have won a victory of victories."

"Thanks to you, Uriah!" someone shouted. Everyone began to cheer again.

"What do you think will happen next? I mean, when these men do not return to the garrison?" Uriah asked.

"What will happen?" someone asked.

"The commander will not be happy. He will send out more men. We will be in the same bees wax again."

"You mean we did this to find ourselves in a worse predicament?" Tokat asked.

"Not if you do something about it. You can make one of three choices. First, you could run like a spooked deer, abandon your homes, perhaps go to Tarsus like I started to and maybe live many more years. The rest of your lives will be lived in the knowledge that you did not protect your families from harm. The once mighty Hatusha will cease to exist."

Someone shouted, "I am not running."

Uriah continued, "Second, you could remain here, build a few fortified positions, you know with dikes and ramparts, set a few ambushes, make more arrows, and face the Achaeans when they return. You might kill a few hundred of them again. But we are too few in number to defend the walls of Hatusha against five thousand trained soldiers. Eventually they will kill most of you."

Another man shouted, "I do not want to die yet. What is the other choice?"

"Attack the garrison at Ankara," Uriah said.

"What? That would never work," said one man.

"They will kill us for sure," said another man.

"We could never get in the city in a million years," another man argued.

"Not if we surprise them. Drive them back to Troy. Ankara used to be an ally of Hatusha before the Achaeans came. Maybe someone there would still help you. What is your pleasure?"

Someone spoke up, "I do not have anywhere to run. Hatusha is my home. My family is all here. Where could I go?"

Another questioned, "We are fewer than four hundred men plus our women and children. Thanks to the gods for the men who were hiding in other places besides the grove. But we can barely even defend our own town. How can we attack the garrison in Ankara?"

"If we stay here we die. If we run we die. If we fight we die. Do we have a choice?" another man answered. "We are either going to die, die, or die."

Another man questioned, "How often would we have to fight them, if we stayed here?"

"Nine times and then a tenth!" another man answered and spat on the ground.

"You are forgetting that we could make the Achaeans die, die, or die. I am for attacking Ankara! If we attack Ankara, we only have to do it once. Whether we win or die, we do it only once. If we stay here we keep fighting again and again until we eventually lose anyway," Tokat said, thrusting his bow into the air and shouting with so much excitement that there was a round of men saying "Me too. I am for fighting! Kill the Achaeans!"

"Do not forget Hatusha has tried twice to defeat the Achaeans but were beaten. You would lose too with your small number of men," Uriah said." They are trained and hardened soldiers, you are farmers and merchants."

"Then how?"

"Send out messengers. Go to all the cities within one hundred furlongs. Tell them you need all their fighting men. Tell them what has happened. Meet at the Cubic Plain northeast of Ankara in a fortnight. Tell them you are driving the Achaeans back to Troy. If you do not get enough help we will all need to flee Anatolia. Find yourselves a leader. I have to go find my sister and mother. I promised them I would go to them. They want to come home again when it is safe."

"We chose you to lead us. We won so far. There is no one else." several men said.

"But my family. They are expecting me. I am the youngest among you," said Uriah,

"They are safe. We are not. We need you more," said Tokat.

The survivors rounded up all the living horses and weapons from the Achaeans. Each man took a horse or two and a few weapons. They may need them later. Then they cared for their dead relatives in the manner of the Anatolians, wrapping them in linen cloth and burying them in the earth, as mourners cried and priests prayed to one of their many gods for protection of their souls.

Uriah wept at the loss of his father. He thought of all the things he wanted to say to him but never did. He thought of the horse he had planned to give him but now never will. He thought of all the times he needed his father and he was always there. He thought that his father would still be alive if it had not been for him. He thought of his mother and sister and what he wanted to say to them. If it was not for him they would still have a home and be a family. Uriah was thrust into leadership and wished he could ask his father for help. He always had a way of saying things to encourage him. Uriah needed encouragement now. He did not want to think about what life would be like without him. His innocent father was killed by angry men, who were deceived by evil men, because of his carelessness.

Why did they have to come to his house? Why did they have to come to his town? Why do so many have to suffer? Why did he sell his ring? Why did there always have to be fighting? The history of man is a history of war. When will this change? Is there not a god who can change it?

But he could not afford those thoughts for long. He had to prepare for the next battle.

CHAPTER FOUR

In Tarsus, a town in southern Anatolia, Annitis and Ravia arrived with other travelers from Yozgat to the market in the center of town. It was mid day. Maybe they could find someone to help them.

"Mother, what are we going to do?"

"I cannot say for certain. I lost my husband, my home, and probably my son. He was a bee keeper, not a soldier. I fear he died in vain. What a useless a waste of a life. We will have to find a new life for ourselves. Maybe you can find a husband among the Hittites in Tarsus and I can live with you," she laughed.

"May the gods give us favor," exclaimed Annitis.

Ravia and Annitis walked down the streets of Tarsus looking for Sisera, concerned about Uriah. Maybe she could get someone from here to help find her son. She stopped a few people to ask the way to the house of Sisera. It did not take long to get directions. Everyone knew Sisera the milkman. When she knocked on the door to Sisera's home, his wife, Diannus, a woman about twice as big as Ravia, wearing her hair pulled back and tied under a scarlet scarf, and an apron of sackcloth was excited to see them. "Welcome to our home. Our home is your home as they say. I do not who they are but they say someone says it. Anyway, what brings you here this early? What brings you here at all? No one visits Tarsus. Many pass through and do not even wonder where they have been. No one stays. Sit down. Have some tea and fig cakes. They are two weeks old and I need to use them up so I can bake some more. Do not worry. They are not moldy? No. Hard? Yes. Just dip them in the tea."

Ravia sat on the wood chair and began to explain, "I am so happy to see you! My son sold his ring to some Assyrians who attacked the Achaeans. The Achaean commander ordered revenge for every dead man so they attacked us and . . . "

"What does that have to do with you? Do not confuse me with politics and war." Diannus interrupted. "That is the affairs of men. We are women! Talk to me! How are your babies? What's the latest news in Hatusha? Do you still make your famous kidney, lung, and liver pie? How is your quilt business?"

"Please listen and I will tell you the news."

"I am listening but you are not talking. Who is confusing whom?"

"May the gods give us favor!" exclaimed Annitis.

"Diannus, I, we, have come here for safety." With those words all the stress of the recent events came on her at once and her voice cracked. She began crying so hard her shoulders were shaking. She lost her husband, son, home, and livelihood all in one night. She stayed one day in Yozgat but this was her first chance to share the experience with anyone. Annitis placed her arm around her mother's shoulders.

"Safety from whom, is your husband beating you? He is just like his brother, Sisera. Sometimes I hate that man. He used to beat me when he was angry until I bought him a dog."

"No, my husband is dead." She continued crying, unable to speak, as her chest heaved under the pain.

"You killed him! My dear, you can hide here. I always said a dead man is a good man, and a widow is better than a bride any day."

"May the gods give us favor," exclaimed Annitis.

"Please will you let me explain? I did not kill my husband. He was a good man. What I mean to say is the Achaean commander ordered his men to attack Hatusha because of his losing ten men."

"But, how do you know all this to be true? How do you know it is not just another fable created by lonely women who have nothing better to do? Or maybe an old star-gazer became moon struck and began forecasting another non-existent crisis."

"My son, Uriah, remember him? He killed a soldier, we ran, they burned our home, Uriah went back to Hatusha, we went to Yozgat, and then we came here."

"We saw it all happen with our own eyes!" exclaimed Annitis.

"My poor dears, let's have some tea and fig cakes, then you can talk to me. When my husband gets home we will talk to him."

"Never said good bye . . . to my husband. Never told him . . . I loved him . . . before he died. Told him . . . to check . . .on the horses. Sent him . . . to his death," said Ravia between sobs.

"Mother, you did not know Achaeans were out there. I t could have been a wild animal of some kind for all you know," said Annitis.

"He was a good man. Caring. Loving. A good husband," said Ravia.

"Good husbands are hard to find," said Diannus.

"Never got to . . . bury him," Ravia cried louder. "How come this is . . . happening to me?"

Diannus put her arm around her and pulled Ravia's head into her shoulder. Ravia rested there for several minutes until her sobbing stopped for a few minutes.

"Uriah is trying to be a man. I am afraid he has been killed. Cannot bury him either. I pray the gods protect him," said Ravia.

"Yes, may the gods give him favor," replied Annitis.

"He was always such a good boy. Cannot think of him not being here anymore," said Ravia.

"He was. Remember when one of dad's horses got loose. Uriah spent all afternoon until past supper looking, until he found it and brought it home," said Annitis.

"Yes. There was the time when our neighbor Aksaray was ill and abed. Uriah worked all day cutting up wood for their fire and gave them free honey until Aksaray recovered," said Ravia.

"He must have been one of a kind," said Diannus.

"That he was. Never believed in our gods. Still, he was the kindest, gentlest person. Never caused trouble. So gentle he could hold bees in his hands without getting stung. Gave most of his honey money to me to help with household expenses, never grudgingly. Now he is gone," said Ravia. "He can never tell me he loves me again. Neither of them can."

Later that afternoon, when Sisera finished delivering his milk Diannus told him, “Ravia your sister-in-law and Annitis, your niece, you remember them, right? The wife and daughter of your brother. They are here with bad news. I mean, all news is good news because it is new news. No one ever stays in Tarsus. But this is new news about something bad.”

“Yes, we need your help. Hatusha was attacked by Achaeans and my husband was killed. Uriah went back to help. He may be dead. The town may be destroyed. We came here for refuge. If it is okay with you, that is. If Uriah does not show up, he is dead. We will move on,” Ravia gushed all in one breath, tears falling down her cheeks.

That evening Sisera called a meeting at the city gate. He explained the situation in Hatusha. “The town of Hatusha was attacked by the Achaeans. My brother was killed. Probably many more men as well.” He spat on the ground. “My nephew stayed behind, to protect, to defend the town. He is a very young but brave man. He may be dead too. Cybele protect him. I need help. I need to help these men fight, or help to rebuild if there is a city remaining. Who will go with me?”

As the word spread quickly through Tarsus fifty men, most of the able bodied men in town, volunteered to help Uriah. A Levite priest and ten families, believers in Yahweh, from Tarsus joined the men. They told Sisera they were feeling pinched by the economy and sought job opportunities in Hatusha. The priest said he hoped to minister the Torah to those ten families and the people in Hatusha to tell them about Yahweh.

Sisera told Ravia and Annitis to remain in Tarsus until he returned with news of her son. At least stay the one month Uriah asked them to wait for him.

As Sisera and his entourage traveled northwest toward Hatusha they told their story. More men joined them at each town and village. Sometimes other families would join them. By the time they arrived in Hatusha there were five hundred men and fifteen families. Many of these men had been mercenaries for Egypt, Israel, and Assyria.

In addition to the five hundred men who joined from Tarsus to help Uriah, over a thousand came from the nearby villages. When they arrived in Hatusha, Tokat told them about the about the three hundred Achaean attackers and about their plan to meet on the Cubuk Plain. Everyone began shouting “Uriah! Uriah! Long live Uriah the Hittite!” and set off to join him.

CHAPTER 5

Uriah worked and trained vigorously, sunup to sundown. He told the mercenaries, experts in warfare, to begin training the men to fight with swords, bows, and spears. Not knowing what to expect they taught personal defense and team fighting. Uriah practiced until the fighting movements became as natural as taking honey from a hive. He knew they would have only one chance and they could not fail.

Uriah sat under the shade of a willow tree on the bank of Cubuk Creek on the Cubic Plain. As he leaned against the tree he allowed the breeze and the shade cool and calm his thoughts. Less than two months ago he was a bee-keeper from Hatusha. Now he was in command of an Army of over fifteen hundred volunteers facing an army of about five thousand. All the mercenaries and even his uncle agreed to serve under him. And he was the youngest of all of them. He remembered not long ago asking himself why he could not be in charge. He laughed and thought, "I guess I am in charge now!" Then in panic he thought, "What am I doing here?" All the towns in nearby Anatolia had sent fighting men and were willing to face the Achaeans. The men from Tarsus had arrived after riding hard for several days. Everyone submitted to his command. Everyone was in training.

They had trained for only two weeks but Uriah knew he had to attack soon before he was attacked by the superior forces of the Achaeans. He began reviewing the training and preparations he had made. Not knowing how he would attack or how the battle would go, he trained the men in as many fighting tactics as he could in only a few weeks.

Uriah organized his men into two basic divisions. The Camel Division would be his trusted men from Hatusha and surrounding cities. The other division, the Horse Division would consist of all the men from Tarsus who joined them.

Uriah decided to use the two hundred mercenaries. These would become corporals, (leaders of tens), sergeants (leaders of fifties), captains (leaders of thousands), and generals in charge of each division. Uriah would be supreme commander.

He divided the men into groups of fifty for training. One group practiced movements and battle techniques for double edged swords. Included were the wedge, diamond, square, and line formations with techniques to pivot the battle line right, left, or divide it in two. They were taught how to enter and clear buildings where the enemy may be waiting. Swords were held in the warrior's right hand and a shield was carried on the left forearm. Training consisted of tactics for five man, ten man, and hundred man unit formations for defense and offense.

Another group practiced archery. The archers practiced enfilade shooting to stop an enemy on the back side of a hill, and concentrating their arrows into small areas for maximum killing. The archers learned how to form several ranks so large areas could be penetrated by numerous arrows falling in larger areas on approaching enemy. He invented a formation he called the half moon consisting of a large semi-circle of soldiers armed with spears and daggers while the archers lined up centered behind them and fired missiles of arrows into the enemy. Archers were able to hit their targets up to a half a furlong. Marksmanship was demanded and only the best marksmen were selected as archers. When they were in closer range, one arrow had to mean one kill. They could not afford missed shots.

A third group practiced spear throwing. They were taught how to hit targets while kneeling, standing, or even running towards or perpendicular to their enemy. The spears were about one cubit longer than the height of the warrior and made from ash wood. They were carried with the hilt of the spear near the left foot and the blade pointing upward beyond the right shoulder when they were marching. From this position they could be easily lowered and thrown with the right hand. Offensive and defensive movements for impaling the enemy became the most enjoyed subject, even though they only practiced with wood spears that had no blades or points.

Another volunteer from Egypt taught the fourth group urban warfare, choosing battle sites, and deployment. They learned how to select positions for maximum defense, how to funnel the enemy into kill zones, how to make escape routes if retreat was necessary, how to identify likely avenues of approach of the enemy, how to conceal themselves until they were ready to kill, and how to noiselessly move for surprise attacks. Throughout all the phases they were taught how to communicate, care for wounded comrades, and field hygiene. Practice was twelve hours a day. After four weeks the men felt confidence in their abilities.

As he sat by the river Uriah knew there were three ways to conquer a city: attack, siege, or ruse. He knew he did not have enough men to do either of those. He thought I cannot just attack the city with this many men. They would be killed going through the city gates or over the walls. I could try a ruse and build a dam in the creek to divert or stop the flow of water to the city. But if I did that, they would be alerted when the water stopped, and everyone would come out to attack us. If I tried a siege, we would all be killed for nothing because we are not strong enough to maintain it and have no siege equipment. Those thirty foot walls were too difficult to go over. If we stay here very much longer we will be seen by the scouts. Many will be killed if the soldiers attack. He knew he needed to attack small groups because they could not defeat five thousand with their number of men.

He was beginning to doubt the idea of an attack on Ankara when he fell asleep. As he slept he began to dream. In his dream he saw ten water fowl land on a body of water and begin to swim in the same direction. As if looking for food all ten birds plunged their heads under water but then they disappeared. Four pillars of fire appeared where the birds had been. Mesmerized, he watched as hundreds of snakes crawled towards the fire, and seemed to disappear under it. Waking with a shout, his clothes soaking wet, he realized this was more than a nightmare—it was a message from the gods. Which god?

He gathered his men in formation on the Cubuk Plain ten miles northeast of Ankara to tell them his plan. "This is summer and the Cubuk Creek is lower than usual due to the dry weather. A squad of ten men armed with swords and daggers from the Camel division will enter the city through the water supply by going under the wall where the creek flows into the city, overcome the guards and open the gates. The rest of the division, with swords and spears will go through the gates after they had been opened. They would leave at sunset, everyone get some sleep today. The Horse Division with bows was to take up positions on roads leading into Ankara to protect the Camel Division"

At sunset Uriah gathered the men into formation and told them, "Death is the worst thing that can happen to a man. Let us prepare for the worst."

Someone said, "It is second to being married."

Someone else said, "It is worse than not being married."

Uriah continued, "Since death is something that we all must face it is more blessed to die for our friends, our town, and our country. Our families lived here before the Achaeans. Many of them died for this land. It is time to remember our ancestors and free our land of this scourge. Some of us gallant men may die today but our actions may give freedom to our wives and to our children and grandchildren for hundreds of years. The Law of Nature says that those who oppress others do so at their own peril. Today, you will fulfill that law."

"I am all for giving freedom to my wife," a couple of men stated.

"Those who survive will honor our names among our people. Our wives will honor us. Our posterity will honor us. If we must die tonight, let us die for freedom!"

"For freedom!" everyone shouted in unison as they thrust the weapons over their heads.

When Uriah finished speaking the men began moving along Cubuk Creek—silently, as their destiny called them.

They stopped eight furlongs from the city walls. Uriah dispatched ten men to continue along the creek, while the rest of his army headed west to the main road leading into Ankara. When they reached the main road they turned toward Ankara. Two furlongs from the city gate and out of sight of the guards Uriah positioned the Camel Division in units of five hundred men each. Two men were sent ahead to the crest of the hill as scouts. They waited. In the darkness Uriah knew his men would not be seen. While they waited, the Horse Division set up a secure perimeter around the site and protected their escape route.

The ten men moved along the creek until they found where it flowed under the city wall. The men swam under the wall in single file. No gate blocked the river. One by one they went under water into Ankara. Inside they formed a semi-circle with their backs to the wall. They waited. They listened. Seeing and hearing nothing, one by one they began moving in the direction of the city gate.

They stopped every few feet to watch and listen. From one house came the sound of loud arguing over who drank the last of the wine. No one else was up, it appeared they had all fallen asleep in a drunken stupor. They saw the tower over the gate. Three guards spaced about two reeds apart along the wall provided security. They all appeared to be sleeping. Soon, the ten heard footsteps and quickly found concealment. The captain of the guards was making his nightly post check. When he found the first guard asleep he began to reprimand him.

"Wake up! You son of camel! You not fit to wear uniform. You want to get us killed? How you know we not be attacked tonight? You know patrol overdue to return.

Worthless piece of human flesh! Your mother wasted sweat giving you birth! Keep both eyes open!" Then he slapped him on both cheeks and spat in his face. "Now stay awake. You are Achaean soldier, not Anatolian dog!"

The soldier standing at attention, a fear in his heart, his mind knowing he could be killed, sentries do not sleep on duty, said not a word except "Thank you, sir" when the officer left. The other two guards heard what was happening and jumped to their feet, escaping the abuse of the officer. After the captain completed his post check the guards sat down but went back to sleep.

When they were certain the guards appeared to be asleep the ten moved to the tower. Three went inside the tower and began to open the gate. Thankfully it did not creak when it opened. Three went up the walkway along the wall and cut the throats of the three guards. They should have listened to their captain. The other four climbed to the top of the tower above the gate and lit four torches as a signal they were inside. They thought of the saying, "Strong gates alone cannot save a city without strong men to defend them." These were not strong men. They opened the gates and waited for Uriah while watching to see if the captain returned.

The two scouts saw the torches and ran back to Uriah. "The gate is open."

Uriah gave the command and everyone moved. They entered the gate in two files. Over a thousand men like snakes went through the gate. Inside the walls of the city Uriah's army spread out in teams of ten men each and began entering every building. Any Achaean they found was killed. Spreading out in concentric circles building by building, block by block they cleared the city. No one heard. No one saw. No one had a chance. Residents of

Ankara told them the Achaean barracks was on the hill in the center of the city. Uriah's warriors entered the gate and went in all directions pouring into the encampment, the barracks, and the headquarters of the Achaean army. The Achaeans attacked Hatusha while they slept. Now the Hittites attacked them while they slept. Most never knew what happened.

Near the temple to their god Uriah's men encountered about five hundred soldiers who had been alerted and were prepared to defend the city. He ordered his men to move into the half moon formation. Archers sent arrows into the mass of soldiers killing more than half of them with their first volley. The soldiers charged but were dealt fatal injuries by the spearmen forming the front of the half moon.

In the city center were about fifty soldiers standing, talking, and laughing with each other. Some appeared to be intoxicated. The captain of the guard had just told them about his recent post check and everyone laughed again. "This must be the response team to help the guards at the tower. The captain of the guard is with them." One of the ten exclaimed.

Uriah -- upon seeing the men laughing and remembering his dead father-- exploded. Enraged he began running towards them alone shouting, "Do you know what you get when you line up fifty dead Achaeans in a row? Dog food!" He drew his swords in both hands and taunted the soldiers. Startled, they lost all military bearing and charged him like a pack of wolves. As he began to slash, parry, strike, and lunge again other men joined him. He could not believe what was happening. "Did I learn to do this?" He wondered. Jumping and flipping forwards and backwards, he struck inside, outside, high and low. Kicking and dodging, punching and blocking, he killed people two handedly with the two swords in his hands. He placed the swords in their scabbards and drew his dagger from his belt. It seemed to give him extra energy. He seemed surreal. The soldiers could not touch him. Arms, heads, and legs were falling all over the field. Blood spewed everywhere giving Uriah a boost of adrenaline he had never felt before. They died headless, armless, and breathless, outmatched by a God-gifted warrior. He used the dagger on the captain, a man old enough to be his father, as he let him feel the entire blade sinking deep into his chest.

When it was over some men said to him "I never saw anyone do the *dancing eagle* or the *diving swan* as well as you did. When did you learn to make those moves?" they asked.

"Never!" he answered. "It was natural. I was overwhelmed by it. Not only could he use the sword both right handed and left handed. He could use the spear and dagger like the skilled warrior he had become. By mid-day the Achaeans counted four thousand six hundred dead Achaeans. Three hundred had been killed in Hatusha. Either the rest escaped or were on leave. Everyone celebrated the amazing victory and heroism of Uriah the Hittite. The citizens of Ankara came into the streets shouting praises to the Hittites.

After a day to rest Uriah called the men into a formation back on the Cubic Plain. "Men of Anatolia, We have made our town safe to live in again. I am going to Tarsus with my uncle and the others who joined him. I must join with my mother and sister. Some of the families who came to help are remaining here. You must select leaders to govern you and defend you. Continue to practice the tactics you have learned this past month. We did not use most of what you learned this time but you may soon need to use them. Maybe sooner than you think."

"We want you to be our leader," Tokat stated.

"I cannot stay here now. My duty is to find my mother and sister. I promised them I would go to them within four weeks. I am already late. My uncle told them to stay there until he returned but you know how well women do what men tell them. I fulfilled my duty to you. Some of the mercenaries who helped us will stay here. Do not remain independent city states or the Assyrians will rule this land. Form some type of organization for mutual defense. The Achaeans may come from Troy and do not trust the Assyrians. Use the training you received to form an army, be ready to defend yourselves. You will need to rebuild your homes in Hatusha. Help each other. May your gods give you favor. Go to the gorge and begin to dig an underground city where you can hide and live in case of future attacks. Troy may come against you, or Assyria, or someone else. Make them large to hold all our people."

As he rode off with Sisera and the men from Tarsus the warriors shouted, "Uriah! Uriah! Long live Uriah the Hittite!"

The men of Hatusha returned home and celebrated their victory with dancing and singing. While most rebuilt their homes some helped the fifteen new families. Someone carved a portrait of Uriah into a large limestone rock at the gorge at Yazilikaya. He had a sword in one hand, a sling in the other hand, a bow was over his shoulder -- and a dagger was in his belt. Under his image were the words, "Uriah, the Hittite Warrior!"

On the way back to Tarsus Uriah heard the sounds of women screaming. He rode to the sound as fast as his horse could run. As he came into a narrow place in the trail the screaming became louder. Then off to his right he could see four men wrestling with two women, and the women, clothing ripped, were losing. Ravia and Annitis he thought. Off his horse he jumped, dagger in hand, heart in throat. Uriah began slashing and stabbing with his dagger as if their lives depended on it, because they did. Seconds later the women were free and the four men were dead.

"Thank you for helping us," said one of the women.

"No problem. I thought you might have been my mother and sister. Glad to help anyway," said Uriah. "What happened?"

"We were going to Tarsus when as we reached the narrow part of the path these men attacked us. We could have been killed or worse if you had not come along," said the second woman.

"The Law of Nature says women should not travel alone even though my mother and sister traveled alone to Yozgat. I hope they traveled with others to Tarsus. I am Uriah. Come with me and my friends. You will be safe with us."

"Uriah! Uriah the Hittite Warrior?"

"I have been called that, yes."

"We have heard about you," said the first woman.

"It was worth being attacked, to be rescued by you," said the second woman. "I cannot wait to tell my friends I was rescued by Uriah the Hittite Warrior."

PART TWO

CHAPTER 6

David, once a shepherd and now the king's musician, played peacefully on his harp the tunes he had taught himself while singing to his sheep. He could not believe his good fortune. Yahweh had blessed him. Instead of singing sheep to sleep, he was singing the king to sleep. While his brothers slept in fields and battlements, he slept in the king's home. He was blessed to be able to play for King Saul, the man God chose to lead His people.

David sang of the blessings and promises of Yahweh: a Promised Land and a progeny to Abraham. Then Yahweh repeated His promise to Abraham's son Isaac, and grandson Jacob. Even when they became slaves in Egypt, Yahweh did not forsake them. He blessed them as Moses led his people to Canaan with signs and wonders performed with his power. For many years Yahweh blessed them with wise, and sometimes unwise, men and women who served their people. Now they have a king chosen by Yahweh and anointed by the prophet. David sang these stories in psalms to his king. Could life be better?

Then he thought of Michal, the king's second daughter and wondered if she would ever be his bride. Maybe life could be a little better. He smiled as he thought about her. But how could a shepherd boy marry the king's daughter? How could even the king's musician marry the king's daughter?

When the king appeared to be sleeping David finished playing and departed for his room. The king's home was a large rectangular stone, granite, and marble building of three stories with many rooms around the outside walls. The interior contained a large botanical garden of lilies, orchids, and roses, juniper and mulberry bushes, herbs and spices, pistachio, almond, and fir trees, and decorative grasses divided by foot paths. David had to cross the garden to go from the king's living area to his own room. He loved the garden for the sweet aromas emanating from it. He loved the garden because from the center where the paths intersected, David could see the door to Michal's chambers. While he stood gazing at her door, he heard someone in the garden. Startled, he thought it was the king. He did not the king catch him staring at the door to his daughter's chambers. But when he turned he saw the king's cupbearer and baker approaching him, presumably on their way to their rooms, he thought they would pass by him. But they stopped.

"You look for Michal. She love you. Want to be your wife," the cupbearer whispered, putting his hand to the side of his mouth as if he wanted no one else to hear. "She talk about you with her attendants. They tell us."

"That be true," agreed the baker nodding his head as he handed David some fresh bread and cheese, glanced at the cupbearer as if for agreement, then up toward her window. "There be no secrets here."

"Do not be ridiculous, I cannot be the son-in-law to the king. I am a shepherd, a musician, the youngest of my family. I have no bride price, no future, nothing to offer." David answered looking them in the face to determine whether they were serious or mocking him.

"We know how you earn bride price. You see how angry king be when he think about those Philistines?" asked the cupbearer looking around as if to see whether anyone else was listening.

The baker agreed, "He hate them so much, if you bring him one hundred foreskins of those uncircumcised dogs, he give you Michal as your wife. If he do not, I bake you bread every day. You rather be king's musician or king's son-law-law? Think about it. If you were his son-in-law, maybe you be king someday."

David choked on his bread when he heard of circumcising Philistines. "What are you trying to say?"

The baker continued to encourage him "I overhear king talking with Adriel the Meholathite, king's son-in-law, at dinner last night. You know I cook king's dinner. He hate Philistines so much he say he give Michal to anyone who kill a hundred and give him foreskins."

"A hundred foreskins? How would I get a hundred foreskins?" asked David.

"First cut off Philistine's head, and then cut off foreskin," said the cupbearer.

"Small price for one beautiful as Michal, yes?" replied the baker.

When they were certain David believed them, they wished him good night with a wink and a nod and went straight to King Saul.

When the baker and cupbearer told the king what happened he said, "Well done. I long to be rid of him. He is everything I am not: he's young, good looking, courageous, all the women sing about him. My own son and daughter adore him. But most of all he has the Lord's heart -- that is what I hate the most. That's why I did not give Merab to him. Michal is beautiful but brazen. I pity any man who marries her." Saul was gloating over the good news. "David will either be killed in battle with the Philistines or he will have Michal as his bride. Either way, he loses. But I doubt he will try to kill the Philistines. I may have to find another way to make him disappear."

"He be killing lions and bears with his bare hands and killing Goliath with his own sword. Remember how many Philistines Samson killed? Perhaps he surprise you, king," said the cupbearer.

"Do not count on it. How many Samson's can there be? Anyway, I doubt that David is another Samson and Michal is no Delilah." Then they all laughed. He gave them each a denarius and a fresh wine skin, and went to bed.

CHAPTER 7

Uriah counted the days before telling his mother and sister what had happened. They would be surprised. Sisera and Uriah had rehearsed the battle many times on their way back to Tarsus. He had escorted the two women he rescued to their destination safely. Now he could hardly wait to tell his mother it was safe to go home again and let them know he was okay. Running into the house he found Diannus but she told him they were not there. They had waited for only three weeks and when Uriah did not come they joined a caravan going to Gibeah. They want him to join them. She said that they heard that King Saul had a reputation as a man who would tolerate no violence in his country so they went to Gibeah, where the king lived, in search of peace and possibly a job. Ravia wanted to wait for Sisera to return but Annitis wanted to move from Tarsus. No one ever stayed here. Diannus had given them provisions for the trip and promised she would send Uriah. The town ruler also wrote a letter of recommendation for them. Perhaps they could work until Uriah found them.

Diannus explained to Uriah that no one knew when he would arrive and his family wanted to leave Tarsus.

Everyone thought he was dead -- killed by the Achaeans. Besides, she explained, no one ever stays in Tarsus. No one ever comes to Tarsus. His mother and sister, they thought they would be able to start life again in a different town. After all, they thought they would be waiting for nothing. Uriah wondered, how could they think he was dead? They must have thought he was another Hittite god. Why go all the way to Gibeah. Life was getting out of his control again. What are the gods doing he wondered.

Uriah remembered the time his dog came up missing. Every day he would look for it, call it, and expect it to appear. Everywhere he went he always kept an eye open for his dog, and even called it when there was not even a dog in sight. He missed it! Then one day he heard that a friend of a friend of a friend had found a dog like his. Uriah identified the dog by the white spot on its forehead and white tip on its tail. He was so happy to have his dog again he told everyone he met that he had found his missing dog.

Now his mother was somewhere. He must find her. All his excitement in seeing her again was crushed when he heard she was not there. He never knew he could feel so alone without her. He missed her many times more than he remembered missing his dog. He felt shame for leaving her for so long. He should never have left her, but how could he not leave her? He had to do his duty.

Sisera and most of the men who fought with him in Ankara returned to their homes. When they arrived home they began talking about the adventure they had with Uriah. Soon every traveler moving through Tarsus, no one ever stayed at Tarsus, or central Anatolia knew the story. Each time it was told, it grew. As it grew it spread. Before long everyone from Gibeah to Troy knew of the wonders of Uriah the Hittite Warrior. He quickly became a folk hero, a legend, a topic of daily conversation. All the little boys wanted to be Uriah when they played together.

Uriah continued to look for his family. He stopped in every village to ask about them. Had a caravan come through town heading to Gibeah with two Hittite women? He looked into the faces of every woman he saw, trying to find them. Some of the women did not understand why Uriah looked so intently at them. Some raised their eyebrow invitingly and smiled. Some cursed him and turned their heads. Most ignored him. There were a few caravans but no one had heard of them. They all knew of him. When the villagers learned who he was people gave him respect. More than a few young women wanted to become his wife so they could have his children. Uriah was not interested. He thought it strange that even in Canaan they would bestow such honor to a foreigner. But his goal now is to find his family.

His followers had increased in numbers to over forty people. Some were curious, some were woman, and some wanted adventure; those who wanted to see what Uriah would do next continued with him towards Gibeah. They believed that if something new was happening in the world, it centered on Uriah, and they wanted to be a part of history. Uriah was looking for his mother and sister, but they were looking for their future.

Uriah's entourage had traveled a few days from Tarsus when they were ambushed by a handful of criminals. Caught off guard, and with weapons sheathed, some of Uriah's men were killed.

"Draw weapons and counterattack!" shouted Uriah as he drew his dagger from his belt and engaged in the fight.

The dagger seemed to activate his adrenaline as he sliced his way through the attackers. Within minutes they were all dead or else they fled. Either way, the fighting was over. Uriah had lost five men. Ten attackers lay on the ground, not breathing.

"Where are the gods when we need them? Travel with your weapons in your hands from here on, "said Uriah. "Since no god can protect us we must protect ourselves."

"What do you think made them attack us?" asked one of his men.

"Not sure. Tarsus was built as an escape from the flood the same time Hatusha was built. Some of the people who fled there were violent. The violent nature was passed down through generations explaining why no one ever stopped in Tarsus. Everyone only passed through," Uriah told them that's what Uncle Sisera had told him.

"They should have known to not mess with Uriah the Hittite Warrior." said another man.

David paced the floor of his room that night, trying to relieve the pain in his heart and figure out what to do. He began praying.

"I love you, Yahweh, the God of the Army of Israel, with all my strength. You helped me kill Goliath. You made me the king's musician. Would you justify my killing one hundred innocent men of our enemy to have a wife?"

"On the other hand, I love Michal, the woman of my dreams, with all my heart. I would do anything to have her. But I am only a shepherd boy and not worthy of her love.

Do I love her enough to kill for her? Does she love me enough to be my wife?

"On the other hand, I hate the Philistines with all my soul. I have killed Goliath and maybe I could kill a Philistine just for fun, wife or no wife. Besides, killing a Philistine is not the same as killing a person, or is it?"

The thought of having Michal for a wife gave him so much adrenaline his mind could not stop racing. He would think about her then plan his attack on the Philistines. Then he would think about the attack again and wonder how Yahweh would view the situation. Would he approve? Would she approve? Would the king approve? Did the baker and cupbearer speak the truth? He knew he could not prevail against the Philistines unless Yahweh helped him.

Between planning battles and thinking about Michal, he prayed again. "Let God arise and let his enemies be scattered: let them also that hate him flee before him. As smoke is driven away, so drive them away: as wax melts before the fire, so let the wicked perish at the hand of God. But let the righteous be glad. Let them rejoice before God. Yes. Let them exceeding rejoice."

At one point he was so restless he had to get up and walk around the garden, looking at her door, feeling the cool breeze, trying to relax. How could he relax after what the baker and cupbearer told him? When he looked towards her door he was ready to kill five hundred Philistines. He had already killed Goliath. Why not kill a few more? He wondered whether the king had said that or was it only fables from the servants. Maybe the servants were jealous of his close contact with the king, and they wanted to get rid of him. The king never really told David to kill the Philistines. Who cares? Any reason is a good reason to kill a few Philistines. He wrestled in his mind all night. He wished Yahweh would just tell him what to do.

He began to remember Goliath, the Philistine giant who mocked the king while no one did anything. The king said he would give his daughter to the man who fought the giant, but no one fought him. If the king was willing to offer his daughter then, maybe it was true he would do it again. David was too young for a wife then. He thought about asking for Michal as a reward for killing Goliath. But somehow the king's promises offered on impulse are soon forgotten and seldom kept. If David came to him with a hundred foreskins, he could not forget that.

David angered at the thought that if the followers of Moses had done their jobs there would be no Philistines to fight. Yahweh said to occupy the land and kill all the inhabitants, including the Philistines. Now, hundreds of years later, they are still fighting them. Then David remembered something else. The Law was given to guide people and tell them what to do. He tried to think what the Law would say about this situation. He thought about Moses. When the Egyptians were chasing him and the Red Sea was in front of him he lifted up his arms. God parted the sea.

He decided that he would attempt to face the Philistines tomorrow. If God parted the Philistines for him and gave him victory, he would know it was God's will to kill them and have Michal for his wife. But what if he was killed? It would be worth dying to be killing Philistines and possibly winning Michal as his wife.

Michal had sung herself to sleep. David played such beautiful music for her father. But when she caught him looking at her, she thought he played for her too. How could she tell her father? She could not walk up and say, “King, father, I love your musician. Can I marry him?” Women did not choose their own husbands. It might make her father tell David to leave, or kill him. She would be stuck with whoever had the highest price for her. Maybe she could ask her father to give her to David for killing Goliath. But daughters do not chose who they marry -- even daughters of the king.

Her sister told her the king had offered her to anyone who would kill a hundred Philistines. She would end up with some brutal warrior who would treat her as a prize in battle. Great! Not exactly the kind of husband she wanted. He would probably grab her by her hair and pull her to their bed whenever he needed her. Maybe he would kill her and hang her head on his wall. Maybe it would be nobody. After all, who could kill a hundred Philistines, or was it two hundred? What if it was someone from another country, someone who could not speak her language? That would not be a good marriage. She put that out of her mind.

David’s songs about Yahweh stirred up belief in her that Yahweh was a good God. She prayed and sung David’s songs on her pillow. His words seemed so true and so reassuring. They calmed her father. They calmed her as she lay there. She believed everything would be okay. One day she would wait until David finished playing and her father was at peace. Then she would ask him to let her marry David. She thought she heard David talking to someone in the garden and wanted to open the door to look. But, no, he would not be in the garden this late.

Saul stared at the ceiling, his anger keeping him awake. He hated David. He needed David. His music was soothing. But this outsider had won the hearts of his son, his daughter, and even his people. He had killed Goliath and saved his army. They treat him with the respect of a king. They make up songs about him. Saul's son Jonathon would rather be with David than be with him. So would Michal. It was time for him to leave. If he does not try to kill those Philistines by the end of the week, he would give him Michal anyway, and send him back to his father. He would find another harpist in Israel. Then he doubted whether there was another harpist as good as David in all of Israel.

CHAPTER 8

The caravan stopped at Jabeth-Gilead so the camels, which had become lame, would have time to heal. They would not be traveling again for several days. The same man owned all the camels and did not want to split them up so they remained where they were. Discouraged, thinking their idea to go to Gibeah was not so good after all, Ravia and Annitis located an inn where they spent the night. They were explaining their situation and why they were in Jabeth-Gilead to one of the maids of the inn. She told them there were job vacancies at the inn if they wanted to stay there for awhile. Upon learning of some vacancies in the staff at the inn they presented their letter from Tarsus. If they had to stay they might as well work. After reading the letter of reference, the inn keeper hired Ravia and Annitis to work in the kitchen. With a salary of two meals a day, a shared room, and two denarii a week, the mother and daughter could not be happier. Then the innkeeper commented, "I see you are Hittites. You know the legendary Uriah the Hittite, do you not?"

"How come? And what do you mean about legendary?" asked Uriah's mother.

"He is a great warrior. He helped liberate Anatolia from the Achaeans. According to legend he attacked the garrison at Ankara with only three hundred men and destroyed the entire Achaean army. He killed over one hundred men by himself as a matter of fact. Even rescued two kidnapped women. Why, it is even rumored that the dagger he carries gives him super human abilities. The king would like to meet him I am sure. He would pay him well to be a leader in his army."

Ravia replied, "There are several Uriah's among the Hittites. I am sure I do not know this one."

"May the gods give us favor," remarked Annitis in disbelief.

"Uriah, be careful." Ravia cautioned just under her breath.

Ravia could not believe her ears. When did her bee keeper so become a Hittite warrior? He was the only Uriah in Hatusha. At least he must still be alive. Then she wondered if he would find them here. He probably went to Tarsus and is now looking everywhere for them. She hoped Diannus had given him correct instructions. She thought they should have stayed put. Instead of getting where they were going they are stuck somewhere else. Fate, or the gods, always throws surprises into her life. The gods seem to make a game of surprising her with unpleasant or unexpected events.

As if she could read her mother's mind Annitis said, "A lot of travelers come through here. We could join them and try to get to Gibeah. Or, maybe if we stay here someone will tell us something about Uriah. We could just go back to Hatusha. It is probably safe there now if these stories are true. I am sorry I made you leave before Uncle Sisera returned. Uriah may have been with him."

"Except that if we went back to Hatusha, Uriah could spend months looking for us here. We will wait. If we stay in one place long enough, he might find us. We need to stay here and be patient this time. If we keep moving and he keeps moving we will keep missing each other. This seems like a safe town where not much happens."

"You are right, mother. The most exciting thing in town is what is on the new caravan."

Uriah and his men bypassed every town and village between Tarsus and Gibeah, failing to stop at Jabeth-Gilead. When they arrived at the gate of Gibeah, Uriah asked," Has a caravan arrived from Tarsus in the past two weeks?"

The men at the gate told him. "There are several caravans a week, one of them may have been from Tarsus."

"I am looking for my mother and sister, two Hittites. They came here hoping to work for the king."

"As a matter of fact, I think I remember someone saying two Hittite women left the caravan at Damascus," one man said.

"Yeah, you are right. Two of them, Hittites. Looking for work, they were," said another man.

"Damascus, one place we have not been to," said Uriah.

David and his men turned around and went north towards Damascus.

"That was an easy way to get rid of strangers," said one of the men.

"Sure was. How can anyone be so naïve?" said another.

The trip took two days. When they checked in at an inn, Uriah asked the innkeeper, "Have any new Hittite women came here, you know, to work."

"Yup, two of them. Came about a month ago. Work at the market they do. You can see them in the morning."

The next morning Uriah went to the market and inquired of the women. He was directed to a table of figs in the center of the market, surrounded by busy shoppers. When he got to the table the women had their backs to him. They had on scarves and cloaks that he thought he recognized. In his excitement he was sure he saw his mother. Walking up behind one of them he put his arms around her saying, "Mom, I told you I would find you."

When she turned around she said, "Mom? I am not your mother. Are you crazy? Leave me alone."

"I am so sorry; I thought you were my mother. I have been looking for her," said Uriah.

One of the men at the market saw Uriah hug the woman and heard her holler so he came over to help her. "Listen pal, leave this woman alone, or else."

Uriah said, "Listen pal, leave me alone, or else. This is not your business." Emphasizing the word pal.

The man drew his sword and swung at Uriah, nearly hitting a couple of shoppers. Uriah drew his dagger, did a double back flip, a *dancing eagle,* and came up with his dagger in the man's stomach. Other men in the market joined in to help their neighbor. Uriah's men drew their swords and instantly there was a full scale battle at the market-- Uriah and his men against the town.

Several fruit tables were knocked over or covered with blood. Shopping was over for that day. Meanwhile Uriah and his men were able to retreat out of town with nothing but a few scratches. Twenty men were left lifeless at the market. His mother, apparently, was not in Damascus.

Uriah returned to Gibeah. This time there were different men at the gate.

"Hittites? We have not seen any Hittite women. If they were working for the king, David might know. Ask him."

"David? You mean the one who killed the giant?"

"That's him. He is the king's musician now."

"From giant killer to musician – how strange. How do I find him?"

"He left, maybe a few hours ago, heading southwest, he was. Seemed to be in a hurry. You could try to catch him, or wait until he gets back. Of course there is no telling how long he will be gone. Could be a day, maybe. Or longer, no one knows what David does. Strange fellow. Grew up among the sheep."

David arose early, gathered his weapons, and went to join his men. Ten brave men, including Ahithophel his advisor and his son Eliam, Joab his nephew from his step sister Zeruiah and Joab's brothers Abishai and Asahel prepared to go with him. These five men were David's right hand but even they had not been told where they were going. They had traveled until about noon when they stopped in a thicket of acacia trees for lunch: a loaf of bread, some figs, and a piece of cheese.

Ahithophel was an astrologer, a Gilonite from the Judean hills, who planned his life based on the stars, believing the heavens declare the handiwork of Yahweh. He believed that if we look to the stars they will guide us in his will. He often gave David advice based on the stars. Sometimes it was good. Sometimes not so good. He balanced what Ahithophel told him with what the others said before he made a decision. Eliam did not believe in the stars and wished his father was not so public in his beliefs, especially when he was wrong. Ahithophel always said the stars were not wrong; it was only his interpretation that was wrong.

"Truth be known, today is a day of great significance, David." said Ahithophel between bites.

"Does that mean I live through it?" David asked and the others chuckled.

"The stars tell me that because of today, two people will influence the rest of your life."

"Dad, please. Not now," said Eliam.

"Are these people I already know? Are you one of them, or Joab?" asked David.

"I cannot say for certain but when the middle star of the bear constellation is straight up on the exact same day that the moon comes up directly in the east, in the center of the lion constellation, these two events, the star and the moon, signify two people coming into your life."

"How do you know it will be today?"

"Tomorrow the moon will not be directly in the east and the middle star will not be straight up. I do not know whether this is good or bad news. I only read what it says. One will be like a bear, the other like a lion."

David had not told his men about Michal. He was trying to figure out an easy way to tell them why they were heading towards Philistine territory. He wondered whether Ahithophel's warning included her. When they heard riders approaching from the northeast, they all picked up their weapons and turned toward the sound.

David shouted, "Stop. Identify yourselves. State your name and your purpose."

"Uriah, the Hittite, looking for David the king's musician to inquire of my mother and sister. These men are my friends."

"I am David but I do not have them," David said as everyone laughed.

Abishai and Asahel looked at each other in disbelief, Uriah the Hittite?

"I cannot believe it! He really does exist!" said Abishai.

Uriah asked, "Who did you say you are?"

"I am David, the king's musician and armor bearer. I am the one you look for. You seem a little old to be looking for your mother. You can put away your swords. We are friendly."

"Very funny! They went to Tarsus where they were supposed to wait for me. I promised to meet them there. When I did not arrive they left by themselves. Someone told me they may have been going to Gibeah. In Gibeah I was told they might be in Damascus, but when I got there, they were not there. I went back to Gibeah and was told you might know if they were working for King Saul."

"A man should not keep his mother waiting, I have heard. Do you come in peace?"

Uriah could not believe his good fortune in finding David so soon. "We come in peace. As I said, I am looking for my mother and sister. When I find them, we will return to Hatusha. We mean to cause no problems."

"Hatusha? Can anything good come from Hatusha?" asked David. His men chuckled.

Abishai looked at Asahel and said, "I cannot believe it." when he saw Uriah. He expected someone with bulging muscles and in his late twenties. But here was Uriah the Hittite, standing over four cubits tall and weighing just over two talents, directly in front of them. His face was skinny and his features were sharp. He looked like the youth he was. Long dangling arms and wiry legs made him look like some type of bird. His hair was shoulder length, black and wavy, tied back with a leather strap. His immature beard revealed a boyish complexion. Abishai thought Uriah did not look like he could find the hilt on a sword, let alone use the one in his belt. Could all the rumors be true?

Uriah sized up the men in front of him. Joab looked like a general. He had hard eyes, a square jaw, and looked like he had been in many battles even though he could not be thirty years old. Abishai and Asahel looked like twins, except they were not. Neither of them carried a weapon in their belts but had swords in scabbards on their right hips. They both wore leather kilts and black woolen pull-over shirts. They wore sandals laced half way up to their knees. Their hair was pulled back and tied with a cord; their beards were full and dark. They were slightly shorter than Uriah and they were sleek, like they could run all day and not get tired. Joab's deep and husky voice was reassuring to Uriah. He believed he could trust him. Maybe these men could be trusted. Uriah felt that he belonged with them.

"Someone said you all might know of two Hittite women who could be working for the king," said Uriah.

David said," I have not heard of any. But I promise if you stay with me until we returned to Gibeah, I could check on them."

After Uriah got comfortable on a rock Abishai asked, "What was it like when those two hundred Achaean soldiers attacked you in Ankara? I cannot believe it. How did you defend yourself?"

"Two hundred, it seemed like at least five hundred! But someone told me later it was only fifty. And I had help," Uriah smiled and motioned to the men around him. "I do not know what came over me. They were looking so unlike soldiers that I became angry and ran into them. Before they could form a defense or counterattack, the fight was over. It was nothing that any of you could not do."

"I heard it was not so easy in Hatusha." replied Asahel. "How did you kill all the Achaeans?"

"I had one hundred men whose wives and mothers were with us. It was easy to motivate them. All I did was told them what to do and what would happen to their family if they did not fight." Uriah explained.

Uriah asked, "How do you happen to be here?"

This was the moment David dreaded. "I had a conversation with the king's baker and cupbearer last night."

"What does that have to do with us being here? I wondered why we were going in this direction. What are we here for," said Joab. "They send you out here on an errand."

"Sort of," said David.

"What do you mean, sort of? Did they or not?" asked Eliam.

David said, "They told me that if someone would bring the king one hundred foreskins of Philistines, he would give that person Michal as his wife. I was hoping you would help me."

"I cannot believe this," said Abishai. "You brought us out here to help you kill Philistines so you could have a wife?"

"I would kill some too. It is only one hundred. Now with Uriah and his men that is only five men apiece. It should be easy," said David.

Uriah laughed in disbelief, "Kill one hundred men to get a wife?"

Joab said. “Have you lost your mind?”

Eliam said,” He may have lost his heart too.”

Abishai said, “I cannot believe it. He has lost his heart alright.”

Ahithophel asked, “Have you thought this through? You are really going to kill one hundred men?”

Eliam asked, “Are you really going to marry Michal?”

“What is wrong with Michal?” asked David.

“Nothing. I was curious,” said Eliam realizing his mistake.

David said, “If I had told you where we were going you would not have come. That would leave me to do it alone and receive all the glory. This way you share in the glory.”

Ahithophel said, “What glory? We cannot marry her too.”

Joab said, “You should have told us and let us make that decision.”

“You believe this tale? What if it was a prank?” asked Eliam.

“You will get the best seats at the wedding banquet. But, you are free to leave if you want. I will not care. The decision is still yours. If it’s prank, we still have the fun of killing Philistines,” said David. Then he turned to Uriah and said, “You do not believe me. Do you care to join us? It could be fun.”

Uriah stated, “You are serious? I am looking for my mother and sister and not a fight with some Philistines. I will go back to Gibeah to look for them. We can talk when you return. They may have the fun of killing us.”

Abishai assured him.” If you can believe it, there have been no caravans from Tarsus in the past week. You might as well join us. There are no new Hittites in town either.”

“Us? That means you will help?” asked David.

"I need to keep looking for my family. They are probably worried, wondering what happened to me. They probably think I am dead. The caravan left Tarsus but if it never got to Gibeah they have to be somewhere in between. I need to find them," said Uriah.

"I cannot believe this. Of course we will help you, Uncle David." Turning to Uriah he said, "Are you afraid we will discover all those stories about you are lies, Uriah? Make us believe you. Come show us the truth." Abishai mocked.

"Let the truth be known," said Ahithophel.

"Okay, I will! But only because I want to see whether this shepherd boy turned musician can do what the rumors say about him! When this is over I need you all to help me find my family," stated Uriah.

"I will help you if you can answer one question," said David.

"What is that?" asked Uriah.

"What do you get when you cross a camel with a dog?"

"I do not know."

"A Philistine!" That brought a round of laughter.

"What do you get when you cross the king's baker?" asked David.

"A ninety day belly ache," replied Joab.

Then David asked, "What do I get if I cut off one hundred foreskins of those half dogs, half camels?"

"More woman than you can handle." Eliam jested. By now all the men were into the act.

Uriah asked David, "How do you kill one hundred Achaeans?"

"I do not know, how?"

"You cut off their heads."

Then Uriah asked, “How do you kill one hundred Philistines?”

“I do not know, how?”

Uriah answered “Same way, you cut off their heads. Let us go find some headless Philistines!” All the men rolled with laughter.

Ahithophel thought this must be one of the people he warned David about. He planned to tell when he had a chance.

CHAPTER 9

David determined to kill one hundred Philistines, his king's despised enemies, and throwing caution to the wind rode hard into Gaza, where he expected to find at least one hundred men. By now the conflict in his heart was over, but it still raged in his mind. His hatred for the king's enemies and his desire for Michal blinded his love for Yahweh. He eased his conscience by thinking that since Yahweh ordained Saul to be king, killing his enemies is serving both Yahweh and the king. He determined if he died trying to win Michal, it was better than not trying and never having her.

One hundred women who woke up with husbands, sons, or brothers would find grief today if he had anything to do about it. But one princess would become a bride. He smiled. With his new friends, if their reputation is true, David knew this would not take long. Besides, even though Eliam asked how he knew the cupbearer and baker were telling the truth, he could not have second thoughts now. His plan was simple, go into town and start killing until there was no one left to kill. He would let Yahweh part the sea again.

David and his men rode into the town of Geba and dismounted from their horses. He had ten men and Uriah had twenty. They would each kill three or four men and be on their way. David shouted, “I am David, the man who killed Goliath.” All the men charged toward him like they were demon possessed, with any weapon they could find: swords, daggers, clubs, others only stones.

David’s men had swords, daggers, spears, and bows. They formed a circle and each man defended the man on his right. The carnage was swift and merciless. The disorganized Philistines, who seemed to be coming out of thin air, were superior in number but outmatched in skill and weaponry. They charged in off balance, unorganized, and fought as individuals. David’s men were skilled, organized, and disciplined, working as a team. The fight was unfair. Within minutes, piles of bodies and body parts lay everywhere, none of them were David’s or Uriah’s men.

Eliam said, “The legend about you Uriah is not exaggerated. You and your men can stay with us as long as you want. Most of us stay in the Cave of Adullam. It is a large cave on a grassy plateau. We camp in the field and take shelter in the cave. It is pretty nice, even has a few trees to conceal the entrance. We will show you where it is.

“The legend about David is true also,” said Uriah.

Then after looking into the eyes of his men, he agreed,” Alright, we’ll stay with you while I search for my family. I will use your cave as a base to operate from.”

David said, “Good, let us finish this job and circumcise these animals.”

Joab said, “I count six hundred dead men.”

David said, “Cut off all their heads. We will circumcise two hundred, and take whatever bounty we can find. We will give the heads, foreskins, and bounty to King Saul.

Joab said, “Maybe you will get two wives, David, since you doubled the bride price.”

David said, “I only want one for now.” The men laughed.

Uriah joked that if David did not want two, he would take one for himself if Saul had any more daughters. More laughter.

Joab said, “If I had a daughter you could have her, Uriah.” More laughter.

Eliam said, “Uriah, I have a daughter. If you want her, you can have her. Her name is Bathsheba, my seventh daughter. She is the only daughter I have left at home.” Laughter stopped. Everyone turned their heads toward Eliam and listened.

“I do not have money for a dowry. I cannot afford to give you anything for her.” Uriah protested. “Besides, I was joking, I am not looking for a wife. I am looking for my mother and sister.”

Eliam exclaimed, “I do not need your money. Your pledge of fidelity and faithfulness to Bathsheba, to David, to our cause, and to our god, Yahweh, is the only dowry I need. You came looking for two women and will find three. How bad can that be?”

Uriah laughed, “In that case, you have a deal of deals.”

Ahithophel commented to Eliam as he reached out and touched him on his forearm, “You may want to see how Bathsheba feels about this arrangement. I think she has other plans for her life. And I think Uriah is one of those two people I told David about.”

Ahithophel was medium height but had a large torso. Gray hair grew past his shoulders. An old wrinkled face was accented by a white beard that extended halfway down his chest. His bushy eyebrows were as furry as cattails. He always wore a sheepskin vest no matter the weather. At first glance he looked like a lion. His voice was deep, he talked slowly but wisely. A believer in astrology he was always looking at the sky and making predictions that sometimes did happen. But he had a heart that could hear a hurt, wisdom to discern the times, and a love for Bathsheba that would last beyond a lifetime.

"She is my daughter, what can she say?" Eliam answered.

"Truth be known, she might say she wants to marry a Hebrew man. She might say she wants to marry a rich man. She might say she wants to marry a man who will be remembered in the future. She might say she wants a man who will be living five years from now. She probably would not say she wants to marry a Hittite."

"What are you saying, father? Bathsheba would not say any of those things."

"What if I told you she may even want to be a queen someday? Would that surprise you?"

"You have not been filling her head with star stories again have you?"

"Just talk to her that is all I am saying."

"Did you say she wants to be queen?" asked David.

"It is just an old stargazer's imagination," answered Eliam.

When they returned to the Cave of Adullam, David sat in the shade of one of the trees in front of the cave and wrote: "I will praise you, O Lord, with my whole heart. I will show forth all your marvelous works. I will rejoice in you: I will sing praise to your name, Oh God most High. When my enemies are turned back, they shall fall and perish at your presence, for you Oh God have maintained my right and my cause. You sit in the throne of judgment. You have rebuked the heathen. You have destroyed the wicked. You have put out their names forever."

When he finished writing David explained to Uriah how Saul had been anointed king by Samuel. He had been chosen by lot from the son of Kish, the family of Matri, the tribe of Benjamin. But, he lost Yahweh's blessings by offering a burnt offering, when only Samuel the prophet was permitted to do so. The Israelites had been fighting the Philistines for years, and they were looking for a king who could bring peace. They thought Saul was the man, but now Samuel has anointed David.

When David finished the story, Uriah, intrigued, committed to learn more about Yahweh, this god of the Hebrews. After all, he told David, if he was to marry a Hebrew he must learn to live like a Hebrew.

"David, I give you my pledge of pledges: I will serve you with my dagger and sword until I find my family and we return to Hatusha." Uriah and David grasped each other's wrists in agreement. Maybe a God ordained bond had been made.

Uriah wondered where his mother and sister were. Someone gave him a rough map of the area. There were many small villages between Tarsus and Gibeah. They must be in one of them. When they return to Gibeah he planned to take his men through all those small villages until they find them. As soon as he found them they were going back to Hatusha to rebuild their home -- unless circumstances changed his life again. Would Bathsheba marry him? Would she go with him?

CHAPTER 10

Uriah sat under a tree reviewing the past two months of his life. Wondering about the power, that unseen essence, that overcame him at the Halys River and gave him warrior skills, he thought about this new god, Yahweh. Had Yahweh touched him? Maybe He is a true god. He fell asleep thinking about Him. The next morning he found David preparing to take his bounty to the king.

"How can I learn more about your God, Yahweh," asked Uriah.

"The best thing to do is to find the king's scribe, any day but the Sabbath, and ask him to read the scrolls to you." David suggested.

"What is the Sabbath?" Uriah asked.

David began at the beginning. He explained that Yahweh created everything in six days and rested on the seventh day, so men have to rest on the seventh day, called the Sabbath. He talked about the flood, Moses, and Abraham. Uriah commented he had heard of the flood but did not know it was worldwide. Tarsus and Hatusha are two towns started by refugees of a flood. David told of the blessing promised by Moses to those who love the Lord.

Then He told him about the commandments. Have no other gods before me. Make no graven image. Take not the name of Yahweh in vain. Keep the Sabbath holy. Honor your father and mother. Kill no one. Commit not adultery. Steal nothing. Lie not. Desire not your neighbor's wife, animals, or anything that belongs to him. Then he explained about the feasts and the sacrifices.

Uriah stated, "I believe the only thing good in life comes from virtue. Virtue comes from obeying the Laws of Nature."

David explained, "Yahweh asks for our obedience to Him. Virtue comes from obedience to the Law of Yahweh."

"Then what about all those men we just killed. Was that virtue?"

"Virtue is obedience to Yahweh. He commands us to obey our king. It is up to the king to be obedient when he gives the orders. The king gave the order. I obeyed." David was not used to being questioned like this and his voice became a little louder. This Hittite was getting under his skin.

"The way I see it, this was not an order but an offer by the king. You acted on your own for your own interests and brought us with you. It seems the king was setting you up to be killed. If the king even said it. You would risk losing your life, your men, and create six hundred widows just so you could get a wife?" Uriah asked.

"Uriah, you may serve your gods your way, but I will serve my God my way. He helped Moses kill the Egyptians, he helped me kill Goliath, and he helped me kill the others like he parted the sea for Moses. It was after I killed Goliath that King Saul took me into his home. I knew Yahweh would help me kill these Philistines. No one was at risk. None of us died did we? He is a God of war. He is the God of the Army of Israel. He cannot be defeated."

"I know very little about your God, but in Hatusha the Law of Nature says any man who sends another man into danger has made a fool of both of them -- and he has no love for either of them. King Saul has made a fool of you and you have made a fool of us. We could all have been killed. You are a fool of fools. Another Law of Nature says the triumph of the foolish is short."

"You know what do with your laws of Nature! I know Yahweh as a God of war. That is how I serve him. I know He is real because I feel his anointing when I am killing, or when I am singing to him. He has chosen me to be the next king of a united Israel. Be careful how you talk to me," David warned. "I win my queen anyway I choose."

"Careful. You may need me to help you. How do you know Yahweh has not sent me to you? Would you have survived trying to kill the Philistines if I had not arrived? Did you choose this way or did King Saul? I suppose Bathsheba is my reward for being a fool for you," Uriah snapped.

"Bathsheba? If you cross me, she could be mine and you could be dead!" David warned.

"Oh yeah! Is that how you get your women? Killing people! All you seem to think about is killing and women! The way I see it, you are certainly not obedient to your God!" Uriah felt his anger taking over. "Which of your commandments says you may kill another man to get a wife? You violated your own laws plus you violated two Laws of Nature. You killed other men so you could have wife, and you sent other men possibly to their death to kill for you."

I know Yahweh as a war god. He is the God of the army of Israel. I know He expects obedience," David concluded. "And I expect obedience! That is the two laws of my camp. If you plan to stay with me, you will follow them too."

"I will follow you only as long as I need to find my mother and sister," Uriah countered. "Then, I am gone."

"Do not expect to ever find them. Let your Law of Nature help you," David sneered. He stood to his feet with his sword in his hand and began approaching Uriah.

"What? Now you are breaking our agreement? What kind of man are you?" Uriah asked him.

"You remember Samuel has anointed me to be king after Saul. I can take your life like this." David stated as he snapped his fingers on one hand and made a threatening gesture towards Uriah with his sword.

"But you will not, not yet, because I do not have a wife for you to steal," Uriah snapped.

David faced Uriah with his sword in a challenging position. Uriah was on his feet and faced him ready for combat. It was a comical scene. Birdlike Uriah faced a strong and godlike David. Eliam thought this was Uriah's last day on earth. He would not have to give his daughter away after all. David lunged at Uriah but Uriah executed a *diving swan* so fast David dropped his sword. The *dancing eagle* put David on the ground, defenseless. Uriah looked down at David and thought of driving his dagger into David's abdomen. He thought he might kill David and become the leader of these men. Then he realized he did not want Saul's daughter.

Uriah placed the tip of his sword on David's throat, "This is a sword of swords. It will serve you until I have found my family. Then I will leave with or without your permission. But remember, when an ant is struck it bites back, and on the hand of the one who struck it."

"As you wish, anything you say!" David replied. He picked up his sword and finished gathering up his bounty to present to King Saul.

"I cannot believe this," said Abishai.

"Truth be known, Uriah is one of the people I told you about," said Ahithophel.

"Great!" said David.

"Life just got more interesting," said Joab.

CHAPTER 11

Uriah decided he would listen to the scribe someday to learn more about Yahweh. He had no other options. David did not know anything about the whereabouts of his family. The caravan from Tarsus had finally arrived but there were no Hittite women. No one seemed to remember them or knew where they were. The Law of Nature taught that men should live in peace, respect each other, and remain loyal to their leaders. David teaches Yahweh approves murder to steal a wife, sending men to danger for the sake of another man's vanity, and respecting no one. This was another situation getting out of control.

Uriah did not like feeling out of control, with no other options. When circumstances occur that force him to act a certain way, they cause anxiety and frustration. When the Achaeans came to his house to kill him, he was forced to act. He remembered that once one of his father's horses got loose and was running straight at him. He had to get out of the way but as the horse approached, he froze. At the last second he fell to the ground and the horse galloped over him. Another time his bees attacked him. He swatted at them and tried to get free but they swarmed from every direction. He got away by running from the hives and jumping into the river He still dreams about the bees. In his dreams he cannot get away, they cover his head until he cannot see. Then he wakes with a start.

This same type of fear came over him when he heard about the Achaeans. When that unseen essence told him to go back, he felt his choices slip away. His fear is that someday, someone is going to put him in a situation where he has no options, no control, and it will cost him his life, or the life of someone he loves. He already lost his father, he wondered who is next? What about his mother and Annitis? They supposedly were escorted to Gibeah, but he is not certain where they are now. He needed to know where they were. They are the only people he knew who had never failed him. His sister was his closest friend as children, and he had always been closer to his mother than his father. Now with his father dead, he felt responsible for his death. He felt he had to care for them, but he did not even know where they were. If he failed to find them, he failed as a son and a brother. He must keep looking for them.

He needed to trust every person in his life to prevent the feeling of losing control. He needed people around him who would not put him in harm's way. He knew the men who came with him from Ankara were trustworthy. He wondered about David and his men. He had pledged his support. Was it premature? Was this new god, Yahweh, leading him?

In trying to find his family he ended up with David. The only thing to do is to stay with him. If David is correct about his god, there will be a lot more fighting. Was meeting David an obstacle in the path of him finding his family? Or was finding David the stepping stone to the next phase of his life? He was having difficulty understanding his god. Do not kill unless you are killing for a wife. Confusing! Perhaps Bathsheba could explain it to him. Bathsheba! He nearly forgot, he had been promised a bride by Eliam. He must speak to him about her. He wondered when he could have her. He got up from the rock he had been sitting on to go find him.

When Uriah found Eliam he was sitting on a log and chewing on a piece of venison. "Get something to eat before it gets cold." Uriah grabbed a large piece and began eating. In between bites Uriah asked, "When do I get to have Bathsheba? You were serious were you not?"

"Let me go home first, you wait here. I will tell her the good news. Let her get used to the idea, you know. Then we'll set a date. I will come and get you," Eliam offered.

"This is not a brush off is it? I made a pledge to you which I intend to keep. I hope you keep your pledge to me," Uriah countered reaching for another piece of meat.

"Just leave it to me. You are as good as married already."

"Right, just leave it to you. No problem," Uriah stated as he thought that he just allowed another person to control part of his life.

Uriah practiced his religion of virtue. When he made a pledge, he kept it. Up until now he had been driven by trying to locate his mother and sister. It seems he would soon have another woman in his life. His father was devoted to his mother until his death, and Uriah intended to be like him. If Yahweh had a plan for him, he would have to remain faithful to those people who were close to him.

He wished the prophet would come again so he could ask him some questions. One thing that Ahithophel added to David's teaching of the Hebrew religion: the just shall live by faith. He said that Bathsheba had faith Yahweh was going to use her for some great event someday. He wondered if that was the same event God had planned for him. What does Yahweh, if he is real, have planned for him? Does the god of the Hebrews even make plans for Hittites? He wondered.

David gathered all his bounty into five borrowed ox carts and presented it to King Saul.

"Yahweh has blessed you again, David. It appears even without a jaw bone, or a slingshot, you had a formidable advantage. Well, son-in-law, you have done your part, now I will do mine. I still doubt you could kill your ten thousands. For now, you need only to marry my daughter, Michal, whom no doubt, you will". Saul was disappointed that David was still alive but he was happier that the Philistines were dead. He decided to face one problem at a time. Today a wedding, tomorrow, or another day, he must deal with David.

When David heard these words he began doing cartwheels in the street, shouting with his loudest voice, and laughing until tears flowed down his face. Michal ran from her chambers, through the garden, and jumped into David's arms. Neither could believe what they had just heard. His love gave him strength to kill for her. He was willing to die for her. Now he just wanted to live for her. She could not stop kissing him all over his face. She could not control her tears of joy, her excitement, her happiness. Saul told them to skip the one year betrothal period since they had known each other for a few years anyway, so they were married that evening. No one saw either of them for a week but everyone enjoyed the celebration too much to notice.

Sometime during the week of celebrating, David remembered that two people would enter his life that would make a significant change. Sometimes Ahithophel is not even close in his predictions so people ignore him. Was he accurate this time? Are Michal and Uriah the people?

If they are, how will they affect him? Who is the lion and who is the bear?

Upon returning to Gibeah Uriah and his men began a slow search for his family. They began in Gibeah and systematically went to every village inquiring of any Hittite women. When they heard there were Hittite women in town they went to meet each one. They would not stop until they had gone all the way back to Tarsus. If his mother and sister were here, he would find them or die trying, taking time out to be married of course. He wondered what Bathsheba looked like.

PART THREE

CHAPTER 12

"You want me to marry who?" Bathsheba yelled at Eliam. She placed her hands on her hips and glared at him.

"I told you. Uriah the Hittite."

Throwing her hands up in the air she asked, "How could you do that without even asking me? I am thirteen years old. Do you think I want to be married already?"

"Well, you were not exactly there when the thought occurred to me so I could not very well ask you!" Bathsheba could hear the frustration in his voice.

Placing the palms of her hands on her forehead then running her hands through her hair and wiping them on her apron she asked, "So you gave me away on impulse? What am I a sheep, a dog, a piece of meat, or your daughter?" Bathsheba felt her own temper rising.

"It was not on impulse, it was after killing several hundred Philistines. He is a great warrior."

"So you decided to punish me because of his crimes? You gave me a life of slavery and drudgery because of him?" Bathsheba was near tears. She turned away to conceal them.

"No, I decided to reward him for his heroism." Bathsheba heard her father getting angrier.

She turned towards Eliam and said, "Reward him! For heroism? What about rewarding me with some respect for my years of being your daughter? " She could not hold back the tears that began trickling down her cheeks. She turned away from her father again.

"I am rewarding you with a good man." Eliam explained.

"Good man! You do not even know him. Everyone is talking about him. He is a killer. You do not know me either if you think I will marry him." Bathsheba turned and glared at him so fiercely he was taken back.

"He is not a killer. He is a gifted warrior. He is a better man than what your sisters have. I do know you want a better man than they have. Right?"

"I want a wealthy man, someone who would buy me nice things, someone who would come home every night and tuck me into bed. I want a Hebrew man! Why cannot I have a Hebrew man?"

"Uriah is becoming a Hebrew. I believe he was sent here by Yahweh himself. If Yahweh had not sent him he would not be here."

"You believe that? How could you know that? Have you ever met a Hittite who told the truth? You know that is why Yahweh told Moses to kill all the Hittites when he led our people to Canaan hundreds of years ago. It looks like we missed one. Do I look that stupid?" Bathsheba stared into her father's eyes. The sarcasm in her voice was not helping her case, but it did express her true feelings. She thought she sounded just like her mother. Her mother and Eliam had just had this discussion.

"Do not get sassy with me. I am the father. What happens in this house happens because I say so. I gave my word and what I said will happen."

Bathsheba knew he was the father. He chose the groom for the bride. Period. That was their custom. That was how things happened.

"I am not being sassy, father. I am desperate. I am tired of being number seven. I never get noticed for anything because my older sisters are always in the center of attention. Can you name even one thing that I did, or that I like? Can you? I do not think so. Look at my sisters. Ester married a metal worker. Soloama married a carpenter. Jerusha married a stonemason. Sarai married a butcher. Deborah married a milkman, and Sytle married a tailor. They are all Hebrew men who come home every day to their families. They will struggle their entire lives to merely exist and then they will never be remembered ten years after they are gone. I do not want that for me. I want to be remembered. But you want me to marry a homeless warrior. A foreigner! A Hittite! Where would we live? Where would I call home? Do you want me to be lonely all the time? Do you want me to raise my children by myself? Do you want to send me away to the Hittites? Do you want me to be a young widow? Why are you doing this to me? What did I ever do to you to deserve this?" When she finished she burst into tears and tried to run from the room as she usually did when she realized she lost the argument.

Eliam grabbed her arm, "Why are you so upset about this?" His voice sounded calm again.

When she could talk Bathsheba told her father, "Since David first came to live with King Saul I wanted him to notice me. Soon after he began playing his harp for the king

I loved him. I dreamed about him. I hoped you would let me marry him."

"I never knew. Why did you not say something? You were only ten years old when he came."

"My grandfather Ahithophel is David's advisor. You are one of his warriors. It seemed to me that one of you would mention me to him. I never wanted an ordinary man. Remember grandfather saw a revelation in the stars that someone in his family would be on the throne of Israel. I could be queen. I could even be the mother of the great prophet talked about by Moses. None of my sisters have married someone in line to be king. If I became queen, or gave birth to the great prophet, people would remember me. Now you want me to marry a foreigner, a Hittite. Everyone knows Hittites are smelly, lazy, greedy, pagans, and liars. I do not want to be queen of the Hittites! You ruined my life, father! None of my dreams will ever come true because of you. I will never be queen of Israel. I will never give birth to the prophet. I will never be remembered. Instead, I will be a young widow. Who would want me after I become used baggage?" she burst into convulsive sobbing again.

"Your grandfather is always finding strange things in the stars. Do not believe any of them. And we do not know when this prophet will come. Besides, David loves Michal. They were married today. He can never be your husband."

"That cannot be true! I cannot believe it!" she cried out loud. Her tears of anger turned to tears of grief, then anger again. "Father, did you never once even suggest to David that you have another daughter? You could not mention me to a man who could be the next king of Israel, but instead you give me away to a foreigner? Is that all I am worth to you, father?"

Eliam shook his head, his eyes looking at the floor, tears welling up in his eyes. The look on his face and the turning of his head said he did not know and he did not talk to David about her.

After several moments of silence Eliam softly said. "I am sorry, but it is all set. Michal is David's wife. You will be Uriah's wife."

Bathsheba felt as though her best friend had just died. She freed herself from Eliam's hand. "Give me two months to enjoy being a single Hebrew woman, and then I will enter the one year betrothal period, but on one condition. You say he is becoming a Hebrew. Let him get circumcised before we get betrothed!"

Eliam muttered, "Oh yes. I am sure he will love to be circumcised!"

Bathsheba went into her room and lay weeping on her bed. She believed in the stars. She believed in her grandfather. She believed in the core of her soul someone in her family would become queen. None of her sisters married the right person, why should she not be the one? What more deserving person to be mother of the Prophet than the Queen of Israel? Surely her father or grandfather had mentioned her to David at least once. Why was he not interested in her? Now her father has told her she will marry a foreigner. How can marrying a foreigner help her to become Queen of Israel and give birth to the Prophet? It cannot! Her dreams were shattered. Her life was over! How could a father do that to a daughter? She must be married to a Hebrew man if she was going to achieve her dreams. She would rather never be married than to be married to a Hittite. If she was not going to become queen, she did not want to be wife of a heathen. She hummed to herself, "Man of my dreams, you never knew me. King of the land, I am a stranger. I waited for you but you did not come, I will still look for you, man of my dreams."

Then she had an idea. The question is not "Why did this happen to me?" but "How can I make what happened to me help me achieve my dreams?" If she persuaded Uriah to purchase a home near David's, he might see her. If he saw her he might like her. And everyone knows soldiers do not live long. She decided she would marry Uriah, be a good wife, but use him to gain access to David. While married to him, she would use that marriage and his position for her advantage. When he died, she might someday become the Queen of Israel if she could get the attention of the king. If the king had other wives, she'd have to deal with to that too.

She knew she was more beautiful than the average woman. If the king noticed her, he would certainly look twice, then who knows what will happen? She feared being just another slave to another man like all the other Hebrew women. When she looked at them she saw women who spent their entire lives just to have more children, men as property owners, and women as the property. That would not happen to her! Nothing in the commandments says a woman must serve a man. If she had to serve one, it would be one who could give her comfort, prestige, and power. With those thoughts, she fell asleep again.

CHAPTER 13

Eliam rose early the next morning and began a leisure trip back to the cave. En route he rehearsed his conversation with Bathsheba. He did not know her feelings for David, nor did he know that she believed the stories of her grandfather. How could he, he was never home? Now the damage had been done. He ruined her dreams. He thought of telling David about her feelings but what a mess that would be. He would have to go back on his word to Uriah in spite of Uriah's pledge. David could outright accept Bathsheba and marry her and Michal. That would cause problems between Michal and David, and Michal and Bathsheba. The potential problems it would cause were not worth it.

They would be betrothed in two months. Where would they live? She cannot follow him to the cave. If Uriah is not able to find a house for them, perhaps they could live with him. How would my wife like that he thought. She is already upset over her daughter marrying a heathen. How do I dare ask him to live with us? No! Maybe he will not want to get circumcised. That would solve the whole problem. Bathsheba was right. I do not know Uriah either. I met him a few days ago. He is a warrior and a leader. He said he came here looking for his mother and sister. After she found out about Uriah, she threatened to sell the house and move to Egypt while he was gone. She told him to go find Uriah's family and send him home. He asked himself whether he would even have a home to go to. If he was the head of the family, why did he feel like the tail? Taking a man's anger and guiding it to achieve what the woman wanted is an art, and Eliam thought his wife must be the master artist. Pretty bad when one of David's mighty men cannot even control his own home! "When did I lose control?" he thought. "It was the night Ahithophel and her father got drunk and pledged us to each other. I never had control since."

Uriah had asked Eliam to check with the chief of servants for the king to see whether he had seen Ravia and Annitis. The chief did not know where they were. He had heard a caravan had stopped at Jabeth-Gilead with some travelers including some Hittite women. He did not know whether they were who he was looking for. Uriah would be happy to hear that his family may have been found. But he would certainly not be happy that he has to get circumcised. If he is looking for a mother and a sister, he may have found them and a wife too.

The twelve tribes still did not control all the land Yahweh had promised them. Was Uriah sent to help us control that land? Eliam decided that if Uriah needed help to accomplish his mission, he would obey his wife and encourage all of David's men to join in. It is the least he could do for a soon to be future son-in-law.

The hot afternoon sun reflecting from the sandy soil, coupled with the windblown grains of sand which seemed to penetrate even his layered clothing was dissolving

Eliam's strength. He found a shrub that provided both shade and shelter and stopped for a minute to rest. Taking a drink from his water skin, wiping his brow with the back of his hand, he looked back towards home. Maybe he should give up on this idea of helping David and just go back home. He had been married for thirty-five years and was not as young as he used to be. Who knew where all this adventure would lead? If the king found out who was following David, he would have him arrested, or worse.

He raised his eyes to something he saw moving about a mile behind him. He waited and watched. Soon he could tell it was a person traveling alone. He thought it might be someone wanting to join David and he would travel with him, so he waited a little longer. About a half mile away he could see that it was a woman. What woman would travel alone out here in this wilderness? Doesn't she realize the danger? As she came nearer he could not believe his eyes. He thought he recognized the red head scarf with the embroidered grape vines and grape clusters all around the edges and the purple frills the same color as the grapes. Was he hallucinating because of the thoughts he had been having for the past hour? But then he heard Bathsheba say, "Thank you father for waiting for me. It is dangerous for a woman to be alone out here."

Eliam asked Bathsheba, "What are you doing out here? You might have been killed!"

"I know father, but I was thinking about our conversation. You are right. You are my father and I should do as you wish. I will be Uriah's wife. I hoped I would have a chance to meet him, at least." She told him. "So I tried to catch up with you, and here I am."

"You are also right. I do not know you as well as I should. Maybe we could begin to know each other. We can talk as we ride. We still have a few miles to go to arrive at the cave." Eliam, unaware of why Bathsheba had changed her mind, felt good inside now that his daughter had agreed to marry Uriah.

Eliam said, "The news that Uriah the Hittite was in the Cave of Adullam has brought men seeking adventure, refuge, and companions, from all over Canaan. Women come seeking men. They all come to the cave. There may be a lot of people when we get there."

"As long as you are there, I will be alright, father," said Bathsheba.

Ravia had not had time to mourn her husband, did not even bury him before she was thrust into this new life. Her son was beginning to be a legend. She wondered whether he would ever find her, or would she die first. She wondered what would happen to Annitis. She began making a few friends and was learning her new job. Even though she began by being the carrier of the garbage, she was pleased to be working. Someone had to carry the garbage out to the burn pile every day, and this was her job. Annitis was responsible for the clean floor. She collected the garbage dropped by the cooks and gave it to her mother. She dreamed of being cook someday. But in Gibeah only men could be cooks. Women cleaned floors, washed utensils, carried garbage, and brought in wood for the oven. She and Annitis had made friends with some of the other kitchen workers. In a few days they were going together to the market. The cook asked them to buy his weekly supply of vegetables. She was looking forward to shopping here. She wondered whether they had kale.

Soon after his arrival Eliam went to David to let him know he was back. When David met Bathsheba he asked

Eliam, "Who is this beautiful woman? Where have you been hiding her?"

"This is my daughter, Bathsheba, the one I promised to Uriah to wed when he helped us against the Philistines," Eliam told him.

"If you had told me about her earlier, you could have been my father-in-law instead of the king being my father-in-law. Then I would not have spears thrown at me."

Eliam laughed, "Life would be boring with me as a father-in-law."

Bathsheba pretended to blush as she thought I knew he would like me. At least now I've met him and he knows who I am.

Eliam looked at his daughter. She stood there in her flowing woolen gown with black, taupe, and crimson stripes. Gold bracelets accentuated her slim wrists. Her scarf exposed a golden, jeweled headband in her glossy hair. Her cheeks seemed to flush and her almond eyes sparkled. Her lips revealed a coy, teasing smile. David thought, "Love runs after her like puppies." Everyone present exchanged looks, feeling the awkward silence, but no one said anything.

Eliam, sensing the attraction David had for Bathsheba and knowing her feelings about him said, "She came here to meet Uriah. She wanted to meet him before she became his wife. You have to be careful about blind marriages. Look what happened to Joseph."

Ahithophel said, "Bathsheba, I am surprised you would agree to be Uriah's wife. Truth be known, I am even more surprised you would come out here."

"Well, grandfather, a woman has to do what a woman has to do."

Not certain what she meant, he said, "Truth be known, that is true."

Eliam found Uriah practicing his fighting movements and Uriah told him about his experience in trying to find his mother and sister. He wondered whether Eliam might have any ideas where to look. Eliam said he did not but to keep looking. Then he told him, "Uriah, I talked with Bathsheba. She agreed to marry you. You will become betrothed in two months. First she wanted to meet you. She thinks you are a killer. It will take a little time. She needs to get to know you."

"It is strange, I never thought of myself as a killer. I was a bee keeper and did not even kill my bees when they stung me. I may be a warrior, but I am not a killer. Right now I am trying to figure out my plans for the rest of my life. Bathsheba will be my wife. I am devoted to her, of course, but I decided Yahweh will be my God."

"Speaking of Yahweh, you know all Hebrew men are circumcised. This is part of the covenant Yahweh made with Moses. Bathsheba insists that if you are going to be her husband, you must be circumcised."

"What? Circumcising a bunch of dead Philistines so David could have a wife is a lot different than getting circumcised so I can have a wife. You did not tell me that was part of the deal. I have not even seen her. No way will I consent to that."

"I did not know she would be so obstinate. It was her idea. It is part of becoming one of our people. If you are not interested, I can call it off. You do not have to go through with this." Eliam was desperately looking for a way to get out of trouble with his wife. "You can announce the betrothal and you can wait a year as per our custom or you can call it off. Two months to wait for the betrothal is really a good offer. It is your call."

"What other part of the deal will be changed or added before then?"

"I do not know. Look at it this way. We have no betrothal. In fact, we have not even made an agreement yet. You can still walk away."

"Let me talk with her, and then I will let you know."

Eliam found Bathsheba and introduced her to Uriah. Then he went to check on the men, leaving her and Uriah alone.

Uriah, trying to assume control of his situation began the conversation, "Your father told me you think I am a killer."

"Your reputation is well known throughout Israel."

"He also said you would be my wife if I waited two months and was circumcised before the betrothal."

"Yes, that is true. Hebrew men must do that. I want a husband who shares my religion."

Uriah could see her dark eyes, her high cheeks and her full lips. He saw the dimples on both sides of her mouth and after getting his first full look at her, his heart melted. He lost his breath, and he could not believe someone like her was even talking to him. He gushed, "Bathsheba, you are lovely. I would give my right arm to have you for my wife. Getting circumcised is something else. But I have committed my faith to your religion."

"What do you even know about my religion?" as she threw her arms upward in front of her palms upward.

"I already know about the patriarchs, the commandments, the sacrifices and the feasts, but I would like to learn more."

"What makes you so special that I would marry you and not one of the Hebrew men?" she asked almost with cynicism as she turned and took a few steps away from him. She thought she would play him like her mother plays with her father.

"I do not know. I know I am not a Hebrew man, but a foreigner. That is why I must serve Yahweh. I was nobody, yet I believe he chose me. All men are nobodies, until God chooses them. How else would I be here?"

"That is what I am trying to determine for myself."

"Hittites have many gods but none of them ever do anything for anyone. I know Yahweh is real. I need to learn what I am to do to serve him."

"Do you think I am part of his will for you?" she teased.

"I do not know whether you or David, or your father or anyone else is part of the plan. I only know I am here. I do believe we would not be talking if it was not part of some grand plan. So you must be included in Yahweh's plan for me. I have heard that Adam and Enoch walked with God, and that Job and Noah were considered righteous men. I want to walk with God and be considered as righteous as them." He tried to explain.

"How do you think you can be righteous when you have killed so many men?"

"I have become a skilled warrior. I think it may be a gift from Yahweh actually. Warriors kill people in wars. I would never kill someone in anger. Righteousness is a condition of the heart. I do not kill out of anger, only out of my duty as a soldier. But to serve you, or David, or Joab I would walk alone into a score of men and kill all of them."

She laughed at that comment, turned back to him and placed both her hands on his chest, "How do you know this is not some wild dream? Your special skills, I mean."

"No dream could give me the skills I have. I am an expert in movements and maneuvers that I never even heard of before. I am more than I ever could have become by myself. I must learn more of Yahweh. To know him is to know my destiny. I believe that you, David, and Joab all have some important role to play in his plan for my life. I am on quest to find his will for me."

"In other words, you think Yahweh wants you to be my husband?"

Uriah felt as though his heart would burst it was beating so fast," Yes I do. I would be as faithful to you as I am to Him. I would live my life to make you happy. Whether I live a few more months, or many more years, I would be devoted to you as long as I live. Hearts are not made to break, and I will never break yours." He said it with tears in his eyes.

"Why should I believe that?"

"I give you my word of words. I am a faithful person." Uriah stated.

"But how can you take care of me, what did you do before you became a killer?" She walked over to a large rock and sat down, motioning for him to sit next to her.

"I am a warrior, not a killer. Back in Hatusha I was a bee keeper. My bees made honey. Every year, before the snows fell and the day had equal amounts of sunlight and darkness, the fall equinox, we had a celebration to thank Cybele for a good year. We mixed cooked figs with honey and made a sweet sauce. Then we would bake oat cakes and put the sauce on the cakes. We would eat them as we lit the evening candles as a token of our thanks to Cybele. Being a bee keeper made me a vital part of our religious celebrations. It provided a regular income. I could be a bee keeper again." Uriah explained.

"That is an interesting custom. What other custom does your religion have?"

"Well, that is about it, except for the celebration when the snow has melted. Again, on the day when the sunlight and darkness are equal, the spring equinox, we would place pieces of sheep and onions on a shish kabob and cook them. Then before we ate it we would dip it in horseradish and sprinkle it with some olive oil. This was to ask Cybele for a prosperous harvest in the coming warm weather. Queen Puduhepa, wife of King Hattushilish III, of the Hittite Empire was the first to practice this about five hundred years ago and we have done it ever since." Uriah explained.

"Those are interesting customs. They sound similar to our celebrations of the feasts of trumpets and passover which occur during those same times of the year."

"Is that a fact? We have something in common already."

"You are interesting. No. You are an enigma: not like other men. You are not like what I expected you to be."

Uriah laughed and asked, "What do you mean?"

"You seem to be genuine, not a phony. Kind, not a killer. I feel safe in asking whether you want me or are you just trying to keep your bargain with my father?"

Uriah took her hands in his, "I want you. But I need to know before I go through this circumcision and life commitment to you, that you feel the same about me."

"I understand."

"Will you be faithful to me as long as you are alive?"

"You really get down to business," Bathsheba tried to walk away but Uriah held onto her hands.

"Will you stay with me as I serve Yahweh in the plans he has for me? Will you teach me more about him?"

"If we marry your plans will be my plans."

"My parents were married for twenty years until my father was killed. I want to be with you longer than that. But if that is not the sincere desire of your heart, tell me now and we can call off everything."

"I do not think we have to call off anything."

"Am I part of your dreams? I know your father arranged this, but say the word, and we do not have to go through with it."

"We have a saying that men are not to like, men are to have. It may take a little while for me to like you, but someone with your compassion and sincerity is a blessing every woman would want to have. Who could say no to an offer like that? If you want me enough to go through all this, I am sure I can make you happy."

"But, what are your dreams?"

"What are my dreams? Right now my dream is to be your wife." She smiled a deep smile. It was the first time he ever saw her smile like that.

Before he knew it he was saying, "I will tell your father we have an agreement." Then he thought, when did I lose control of that conversation?

Paltiel took Michal by her left elbow and forced her into his home. She threw herself into a chair and refused to talk to him. Paltiel yelled," You are my wife. You will act like my wife. I bought you, and you were not cheap. Now you will do as I want. Get over this attitude. It is you and me together forever, or until I divorce you. That will be never because I do not want your father to kill me."

Michal picked up a vase and threw it at Paltiel but he ducked and the vase broke when it hit the wall." I might kill you myself. Yahweh might kill you. I am already married. If you touch me you are breaking God's laws. God may kill you himself! You cannot have me. I love my husband. I hate you!" Michal shouted at him. She threw a knife at him but he dodged out of the way. "If God does not kill you, and if I do not kill you, when David finds out where I am he will kill you for sure."

Paltiel tried to approach her, "Hah! Saul will kill David before he finds me. Get used to it. Your man is as good as dead."

She tipped the table over between them and ran behind it, "You get used to the idea that I may have to do some things I despise in order to obey our law, but I will never love you. I will be the first to dance on your grave. That is the only promise and commitment I make to you. I will dance on your grave! You heathen!"

Paltiel grabbed her by her wrist, twisted her arm behind her back and forced her into his bed while Michal screamed and fought until she was exhausted.

PART FOUR

CHAPTER 14

Ravia and Annitis had been looking forward to this day for a couple of weeks. This would be the first time they joined some other kitchen workers and went shopping with a list of things the innkeeper ordered. The market was a large square in the center of the town where all the vendors set up and sold their wares. Fruit, vegetables, jewelry, fish, lamb, beef, beverages, bread, pottery, clothing, baskets, and many other things were available for sale. All the vendors were shouting out their wares to passersby and whoever was listening. The smell was nauseating, the din deafening, and the crowd was bustling; much different than the market in Hatusha.

As they shopped they shared stories and gossip. It seemed the king's daughter Michal married a man named David who used to be a shepherd, poor girl. A bunch of homeless derelicts were gathering at some cave outside of Gibeah. That's a good place for them! A man named Uriah had a reputation for killing Philistines but no one knew where he was staying. Saul was planning to raise taxes again to pay for his army. Ravia and Annitis wondered what happened to the bee keeper. That could not be their Uriah, what reason would he have to kill Philistines?

They stopped at the fruit market and bought some delicious citrus fruit, date figs, grapes, olives and olive oil. The green grocer had a special offer on barley grain and corn flower.

"God give us favor mother, have you ever seen a market like this before? Asked Annitis.

"No, never, not in Hatusha or anywhere else I have been."

"This is exciting, right?"

"The most excitement since we left Hatusha. I love it. I am glad we got to come today."

"Me too! I love the gossip we are hearing."

They purchased all the produce the innkeeper needed and decided to go to the fish vendor next, but first they stopped for a beverage of fruit juice. All of a sudden some men entered the market from out of nowhere, wearing hoods, carrying spears, and shouting, "You come with us and no one will be harmed." Then it seemed as though there were spears pointing at them and a handful of other shoppers from everywhere.

Ravia asked. "Is something wrong?"

"If you come with us and do as we say there will be nothing wrong," they replied. Ravia and Annitis and the other women who were with them were taken around the corner where mule carts were waiting. They complied with the order to get on.

Annitis replied, "May the gods give us favor. Where are you taking us?"

"Nahash, king of the Ammonites wants to publicly embarrass King Saul. We are taking you to Ammon until King Saul pays your ransom. We are laying siege on this city. You can thank your gods you will not be part of the siege. You will be hostages instead."

"May the gods give us favor. Hostages? What for would the king pay ransom for a bunch of kitchen workers?" replied Annitis.

When the cart began moving Ravia could see there were only six men guarding as many carts which held five hostages each. She thought that it had seemed like more than that when they stormed the market. They looked dangerous, with bows on their shoulders and spears at the ready. Ravia said," I never knew riding in a mule cart could be so uncomfortable. The cords that bind us do not feel good either. Where was Uriah when she needed him?"

"How far is it to Ammon?"

Ravia spoke softly to Annitis, "Pray that Uriah finds us."

"I have been praying, mother." replied Annitis. "But how is he even going to know where we are? I do not even know where we are or where we are going," said Annitis.

"I suppose one of our gods will have to tell him somehow."

"I have never even heard of the Ammonites. Now I hate them."

"Their king is trying to embarrass the king of Israel by kidnapping some people from Jabeth-Gilead and laying siege to the town. I suppose that makes sense to someone, not to me."

"Maybe the God of the Hebrews will send Uriah to rescue us."

"May the gods give us favor. Those types of things only happen in fairy tales mother."

"Annitis keep watching where we are going. Remember anything that will help us return if we can escape."

“Mother, how are we going to escape? Our hands are bound behind our backs and our feet are bound to each other? Besides, these soldiers ride in front and behind us.”

“I do not know how we will escape, but if we wait to be rescued, we may become married to an Ammonite first.”

“May the gods give us favor. I do not see how we can escape, but the gods must know a way,” Annitis replied.

“Maybe the guards will tell us how to get back, or at least free our hands, if we talk to them Annitis.”

“How come?”

“Listen Annitis, one thing you need to learn about men is they like to talk to women. They will tell us their entire life story if they think we are listening, especially if they think we like them. Get one’s attention and begin talking to him. Make him like you.” Then to one of the guards she called out,” Soldier, can I ask you where you come from? Did I tell you that you have a nice smile behind that spear?”

“Is that so?” asked the guard as he moved his horse to be near them.

“That is true. You cannot be a very bad person to have a smile like that,” Annitis said.

“That is true also. I am really a nice person.”

“You know these ropes seriously hurt my wrists. I promise to not escape if you loosen them a bit.”

“I will make a deal with you. I will loosen your ropes if you tell me why you think I am a nice person.”

“I can see the way you talk, smile and carry yourself, like a professional who is really kind in side but knows he has a job to do. You are just doing yours. Right?

“You are so right. It is like you have known me forever. And we just met. Amazing is it not?”

“Not if you believe the gods can give you favor. They probably arranged this meeting. Do you think so?”

"I know so. I will tell you what I will do because you are right, the gods did arrange this, for both of us. I will leave your door unlocked. When you leave meet me at the fork in the road, and I will escort you to safety."

"What about these three other women on our cart?" asked Annitis.

"I will free them also, if you promise to come with me after you escape."

"We promise."

"Okay. I will leave your lock opened after the fifth night here. I will hide behind a tree along the road you will be traveling. I will join you then."

"May the gods give us favor," said Annitis. "The fifth night?"

"How could Nahash have the audacity to kidnap people from Israel and demand ransom? Who does he think I am? I will give him ransom alright, but not the ransom he wanted!" Saul said to his son Jonathan. He sent word out to all the tribes of Israel for help. When twenty thousand men responded the king gave David and Abner orders to attack the Ammonites, "Divide the men into three divisions, David, you lead one, Jonathan, you lead one and Abner, you lead one. Take six thousand men in each division, free the hostages, and bring them back here to Gibeah. I will take the rest of the men and break the siege."

David had left one of his officers in charge at the cave while he was in town. He rode back to tell them about the change in plans. Arriving at the cave David told them that he had been ordered by King Saul to fight the Ammonites to return some hostages from King Nahash. Joab asked if they could go with him. Uriah, Abishai, and Asahel went with him. David had told his soldiers they would set up a rally point outside the eastern gate of Jericho, near a large sycamore tree. Wait there until he arrives.

"Uriah, I heard a caravan stopped at Jabeth-Gilead about a couple of months ago. That could have been the caravan your family was in. We are going to Jabeth-Gilead now. When we break the siege and free the town, you may look for your mother and sister," said David.

"Great. I will. What if they are among the hostages?"

"You can look to see if they are there when we free them."

The night sky was just beginning to turn pink on the horizon as Ravia and Annitis approached the door to the building in which they were being held. The guard said he would leave the door unlocked for them on the fifth day if they would meet him when they escaped. Today is the fifth day. Ravia did not want to drag along a man but it was the only way he would agree to letting them escape. They found the door unlocked and slipped through it. Moving slowly through the town they were able to use the concealment of other buildings to evade notice. After what seemed hours but was merely a few minutes, they were out of town. Without making a sound they took the road west as the guard instructed; the road that would lead them to Jericho.

They were not surprised when a man came from behind a tree and greeted them. It was the guard who had helped them. He told them that when his commander found out they had escaped, his life would be over. The best thing for him to do was to desert the army and help them. After several hours they arrived outside the gate of Jericho, under a sycamore tree. Once outside Jericho the three other women left Ravia and Annitis with the guard.

The escaped guard told them they would be safe once inside the gate. If they stayed in Jericho a few days they would be able to find a caravan going to Gibeah. He would travel with them for their safety. Upon entering Jericho they blended in with other travelers, begged for food, and waited. While they were waiting for a caravan someone shouted that Saul's army was headed towards Ammon and was going through Jericho.

When he heard the news about Saul's army the soldier told Ravia he was going to try to join Saul. It was his best hope. If he could join with Saul, he would not be killed by Nahash. Ravia asked him to try to get one of the officers to come for them. She believed her son might be with the army and she would be able to find him. The soldier agreed.

When David arrived in Jericho they planned their marching orders for the attack. The Ammonite guard entered David's camp explaining he was a deserter from Nahash. He could lead them to the hostages and the main barracks of the army. He could describe how the city was defended and where he could find Nahash. The soldier said he had two women who were trying to meet King Saul and wanted to leave with them when they returned to Gibeah. They had been hostages but had escaped. David did not think to ask him if they were Hittite women.

At sunrise the next day the three divisions charged from three directions, south, north, and west. David did not attack from the east because he did not want the sunrise to blind the Ammonites. He wanted them to see him coming.

He wanted them to feel terror before they felt death. Without warning they attacked so fast no one could escape and no one could mount a defense. Joab found King Nahash still in bed with one of his wives. "King Saul wants you!" he shouted as thousands of men were sacking the town. He shouted," You steal from God's people and you receive God's wrath. Here is some of His wrath!" Buildings were set on fire, men were killed, and widows collected for slaves. Uriah learned where the hostages were being held, and his men took apart the buildings board by board, and brick by brick. He did not know he had missed his family by only a day.

In the midst of the bedlam, with hostages being set free and praising Yahweh, Ammonites being killed, horses neighing, men groaning, women and children crying, officers shouting, and the smell of smoke, blood, perspiration, and fear filling the air, Uriah began tingling from scalp to toe, the hair on his arms stood up. Uriah, awed by this experience, thought that a few months ago he would have shuddered at the thought of battle, but now he relished it! He knew he was born for this.

Joab brought Nahash, bound, gagged, and still in his night clothes to David as ordered. "King Nahash, I have been anointed to become King of Israel after King Saul. You will have to do business with me in the future. I am giving you a choice. Either you can agree today to live in peace with Israel and I will not destroy your kingdom, or you can die today. By the way, if you die, so does every male in your kingdom. Which do you prefer?"

"You do not leave me much of a choice. I will live in peace with Israel. I will recognize you as the only king in Israel." David, happy that he had peace with the Ammonites -- at least for now, allowed King Nahash to leave. He ordered the men to stop their killing and sacking of the town.

David had forgotten about the man who told him about the two women until he found him dead, an Ammonite arrow through his heart. He could not send anyone to town to look for two women, not knowing who they were or where they were. He forgot about them.

When they returned to Jabeth-Gilead, Uriah spent two days looking for his mother and sister until he met a man that said he thought he saw them working at the inn. With his heart pounding with excitement Uriah hurried to the inn. But the inn keeper said he had two Hittite women but they were some of the hostages taken by the Ammonites. Uriah knew they were not among the people he set free. They were not found among the dead. No one recalled seeing them. After three days of searching everywhere in town he decided to return to the Ammonites and ask them They told him they had held them but they should have been freed with the rest of them. Where could they be? He did not know about the deserter.

CHAPTER 15

The Ammonite guard was right. Within three days they heard of a caravan going to Gibeah. They begged the caravan leader to allow them to travel with them and he agreed. They could not believe their good fortune. Two days later the caravan left Jericho.

Meanwhile, still puzzled about what could have happened to his mother and sister, Uriah and his men left David to look for them. Uriah reasoned that if they were went shopping for the innkeeper then one of two things happened. Either they were captured or they were not. If they were captured they would have been among the freed hostages unless they found a way to escape. So they were either still at Jabeth-Gilead in which case they may have returned to the inn, or they were hostages and escaped. If that was true, they could be anywhere.

He began his search at the inn. "Two Hittite women worked here a few weeks ago, is that correct?" asked Uriah.

"Yes, that is true. But they went to the market for me and were taken by the Ammonites. I have not seen them since then. Thankfully King Saul broke the siege and set us free," said the innkeeper.

"Yes, thankfully," said Uriah. "They have not returned. You said."

"No one has seen them. But three of my other kitchen workers said they heard the two women make a deal with a guard."

"Deal? What kind of deal?

"He would leave the door to their building unlocked if they let him go with them. Apparently he did and they did. All five of them escaped. The two you are looking for are not here but the other three women are."

"So you are saying they were captured but may have escaped and could be traveling with an Ammonite soldier?

"That is what I am saying."

"Great, They could be anywhere from here to Ammon. They could still be there if the guard took them to his home."

Uriah decided to go to Jericho again, and look there. When they arrived at Jericho, there were so many travelers, shoppers, and people in the inns that Uriah knew he was looking for one grain of wheat among a bushel of tares. After three days of asking every innkeeper, caravan leader, street vendor, he gave up. No one had seen two Hittite women possibly traveling with an Ammonite soldier. Uriah decided to go back to Nahash.

In Ammon, the king allowed Uriah to talk to him. "King Nahash, I come looking for my mother and sister. They were among the people you took from Jabeth-Gilead. I know this because they worked for an innkeeper who had others of his staff captured also. He told me they had been taken."

"What can I do to help?"

"I heard a rumor that maybe one of your guards arranged for them to escape if they would let him travel with them. I wondered if you had any deserters or anyone recently discharged who could have done that."

"Nonsense! None of my men would help a hostage. But we did kill one man who was a defector to King Saul's army. We killed him as soon as we found him."

"So you have no idea where these women could be?"

"No idea," he said. "Did you check among the hostages?"

"They were not there."

"Then we did not have them."

"Thank you for your time." said Uriah. He decided to take his men back to the cave of Adullam and wait for further news.

David played his harp, expertly without missing a note, softly as to a sleeping child, lovingly as to his wife; he played as he had never played before. Michal was sitting at his feet, her brother Jonathan was sitting next to her, both enraptured by his music. Living in the King's house, married to the woman he loved who just happened to be the king's daughter, and best friends with the king's son, created a sense of awe in David's heart. He could not believe where he was. He was not only the king's son-in-law, but one of his leaders of a thousand men. He had returned safely from the Ammonites and was handsomely rewarded. The siege was broken and His men returned to the cave. Thinking of his years as a shepherd, he sang as he played: "The Lord is my shepherd, I shall not want. He makes me to lie down in green pastures. He leads me beside the still waters. He restores my soul. He leads me in the paths of righteousness for his name's sake. Even though I walk through the valley of the shadow of death, I will fear no evil, because you are with me, your rod and your staff they comfort me. You prepare a table before me in the presence of my enemies, you anoint my head with oil, and my cup runs over. Surely goodness and mercy will follow me all the days of my life, and I will dwell in the house of the Lord forever." He looked at Michal and added, "I love you, and may you dwell in my house forever."

Michal admired her husband and felt secure in his presence. Happy she actually married the man she loved. She could not stop looking at him all the time. He was a dream come true: strong, handsome, poetic, musical, and a soldier -- he could protect her, sing to her, and care for her. He loved her too or he would not have risked his life for her. More than anything else she desired to be near her husband. The past month was like a dream an angel had bestowed upon her. No, it was a dream of dreams.

No angel could love like she loved, dream as she dreamed, dance in her spirit as she danced, or soar with the eagles as she was soaring. She knew she would do anything he asked, even if it meant leaving her father and brother and starting over in some heathen country. If he took her to a castle or a cave, it did not matter as long as they were together. Even if she had to take sides against her father, it did not matter.

Without warning or provocation, Saul became enraged and threw his spear at David. Michal screamed and David jumped out of the way. Saul had watched his children fawn over this shepherd who had earned their love, and jealousy overcame him. Missing with the spear he lunged toward David with a knife only missing because Jonathan dove in front of him causing him to fall onto his knees. Jonathan prevented Saul from pursuing as David and Michal fled from the house. They ran to their home as fast as they could and bolted all the doors once they were inside. Saul sent a squad of soldiers with orders to kill his son-in-law as soon as he came out of the house.

Michal asked, "Are you hurt?"

"No. What has come over your father?" David shouted, "He tried to kill me!"

"I do not know. I have never seen him like this. You have to leave here or he will kill you." She shouted.

"You are right about that. Come with me now."

"I will only slow you down and get you killed. Send for me in a few days. Maybe he will change his mind by then. Here, let me help you out the window."

As she lowered the rope for him she whispered, "I love you. I will wait for you." Then she blew him a kiss with her hand.

When David placed his feet on the ground she saw him begin running for his life and heard him say, "I will go back to the cave. I will take a roundabout route to get there in case they follow me."

Meanwhile, Michal took one of the household idols, put it on David's pillow, and made the bed to look as though David was asleep. The next morning when Saul came she tried to pretend David was sick. Saul pulled back the blankets and when he discovered David missing, he had Michal arrested.

David had arrived safely back at the cave unaware of what happened to Michal. He told his men how the king had behaved. No one could imagine the king trying to kill his own son-in-law – especially after he had just freed the hostages. Several of the men wanted to mount up and attack the king as soon as they heard it. Ahithophel warned against the foolish act by telling them they could not kill the Lord's anointed without the Lord becoming angry and doing something worse to them. David gave instructions to Joab. "Go into town and send out word. Anyone who is distressed, in debt to the king, or homeless can find shelter here in this cave. I am now a refugee, and will provide refuge to all. Go to King Saul and tell him to give my wife to you, and then bring her to me. Take as many men as you need. Send some men to find Samuel the prophet and beg him to come here. I need some advice from Yahweh."

David knew he had done nothing to the king to deserve treatment like this. I was not David's fault that Michal and Jonathon loved him. He had never spoken ill about the king. Yahweh's blessings were removed because of the king's own disobedience. There is that word again, obedience. David had said that obedience was a virtue. What was does Yahweh want now? Obedience! Obedience to what, which law? Love your neighbor as yourself? Was Saul really his neighbor? No! He was not a friend, he was a relative.

Uriah would obey the Law of Nature. It would be easy for him. What would the Law of Nature say about this? No one should kill the anointed king or risk being killed himself. He knew he had better prepare to move because the king would surely come after him. As soon as he had Michal with him, he would leave.

The next morning Eliam circumcised Uriah, making certain Uriah drank a whole wine skin to ease the pain before he started. His admiration grew deeper for a man who would do this for his daughter. Yesterday he had been talking with Uriah about how he ever got into this situation. Uriah told him that after the Achaeans attacked Hatusha he started to flee when he felt an overpowering essence within him. He knew he had to go back and help defend the town. He would have stayed in Hatusha to help rebuild the town, except his sister and mother had gone to Tarsus, he had promised to meet them there, so he left to join them. Chance caused him to find David and Eliam. At that time Uriah trusted that Nature was leading him so he stayed. Uriah told him that now it may be Yahweh who had been directing his steps all the time.

Eliam marveled that he had never seen a man with so much faith, so much respect for his elders, and so willing to serve his leaders. He had made a pledge to Eliam and would keep it, even if it meant circumcision. Uriah made a pledge to Yahweh and Eliam knew he would keep it even if it meant death. He has the appearance of a boy, but the heart of a man. This man would be a good husband for his daughter, whether she knew it or not. He smiled at his good fortune to find a man like that for his youngest daughter.

His thoughts drifted to his other daughters. The husband of his second daughter decided to stop serving Yahweh and began worshipping Baal. He forsook all the teachings of his youth and forced his daughter to follow him. Neither of them is serving Yahweh and none of their children even know who He is. His third daughter married a man who serves Yahweh but follows the teachings of Rabbi Mordica who teaches that is it okay to work on the Sabbath and eat swine. How blasphemous can you get? Why cannot children just do what they are taught? Why do girls have to marry men who drag them away from the teachings or their fathers? His fourth daughter began worshipping the Ammonite god Molech and had her first child burned in the

Valley of Hinom. His sixth daughter was the biggest problem. She conceived before she was even betrothed! What a scandal that was! Everyone in town wanted to stone her, but Eliam intervened and stopped them. Before long the man involved repented for what he had done and agreed to marry her. The man's family claimed he had become a wolf, totally disowned him, and never allowed him back into their home again. Eliam did not know where they were living. How could any man disown his children?

Eliam smiled. Children are so sweet and precious when they are little. They cause parents to pray every day for Yahweh's blessings of prosperity, happiness, and the right spouse. Eliam wished he could pour his knowledge and values into their hearts. He wished he could pour Yahweh's best for his daughters into their lives. It was hard to watch his children slip away from Yahweh in their own way. How many nights had he spent praying for them? How much had he sacrificed for them? How could they have done these things? Only his first and fifth daughters are serving Yahweh according to his teachings. He felt the urge to shout to Yahweh and ask Him why. What had he done wrong? Then he remembered, no one is totally righteous, not his children, not even himself. At least that is what a wise man wrote. It seems to be true. Thanks to Yahweh that Bathsheba at least has a man who wants to serve Him.

That afternoon Joab returned to the cave without Michal. David, perplexed and annoyed asked, "Where is Michal? Did I not send you to get her for me? Where is she?"

"King Saul claimed that since you left against his will and without her that you had divorced her. He gave her to someone else." Joab reported.

"He did what? He cannot give away my wife! Get our men together. We are going to pay the king a visit!"

"How do you think you can do anything to him? Did you not say he was the Lord's anointed king? You want to be cursed for the rest of your life? "

"Find her! I will kill the man who has her!" David needed a release valve for his anger.

"Why are you going to kill someone else for what the king did?"

Joab knew he was correct but he also knew David did not want to hear what was right; he wanted to hear his wife.

David cried out to God, "How long will you forget me, Lord, forever? How long will you hide your face from me? How long will I have sorrow in my heart daily? How long will my enemy be exalted over me? Consider me and hear me!" Then he stormed off. Joab observed that David spoke to no one the rest of the day.

Joab turned to Uriah and warned him," If your family is working for King Saul and he finds out you are helping David, they could be in danger."

"I know. You are right. It could be bad for them. Is there any way to get information about them?"

"I will keep contacting my sources, but . . . you know, new workers come and go so fast. Most do not even talk about them."

CHAPTER 16

After three days of waiting in Jericho for a man who did not return, Ravia found a caravan en route to Egypt by way of Gibeah. Annitis told her mother the gods must have found favor with them because they escaped the Ammonites just before a horrible battle had been fought there. King Saul's army had killed several thousand people and now they had found this caravan going through Gibeah. They still maintained their original plan to try to work for King Saul until Uriah found them.

The next day Samuel arrived at the cave. The number of men was steadily increasing by four or five a day. At last count there were nearly four hundred men who had joined them. Samuel made his way through all the men and found David sulking. "David, do not be so sorrowful? Your fame is wide-spread. You will be the next king. Rejoice."

"Samuel, Saul is trying to kill me. Not only that but He gave away my wife to another man. I want to make him pay. What do you say?"

"You know you will be the next king. But now Saul is still king and you are considered by him to be an outlaw. If you do the evil things that are in your heart the people will not support you as the next king. Let Yahweh take care of Saul for you."

"I killed six hundred men to have her. Why cannot I kill one more to keep her?"

"You know that you would personally kill anyone who harmed the king. You cannot do what you would punish someone else for doing."

"You are right, of course. How can God allow this to happen?"

"God gives men the right to make their own choices. The events of daily living are the combination of all the choices of men interacting with each other, some good, and some bad. It is not God who does this, but the hearts of men. He allows events to happen but somehow guides them to ensure His will is achieved. You are the victim of evil. Wait to see how God will work this out."

"I do not want to offend God in this matter. I will do as you advise. Though my heart seeks revenge I will honor the king. Speaking of God, did you hear I have a young Hittite in my camp? He wants to learn more about God. Can you talk with him, teach him, or prophesy over him?"

Samuel agreed to meet with Uriah so David took him to where Uriah was sitting on the ground leaning against a tree, and said to Uriah, "This is the prophet, Samuel. He agreed to teach you a little more about our faith."

Samuel asked what Uriah would like to know. Uriah stated he would like to know how men can profess to believe in the one god, Yahweh, and then act exactly opposite of what they say they believe.

Samuel began to answer Uriah's question. "First you must believe there is only one god. Where you are from, you believe in many gods, yes?"

Uriah answered, "That is true. When I came here I did not believe in any god, except the Law of Nature. But it seems easier to believe in many gods, than one god."

"There is one god. His name is Yahweh. He is the God of nature and of history. He is the God of men. Three forces interact to prevent men from obeying him: the devil, the world, and our flesh. Together, these forces cause men to do what they do. While we are mindlessly engaged in pleasurable activities, the noose is being drawn tighter around us until we are trapped in bondage that is almost inescapable. Men who say one thing but do another are men who do not really believe what they are saying. They only think they believe but they are really in bondage to the things they do."

"There really is a devil? I thought he was just a lie of lies to scare children."

"Not true. The devil is our worst enemy. People refer to him in jest. He is mentioned as a joke or slang. We have all heard someone say, "The devil made me do it". People who make that remark are unaware of what they are saying. Perhaps they should learn to be sober and vigilant. The history of the kings and the books of Moses teach us that our adversary the devil is real. He walks around the earth like a lion in a cage pacing to and fro looking for those he can devour. He is not our friend. The enemy of our soul would like nothing greater than to see that all mankind ends up in hell with him."

Uriah asked, "What does he do that for?"

"His plans are to steal, kill, and destroy us and everything we have and everyone we know. He hates us. He will deceive and trick men to believe his lies and catch them in his trap to never let them go. He will use anything to trap us and enslave us. Money, power, and sex are his favorite traps, but he will use whatever it takes, for as long as it takes, to possess our soul. He wants to take us farther than we want to go, keep us longer than we want to stay, and it will cost us more than we want to pay. His three favorite tools are pride of life, lust of the flesh, and lust of the eyes. Recognize these and resist them. That is how to resist the devil. He wants to take us to hell and never let us go."

"I never heard any of that before. I was always taught that everything evil that happened was because Cybele was not happy. Religion consisted of keeping her happy."

"The devil wants us to be confused about him and what we should believe. He wants us to doubt his evil existence. He is always trying to confuse us, to argue with what we know to be true, to lead us away from the truth, to lie to us, to change our belief. He wants to destroy us."

"You said there are three enemies?"

"The world we live in is our second enemy. Sin is everywhere. For all that is in the world, the things that satisfy our fleshly desires, the glittering things our eyes like to look at, and the pride of being somebody in this life, is not of Yahweh, but is of the world. If we did what the world wants, we would have achieved a society where everyone could do what feels good, and feel good for doing it. But thank God, when we remain focused on him, the things of earth lose their appeal in the light of his glory and grace."

"The world does seem to have a strong attraction for some men."

"Our third enemy is ourselves. We like to blame others for our actions but really, we chose to do it. Sin begins in the mind. When we think about something long enough, we begin to do it. We give in to sin. Sinful thoughts lead to death because the wages of sin is death. A mind focused on Yahweh, will not dwell on evil thoughts."

"Then in other words, these three enemies work to keep us from living by faith as Ahithophel told me?"

"That is correct. Men always do what they believe. Our own habits are our enemies. We have met the enemy, and it is us. When our first enemy, the devil, attacks us we can resist him. When our second enemy, the world, tries to dull our senses, we can resist it. When our third enemy, our own thoughts, begins to wander to the things they should not, we can resist them. It can be difficult, but we can win. We need to change what we believe. We always do what we believe."

"Thank you. I must learn to not give in when I face these enemies. I want to live for Yahweh. I want to obey him. No other god ever came to men to tell them what to do."

"God has spoken to Abraham, Moses, and Joshua in our past to tell them what do. Whenever he is up to something on earth, he always tells someone. He has been faithful to others. He will also be faithful to you."

"Who is man that a creator would even want to talk with him or get involved in his affairs."

"You are correct. To be visited by God is an honor. To those who have been given much, much is expected. Let me tell you what God expects from you."

"Whatever it is I will obey him. I feel that when I am obeying him, I can feel Him right inside me. I will not do anything to cause him to leave me."

"He said he would never leave us nor forsake us, Uriah."

"I know. I just do not want to take a chance."

"Draw near to God and he will draw near to you. He wants you to stay with David, help him fight his battles, lead his men, and help him establish his kingdom."

"That is a big job but it is too risky to not obey him. I remember one time I was with my father, when I was young. He was hunting and I was with him. It was getting dark outside and he said it was time to go home. Foolish me, I stayed behind to pick a few berries. When I looked up, he was gone."

"He left you there?"

"Yes. It taught me a lesson. I was so afraid on my way home that from then on I always did what he said."

"It was a hard lesson to learn."

"I learned it well. I learned to obey my father. I will obey Yahweh. I will serve David and Joab as my leaders. I will forever be true to my wife, Bathsheba, if she ever becomes my wife. I will do this. I truly believe in Yahweh. I want to serve him for the rest of my life."

"That is a wise decision Uriah,"

"I feel like I have to give up the Law of Nature to serve the Law of the Jews."

"Yahweh created nature but man invented the law of nature. Place your trust in him not in man's invention. Virtue is good but it comes from obedience to Yahweh."

"Now I understand. Obedience leads to righteousness."

Uriah left Samuel and went off alone to pray. "God, Yahweh. I never knew you. I did not even know about you. Now that I know about you, I believe in you. I believe you brought me to this place. For what purpose I do not know. Help me resist the tools of the devil. Help me resist my own inner thoughts when they are evil. Help me resist the influence of the world when it is evil. Help me to be obedient to you and righteous in your sight. Take care of and protect my mother and sister. Amen."

Ravia and Annitis arrived safely in Gibeah and asked directions to the king's palace. At the palace they met the king's chief of staff and asked for employment. After they explained their story to him, they were hired. Annitis went to work in the vineyards and Ravia went to work weaving material. The pay was about the same as before except now they earned three denarii a week. They blended in with the other foreign workers and no one noticed them. They agreed to stay in Gibeah until they heard something definite about Uriah. Was he the Uriah of legend? How could someone who hated violence as much as he did, become a mighty warrior? It must have been the work of one of the gods.

PART FIVE

CHAPTER 17

David paced to and fro inside his camp, his mind racing so fast he could not sleep. The cool breeze in the night air usually calmed his spirit. But not tonight. The stars. The stars! So bright in this moonless night David felt as he could touch them. He reached up but could not grasp them. He threw a stone but missed them. They looked so close tonight. He thought about the stars. When I consider your heavens, the work of your fingers, the moon and the stars that you have ordained, who am I that the God who made those stars would be concerned about me?

The constellations -- usually his friends -- were his enemies tonight. The lion seemed to be laughing at him, the scorpion seemed to be scolding him, and the bull seemed to be blaming him. Majestic, glorious: nothing superseded the stars in the midnight sky on a moonless night in Israel. The stars not only sparkled, they glimmered. Their radiance was like a thousand candles. Was God up there somewhere looking at those stars too? Was there a secret hidden in the stars to guide men in their life journeys? Ahithophel thought so. What do they say tonight?

He needed this time to relax, but unlike in the past, the pacing only made him more restless. The laughing, scolding, blaming constellations could not calm him tonight. He was overcome with restlessness.

Saul was still trying to kill him, and there was no word on Michal. His anger was so hot the cool breeze did not remit it. He could not sit or stand still. Samuel had said to do nothing. How could he do nothing? He craved for relief like a rabid dog looking for someone to bite, a wasp looking for someone to sting, or a dam getting ready to burst.

David tried to stay busy by organizing food gathering details, establishing camp routine and hygiene. The number of men increased to nearly one thousand. Some even brought their families. Camp smelled like butchered livestock, spices, old fires, latrines, animal dung, and human sweat. Flies and mosquitoes, fleas and lice, mice and rats were everywhere. While his men looked to him for help, he was pre-occupied with thoughts of where to find Michal.

Thank God for Bathsheba and her knack for organizing women. He made a mental note to hire her when he became king. Soon she established a daily routine. Fire wood was gathered, jugs of water were being carried in, trenches were dug for latrines, fire pits were prepared for animal entrails and remains, everyone at the camp had been given a detail to help with the work.

Uriah had healed and David sent him back to Jericho. It seems two Hittite women were seen there. Maybe they were his family. Unfortunately, he could not find them. He did find a small Hittite community there who said they would be alert for any new Hittite women in town. They would contact him by leaving word at the gate of Gibeah.

With camp routine established, David could no longer bear the intense emotions inside his heart. He must do something! He ordered Joab and his brothers, Eliam and Uriah, and about six hundred men to leave the cave with him. His intense anger blinded him. He did not even know where he was going. He had to go somewhere.

By the time he realized where his whereabouts, he was in Nob standing outside the home of Ahimelech, the priest. He had brought Uriah and Joab with him while the rest of the men made camp in a small wood, near town.

At the home of Ahimelech he shouted, “This is David son of Jesse, and my trusted men. I must speak with you.”

Ahimelech, frightened to see David, said “David, go away! What are you doing here? You want me to die? The king is looking for you. You are a wanted outlaw. He will kill anyone who is seen with you. Why are there no men with you? I heard you had an army and were preparing to attack the king.” David could hear the fear in his voice and tried to calm him.

“I just need advice, and some food. The rest of my men await me at a designated place. King Saul took away his daughter he gave to me as my wife, and gave her to someone else -- I do not know who. I love her but do not know where she is. The king is trying to kill me. I do not know why. I must do something. I do not know what. I am supposed to be the next king. I do not know when. The things I do not know about me are more than the things I do know about me. I do not plan to attack the king. What do you know about me? Has Yahweh told you anything? Can you help me?”

“David, you are in danger. I cannot help you. I have only some consecrated bread that you may take but if you do your men must keep themselves from women.”

"One of the rules in my camp is that men must keep themselves from women."

"That is our rule of rules." agreed Uriah.

"In that case, take the bread. No one knows the mind of Yahweh except Yahweh. I can only tell you that Saul is still the king. If you forget that, you will not be king. Please leave before someone sees you and the king kills me."

While David met with Ahimelech, Eliam stayed in the camp with the rest of the men telling them how fortunate they were. Yahweh anointed David to be the next king and he believed he anointed Uriah to make certain it happened. He believed that Uriah had been chosen for a special assignment for Yahweh that would impact the whole world. No one knew what is was but they will find out at God's perfect time. His father Ahithophel even said it was written in the stars. Two people were to have a crucial impact on David's life: Uriah and Michal. The men chose good company and could be certain of many successes if they stayed with David. All the men agreed to remain no matter what it may cost them.

David returned to his men with the bread. "All I learned was that I was in danger, as if I did not already know. This is all the food we could get. Eat it and enjoy." He left Nob and took a few days to go to Keilah. When he arrived in Keilah, Abiathar, son of Ahimelech told him his father had been killed by one of Saul's men. Furthermore, the Philistines were looting and pillaging some of the smaller villages in Judea. David was beyond himself with rage. He turned to Uriah, "Have you healed well enough for some fun? A few hundred dead Philistines might improve how I feel and keep me from killing Saul. I will kill them instead of him".

"I endured the pain of pains, now I am ready to inflict some pain. Besides, I am ready to see if I still have the special anointing. I hope I did not lose it like Samson lost his when he lost his hair. I need to do something besides worry about my family."

"It was not your hair you lost," said David. Everyone laughed.

David located a camp of Philistines half way between Gaza and Hebron. They were laughing and drinking, no one provided security. They were not aware anyone was nearby. David split up his men into six groups of one hundred men each. Then they waited. At dawn, when the Philistines began their morning activities while suffering horrible hangovers he attacked with fury. All the anger he felt towards Saul was vented on the victims. He killed for Michal. He killed for Ahimelech. He killed for himself. He killed Saul vicariously. His men attacked fiercely from six different directions. The rout was total. The confused Philistines began killing each other. David and Uriah killed over fifty men between the two of them, Joab and his brothers had killed at least as many. David wanted more, but they were all dead except those who fled. The Philistines ran in every direction, leaving their livestock, their possessions, and their dead. David turned the possessions over to the residents of Keilah, the livestock he kept for himself. He gave the dead to the vultures.

A messenger warned David that Saul knew his location and had sent part of his army to lay siege to him. David rallied all his men, and left taking the livestock with them. He designated fifty of his men to take the livestock back to the Cave of Adullam, while the rest of his men escaped from Keilah. When Saul learned that David was not at Keilah, he called off the siege. David believed that the men with the livestock would return to the Cave of Adullam safely.

David and his men journeyed to Horeth in the Desert of Ziph but the Ziphites sent messengers to Gibeah to tell King Saul. They fled to the Desert of Maon so Saul followed him there. The king was about the catch them when the Philistines attacked him in retaliation for their slaughter and loss of livestock at the hands of David. Saul called off his pursuit of David in order to fight the Philistines. Taking advantage of the respite, David led his men to the Desert of En Gedi. An informant told him that Saul was pursuing him with three thousand men and that Saul was determined in his heart to find him.

Saul was gaining ground on David, so afraid of being captured, he and his men hid in a nearby cave. To their surprise Saul came into the same cave to relieve himself. David whispered, "This is the day the Lord was talking about when He said he would deliver my enemies into my hands." As he began to move towards Saul, Uriah cautioned him, "Do not take his life." David shot an angry look at Uriah. He crept forward and cut off a piece of Saul's garment. He looked angrily again at Uriah and snarled, "I will decide who and when I will kill."

After Saul had left the cave David followed and shouted to him, "King. You have heard I want to harm you. That is not the truth. Look, this is a piece of your robe. I could have killed you but I did not. You are my father, so I did not harm you. You are my king, so I did not kill you. I have not wronged you. But you are hunting me. You know evil doers produce evil deeds. I have done no evil to you."

Saul replied, "You are more righteous than I. You have treated me well. I know you will be king of Israel. Swear to me you will not kill my father's entire family."

David assured him, "I will give you my word when you tell me what you did with my wife."

"Because you did not kill me I will stop chasing you. But you will never know where she is."

"Then I will not seek to kill you either. But advise your family to stay out of my way."

Back at the Cave of Adullam, Bathsheba grew anxious. She was supposed to become betrothed to Uriah after two months. Uriah spent one month recovering. Then he rode off with David. They had been gone for three months and had not returned. She feared that her plan had backfired. What if David and Uriah were both killed? What would happen to her then? She had expressed her fears to Ahithophel who had remained at the cave, and he told her nothing could happen to those men without Yahweh's approval. She busied herself with the affairs of the camp to keep her mind occupied. Was she worried because she cared about Uriah, or because her own selfish dreams were being threatened? She wondered.

Ahithophel told Bathsheba all he knew about Uriah. He was not interested in horses ever since he almost got run over by one. He had a nasty encounter with bees also, but seemed to enjoy working with his bees. Her grandfather told her how Uriah mostly played alone while growing up. He never got into fights and always respected his parents. She asked him," How it is that he is now a gifted warrior?" He told her that the Achaeans were raiding their town of Hatusha and his father had been killed. Uriah and his family escaped out the back door and were wading down the river to get away. Then Uriah decided to return to town because it was his fault they were attacked. He did what his conscience told him and freed the town from the attack.

Ahithophel described Uriah during their last battle. "He rode on a white horse looking like an angel. He was calm despite the bedlam, majestic despite the clamor, serene despite the turmoil. Truth be known, he is not even my son, yet I am proud of him. You should be too."

Bathsheba saw tears well up and overflow Ahithophel's eyes. She thought maybe Uriah is anointed by Yahweh to save our people. Maybe he has become a Hebrew by faith. He intends to be a faithful husband to her. Maybe the way to become famous is to stay with him. Maybe David will be killed and Uriah will be chosen king. Did she want to be queen so badly she would use Uriah for her selfish interests? After listening to her grandfather, she wondered.

David sat at the camp site, his emotions hardly abated, a stick in his hand that he was poking into the fire and turning his head when the wind blew smoke into his eyes, and aching for the loss of Michal. He did not feel like eating, he could not sleep. He could not even sit still. Raiding and killing enemy soldiers only provided temporary relief. If he knew who had her he would go take her back, but he did not know. He had killed for her, now someone else had her. The thought of someone else with her was driving him beyond his senses. He would rather die than be without her. He put his life on the line to get her. Wine would give temporary relief to the pain, but would not bring Michal back. What should he do?

"Joab, when you talked with King Saul did he say who he gave Michal to?" David asked.

"Not a word. He just laughed and said you will never have her again. He looked like an evil spirit had taken up a permanent home in his heart."

"He is evil alright. What can I do? I cannot stand to be without her, but I cannot go get her. "David paced back and forth as he talked.

Joab replied, "Both Samuel and Ahimelech told you to wait. It seems to me you may never get Michal back. Saul could live for many more years and you may never know where she is. A heart grieving over a lost love has only one cure."

"What is that?" David asked.

"Find someone else. Take another wife. Let her comfort you and ease your pain."

All the others agreed that everyone would be happier if David had another wife.

Uriah stated, "One thing is different this time. I will not help you kill six hundred men for the next one. I will not help you kill even one man for the next one. Sometimes, it is okay to take necessary chances, but you go out of your way to look for chances to take."

"What do you mean by that remark?" challenged David.

"Nothing in particular. Unless you consider that you get your wives by killing people. You even threatened to kill me to get Bathsheba. You can do your own killing." Uriah answered.

"I would kill you for the satisfaction of watching you die if I did not need you. Do you think you would be here if it was not because I need you? You may think you are on a mission from God, but to me you feel like a messenger from Hell."

"You act like someone sent from hell. All you can think about is killing someone because someone else has your wife. Get over her. You are girl crazy. A real king would be thinking about war, not women! Get someone else. You are the next king. You should be planning your kingdom instead of moping, fretting, and stewing over a woman you will never see again. Go kill someone and take his wife as your own wife. Leave me out."

That comment struck David's heart as fiercely as Uriah's dagger could have. David had watched sheep for ten years. He only knew how to fight to protect his flock from animals and other men. God had always helped him. Being the youngest of eight sons and being forced to watch the sheep caused David to hate being told what to do and being challenged by others. He could not talk to women because women were not shepherds. In his new role, David had valued a woman's companionship almost like a religion but had received little training in social skills. He knew he would kill to protect a wife just as he would to protect his sheep. He was strong in the presence of any man but he was weak, even fickle, in the presence of women. Yet, he was angered that he was so transparent, especially to this Hittite. "Say that again and you will be the resident of Hell."

"In your dreams maybe! All you can think of is violence. You think every problem can be solved with the sword. You are nothing but a little boy trying to grow up to be king. Stop acting like a kid, start acting like a king!"

David jumped up to face him. He hesitated for a second remembering what happened the last time he confronted Uriah with a sword. They glared at each, neither flinching, or moving.

Joab interrupted them, “Look, it has been hard for all of us. Fighting with each other will not solve your problem, David. You know the enemy and it is not us. We did not take Michal from you. Do not take out your frustrations on us.”

Uriah walked over to a grassy area away from the rest of them and found a good place to lie down. He thought about returning to Hatusha without his mother and sister. Maybe they were already there. David went to the other side of the camp and lay down also. Everyone felt they had said enough.

Eliam went to Uriah and spoke to him in a whisper, “Why do you put up with him?”

“What choice do I have? He is our leader, anointed by Yahweh to be the next king. We have to follow his orders.”

“Yes, we must follow, but only as long as he is alive, Uriah. Ahithophel would help me if you wanted to become king. We could make an accident happen to David and proclaim you king. Then you could do what you were sent to do.”

“I never thought of being king. Well, I did once back in Hatusha but I was not serious about it.”

“Think of commanding five hundred thousand men and living in luxury. Think of what you could do for Bathsheba. She might like to be queen.”

“I told Bathsheba I would kill any man for her. But just because David feels it is okay to kill to get a wife, does not mean I feel it is okay to kill to become a king. That would be the deceit of deceits.”

“Uriah, how do you think people get to be kings? They kill the current king!”

"Great, then someone else will want to kill me. I would gladly be king for the sake of Bathsheba, but not for myself. Can you hear the people cheering me and following me?"

"They do already. Why do you think there are so many men in David's camp? They want to follow Uriah the Hittite!"

"Your law says to not covet and to not kill. Even though I would be king if it were offered by the people, I cannot kill David to improve my position. I am content as I am."

"You may be content, but what about your wife, my daughter, your future family? What could you do for them if you were king?"

"I cannot believe that if I kill the man anointed by Yahweh's prophet to be the next king, that I would be fulfilling His plans."

"Do you have the mind of God, that you can make this conclusion on your own?"

"No I do not. I only have the heart I was born with. I pledged loyalty to David, to you, and to Bathsheba. I cannot remain loyal to him if I plot to kill him. The Law of Nature says wrath kills the foolish man and envy slays the silly one. I am neither foolish nor envious."

"Uriah, you amaze me more every day."

"There is a story in your writings about the trees. They wanted a king so they asked an olive tree, a fig tree, and a grape vine. They each said in order to be king they would have to stop doing what they were doing, making olives, figs, and grapes. So in desperation they asked a bramble bush to lead them. Which of those trees am I?"

"You made your point. Do what you must."

"I will keep this conversation between us, but I cannot kill David to take his future throne. I am sorry. Samuel warned me about the pride of life. This is certainly a temptation for me. If I became king the world would never forget me. I must say no thank you. God did not give me a gift to be a warrior just to bring glory and honor to myself. I must honor and obey Him!"

CHAPTER 18

Uriah did not want to speak to David. He thought David was angry enough to kill him because Uriah felt the same way about David. He would leave except he thought that staying would help him find his family. Uriah knew they were going in the wrong direction but chose to let David continue with his childish behavior rather than to play the game with him. He had told David that he wanted to get back to Bathsheba so David headed north -- away from the cave. As he rode beside Eliam he said, “I hope this boyish impulsivity disappears before he becomes king. I will help him in his battles. He just acts without thinking. What would it hurt if we went back to the cave now? I believe David or I will end up killing the other if this behavior does not stop. Maybe I should take you up on your offer.”

About three miles south of Jezreel David and his men had to pass through a narrow gorge in Mount Gilboa. The gorge was the only way to get through the mountains and into the valley. Flash floods during spring and fall over the years had eroded the rocks where they cracked, forming this trail and producing pillars and large rock outcroppings about ten cubits high on both sides. A few scrub bushes tried to survive in the hot sun while down in the valley were lush gardens. A few lizards scurried from the men as they approached. The gorge was so narrow they could only travel about three or four abreast. David sent scouts ahead to make sure no ambushes waited for them as they passed through. The scouts gave the all clear signal and some of the men began to move through the gorge.

No one noticed the tribe of about thirty Ishmaelites hiding behind the rocks before they launched a violent attack from the rear. Some of the men were all clustered together waiting to go through while some were already in the gorge. It was a perfect place to ambush. The Ishmaelites took advantage striking hard and fast. The fight, however, was over in a few minutes. David had trained his men what to do in case of an ambush. Turn towards the enemy and counterattack.

Twenty of David's men died in a heartbeat. After the counterattack most of the ambushers were killed; the rest ran for safety. One of the Ishmaelites ran up to David and swung at him with his sword. He tried to block the attack with the sword in his left hand as he plunged the sword in his right hand into the man's abdomen. He killed his assailant but David's arm was bleeding. Though not life threatening -- he had not broken any bones – the deep wound bled freely. His men quickly wrapped it with cloth to stop the bleeding. The loss of blood coupled with the hot sun drained so much of his strength that when they arrived at the city gate of Jezreel, he fell unconscious to the ground. Joab took command of the men and gave them liberty in Jezreel until sundown.

Meanwhile, Uriah and Eliam asked the men at the city gate who was the best person in town at bandaging injuries. The men directed a young lad to escort the three men, David, Uriah, and Eliam, to a woman named Ahinoam saying she would know what to do. Uriah and Eliam had to carry David. Because he was still unconscious, Ahinoam was free to cleanse and bandage the wound without causing any further pain.

"This is a deep cut. No major blood vessels were cut but he will need several days to heal." She told them. "I need to change wrapping daily to keep clean the wound. If he gets infected he could lose his arm or even life. I make of two part olive oil and one part honey a healing balm. That prevents infection and speed healing. "

"Maybe I will not have to kill him after all." Uriah whispered to Eliam.

Ahinoam placed cool cloths on David's forehead and while waited for him to regain consciousness, she also treated the other wounded men. They were allowed to return to the camp Joab had established on the edge of town.

When David awoke, looked around, and saw Ahinoam he thought he had gone to heaven and was facing an angel. Until he saw his arm in a sling and heard Eliam sat, "We need to stay here for a few days, possibly a week or more while you heal. You could get infection that will make the wound even worse than it is."

Ahinoam agreed, "I have a spare room. You may stay there if you like."

Uriah stated," I will sleep with the men."

Eliam reported, "I will join the men also. Send for us if you need us."

Uriah and Eliam left David with Ahinoam.

Ahinoam was there to meet every need. When David was thirsty she placed her hand under his head and lifted him enough to drink. When he was hungry she fed him her best hot stew. When she changed his bandages every day she would hold his left hand in her left hand and wrap the bandage with her right hand, all the time looking into David's eyes. She prepared fresh water for him to bathe and washed his clothing, gave him oil for his hair, and treated him like the king she knew he would be. In fact, she never left his side, even sleeping on the floor beside him at night in case he needed anything.

When he was well enough to travel she said, "I am going to miss not having you around to care for. May God be with you and keep you safe."

"I am leaving Jezreel but I do not have to leave you. Come with us and be my wife."

Ahinoam thought for less than a second and agreed to go with him. She packed the things she wanted to keep, and left with them.

Uriah had met some of the people in Jezreel. When they learned he was the legendary Uriah the Hittite every available woman in town followed him, trying to outdo each other in waiting on him. All the young boys demonstrated their fighting movements to him. They wanted him to stay with them even though he insisted he had to go. When they learned he was actually leaving one young woman in particular wanted to go with him.

"Take me. I will be your wife. You will not be sorry," she said.

Uriah told her, "I cannot take you with me. I have promised to get betrothed to marry someone else."

Joab teased Uriah “There is nothing in our law that says a man cannot have two wives. Take this one. Take the other one too.”

”The Law of Nature says a man should have only one woman for his wife and a woman should have only one man for her husband.”

She pleaded,” I would be happy to share you with someone else as long as I could be with you. I would treat you better than she could. Then I would be your favorite wife.”

Uriah told her, “You could easily find a husband. You do not need me. I made a pledge to Eliam, to Bathsheba, and to Yahweh. I must keep my word. In my flesh, I think you are desirable. But in my spirit, I must leave you,” as he thought of Samson’s warning about lust of the flesh.

One of the men riding with them said he needed a wife. She left with him. Uriah thought of the Law of Nature that said any woman who will marry the first man to come along will quickly leave him for the next man. He left the women for the other men.

They headed towards the Desert of Maon, working their way back to the cave. They found a man who owned a thousand goats, three thousand sheep, and a great deal of property. The man’s reputation said he became wealthy by surly and mean business dealings. Most men tried to avoid him but he owned so much, everyone had to deal with him in some manner. The shepherds watching the man’s flocks reminded David of his younger years. He decided they would stay and help them protect their master’s property. Night and day they made a wall of protection around the flocks. After four months, none of the flock had been lost and none of the master's property had been stolen.

David heard that the man, named Nabal, which meant fool, was shearing his sheep in Carmel. He sent ten men to him to wish good health to him, his family, and all that was his. They were to tell him they treated his shepherds well. Now please help David by giving the men anything he can spare. They gave the message to Nabal in the name of David.

Nabal replied, "Who is this David? Who is this son of Jesse? Everyone is leaving their masters these days. You tell me, what makes you think I would sacrifice my own belongings, and give them to someone from who knows where? Did I ask him to help me?"

David's men returned to him and told him what Nabal had said. Immediately angered, David shouted to his men," Put on your swords!" He left two hundred men with the supplies and told Uriah to be in charge. The other four hundred went with him.

David said, "I watched over this man's property in the desert and made sure nothing happened to him. Now he repays good with evil. By morning I will kill every male that belongs to him."

One of the servants ran to Nabal's wife, Abigail, to tell her what her husband had done and how David reacted. He told her how good David had treated the shepherds and Nabal lost none of his flock. Then Nabal reacted in a rude and belligerent manner to David. The servant asked Abigail to do something or they would all be killed because Nabal, through his wickedness, brought disaster upon his house.

Abigail, fearing the worst and angry at her husband, lost no time. She gathered two hundred loaves of bread, two skins of wine, five sheep, five seahs of roasted grain, a hundred cakes of raisins, and two hundred pressed figs, and loaded them on a donkey. She sent the servant ahead and followed after him without telling Nabal.

When Abigail saw David she dismounted the donkey and bowed down to him saying, "Please, pay no attention to that wicked man Nabal, he is just like his name. Please take this gift and give it to your men. Forgive my offense. May the Lord give you a lasting dynasty. When you become king, remember me."

David thanked her," May you be blessed for your good judgment today. You have prevented bloodshed. If you did not come when you did, not one male would be left in your household. Go home in peace."

After she had left David said to Joab," That woman is beautiful and intelligent. I think she too could make me happy." He raised his eyebrow at Joab. Joab gave him a smile and nodded his head in return.

Uriah did not want to risk another attack by nomads or thieves so he organized a security detail around the camp. A few of the men still rested while they recovered from their wounds. Uriah divided the rest of the men into three response teams and assigned each a sector of responsibility. If any trouble began in their sector they would respond. If more help was needed other response teams would be sent. While waiting, they practiced their fighting techniques and maneuvers. When David returned to the camp with the four hundred, he said they would stay there for two weeks. Joab enlarged the security details as the men continued to prepare in case of an ambush.

Eliam asked David if they would be going back to the Cave when they left here. Uriah would like to have his wife and the men could all use some rest. David muttered something about going back when he was ready to go back.

Ten days later a messenger told them that Nabal had died mysteriously. David sent his servant to ask Abigail to come and be his wife. Without delay she packed her donkey, gathered her five maids, and joined David. Now David had two wives. Uriah was still trying to get back to the one he was promised. More women were joining them daily. It seemed as if the men all found someone who wanted to travel with them.

Uriah approached David and asked," Did you not tell Ahimelech that your men would keep themselves from women whether the battle was holy or unholy? Now look, we have as many women as we do men, and some men do not even have any women! Is this what you call keeping ourselves free from women?"

"Begin training the women to fight. Teach them to care for the camp so men will not have to be left out of the battles. Teach them how to be useful. In that way we will double the size of our force."

"If you are serious, you are mad. You are allowing the men to break your rules because you are breaking them yourself. Now you are justifying it by giving them made up duties. How do you expect anyone to fight when all they have on their minds is their man or woman?"

"Uriah that is my problem, you do what you were told."

Anger filled David's heart as he paced along the stream bank. He contemplated his current situation. It began when Samuel anointed him to be king while he was a shepherd boy. Since then he has killed a Giant, was a musician for the king, fought the Philistines for Michal, won her and lost her, he has two wives, and a foreigner keeps criticizing everything he does. Even though he is content with Ahinoam and Abigail he still ached for Michal. Nearly one thousand men and their women and children are following him, six hundred with him here and the rest back at the cave.

While Israel's enemies are getting stronger, King Saul is ignoring the enemies and trying to kill David. Obsessed with his hatred for David and fearful of the Philistines, Saul refuses to act to protect the country. David refuses to attack Saul because he is anointed by God.

Even though Uriah was right about the women he cannot let him continue to criticize him. Now Samuel the prophet has passed away. Samuel seemed to like Uriah and did not disagree that he was sent to him for a purpose. But Samuel was gone. Maybe it was time to make Uriah disappear too. But the problem seemed to be with Saul. Maybe Saul should disappear. Maybe Uriah is right and the women should disappear.

PART SIX

CHAPTER 19

What is God's plan? David wished he knew. How is it that a foreigner seems to be more in tune with God than he is? How can a thorn in his side be his ram in the bush? Should he start working with him instead of against him? Never! No one who embarrasses him in public will ever be treated as his equal. Where should he go from here? What should he do next? Maybe if he returned to the cave, someone will have foun0d Uriah's family and he could take his wife and family back to Hatusha. That would get him out of his hair. How long will God wait to act?

Abigail found him walking along the stream and took his hand. They sat down together on the grass. Abigail pointed out the lone fig tree growing on the edge of the stream. David started singing softly," Blessed is the man that does not walk in the counsel of the ungodly, nor stand in the way of sinners, nor sit at the feet of the scornful. His delight is in the law of the Lord, and on His law he meditates day and night. He shall be like a tree planted by streams of water that bring forth their fruit in season, his leaf will not even wither because whatever he does will prosper. Not so the wicked, they are like the chaff the wind blows away. The ungodly will not stand in the judgment or sinners among the righteous. The Lord knows the way of the righteous, but the ungodly will perish."

"That is beautiful. What does it mean?" asked Abigail.

"I think it means if I want to prosper I need to listen to Uriah and my advisors."

He lied down in the grass and put his head in Abigail's lap. Soon he fell asleep.

Startled, David heard Uriah shouting, "David wake up! The Amalekites are attacking! That's what happens when women are allowed into camp. The enemy attacks while the men lie about with women!" He looked up in time to see Uriah jump into the stream ten feet from him producing four headless Amalekites. The water turned red as more men joined the battle, and more men died. David killed a man about to stab Abigail and quickly rallied his force into a circle with each man fighting outward. He was surprised to find the women in the circle fighting alongside of the men. An hour later the fighting was over. The Amalekites attacked twice but both times they were beaten back. The battle damage assessment indicated too many men were killed or injured. David had received an answer to his prayer.

"Uriah, quickly choose fifty men who have not been injured and pursue those men who fled! Do not let any of them get away!"

"They are as good as dead already."

Uriah chose his men and began the pursuit. The trail was plainly marked with pieces of clothing, drops of blood, broken branches, trampled grass, and even lost weapons.

Finding the Amalekites at the edge of a wooded area about two furlongs in front of them, they stopped to assess the situation. Uriah sent thirty men around to come in from the rear; fifteen circled left, fifteen circled right. They were checking for any scouts or lookouts as they approached but found none. The Amalekites appeared to be doing their own battle damage assessment and were not aware anyone was approaching. When he saw his men in position, Uriah charged into the clearing and began a feigned attack, all twenty men giving the Jericho yell. Startled by the noise and the sudden appearance of unexpected men, the Amalekites fled into the woods, right into the spears of the men waiting for them. Uriah and his twenty men closed in ensuring no one escaped this time. They rounded up all the dead, placed them on their horses, and brought them back to David as evidence that none got away.

When Uriah joined David and the rest of the Men, Ahinoam and Abigail had bandaged the wounded, while the dead were being buried. Someone had killed some game and hot stew was ready to eat. Sometimes having women in camp is a good thing. As they ate David told them," We have been in the field too long. I have decided to gather all our men together back at the cave and let you have some rest. I need to plan my next move."

David sent out ten men to the left, right, front, and rear to scout for enemy activity. They formed two units of approximately 300 men in each unit lead by Uriah and Abishai. A good furlong separated the two units. They were heading back to the cave. The mere thought of it boosted everyone's morale, including the women. David hoped he was doing the right thing. He prayed, "Show me your ways, Lord. Teach me your paths. Lead me in your truth and teach me, for you are the God who saves me. On you I wait all day."

Feeding his men had meant raiding cattle and sheep, asking for favors, and stealing from caravans. David decided to leave one hundred men at the home that used to belong to Nabal, and now belonged to him, so they could grow fruit and vegetables, and raise livestock to feed David's men.

"I do not care if he is helping David. I want him here with me!" Bathsheba complained to Ahithophel. "He was supposed to be betrothed to be my husband months ago and no one has heard from him since we received that herd of stinking cows. I want to go home. If you will not come with me, I will go by myself!"

"You do not know but he could be here any day. Stay another month and then if he is not here I will take you back home myself."

"You do not know but he could be dead. What then? What about my plans for my life? Am I just supposed to wait for him to come back from fighting? Is that the life my father wanted for me? I am leaving in the morning. At least at home I can sleep in a bed and take a real bath."

"Look Bathsheba, many women with children have joined us. You have a job to do here. These people need you."

"The future Queen of Israel cannot lower herself to caring for dirty, disobedient children from families who are in debt to or are wanted by the king for breaking the law."

"The future Queen of Israel cannot learn how to be queen unless she does learn to humble herself to care for these people. More people like these live in Israel, than rich, law abiding citizens. You need to learn how to work with these, and even less than these, if you are to achieve your dream. Looking like a queen in fancy clothing is not enough. Even your sharp mind and brave heart are not enough. Your sharp tongue will disillusion them. If the people do not see you as queen, you will not be their queen in their minds. Help them now. Win their hearts today, be their queen here. Then when you are queen, they will love you."

"Alright, I will stay one more month! After then, I do not care what happens!"

Bathsheba began by helping some women bathe their infants. Then she helped prepare food for them. Others needed to have their clothes cleaned. Everyone seemed to have a need. Before long Bathsheba realizing there was no order to the activities established routines for bathing, washing, feeding, and caring for the families. She never knew how many women were in the camp and how many needed help. Before long all the women were assigned to a detail designed to help keep order in the camp. With the new details the camp saw a reduction in the number of rats, flies, and sick children.

The route David chose to go back to the cave led through the Desert of Ziph, not the best place to travel but the shortest distance. Some of the local residents recognized David and went to Gibeah to tell Saul. David's men, not knowing they had been seen, traveled until early evening. Before dark they found a few caves to stay in for the night. The evening sun was shining through the opening, reflecting red light off the walls near to entrance. The color gradually changed to lavender, then purple, then black, the further into the cave it went. Uriah noted that even in a cave, God likes to paint beautiful pictures for his people. He thought how he wished he could describe that scene to Bathsheba. Then he wondered whether she would still be there when he returned.

Abishai and Uriah were sharing a small loaf of bread when David burst into the cave. “You will never believe who is down in the valley just below us.”

“I cannot believe it. Not King Saul?” guessed Abishai.

“The one and only. Tonight we rid ourselves of him once and for all. We can make him disappear and I will be king. Then I can defend Israel from its enemies. Who wants to go down to his camp with me?”

“I will.” volunteered Abishai. “Uriah will too, right Uriah?”

“Yes, of course. I would love to go into the king’s camp where it is safe for a follower of David. I am sure the king will not mind. Maybe I will disappear too and you will be rid of both of your problems.”

David ignored the last sentence and said,” Good, meet me outside this cave in about an hour.”

When David had left the cave Abishai asked,” What do you make of David?”

Uriah answered,” I feel loyalty to him. He is the leader of our men and the future king of Israel. I owe it to him to be loyal. I made a pledge to Eliam that I would serve David.”

“I can believe it but what do you think of him as our leader?”

"I know he is anointed by God to become the next king. Right now I think he is impulsive and wears his emotions on his sleeve. Like tonight, we are going to Saul's camp to do what, embarrass him? Kill him? But that does not matter. He will grow and learn. He is older than me and chosen to be the leader. My job is to be loyal, and help him."

"Do you ever feel like you could do his job better sometimes? Joab is the commander of the men. I believe he could do the job better than David."

"No. We know David's secret hiding places. We know his weaknesses. We know his triggers. We cannot betray that or use it to our advantage. To have such knowledge about someone and then to not serve him is a violation of the laws of nature where I come from."

"That is an interesting way to look at it."

"My father told me a story once about how the last king of the Hittite Empire made an alliance with Ramses of Egypt for military help and trade. After Pharaoh had learned of our weaknesses, he sold that information to the Achaeans. The Achaeans used that information against us when they attacked and brought our kingdom to an end. Since I heard that story I always thought it best to die for a leader rather than betray him."

"I cannot believe it. But it's true. We have so much knowledge about David. We could sell it to Saul for a lot of money."

"That is something I would never do. Nor would I ever leave."

"Nor would I. I have gone too far now to turn back."

"We know too much. David would send men after us until he killed us or brought us back. We have a choice. We can stay here, be faithful to David, and possibly get killed.

Or we can betray him and know we will be killed. We could probably escape death at the hands of the enemy. We cannot escape death at the hands of David."

"Is that why you are so loyal to him?"

"No, I am loyal because the more I think about it the more I believe Yahweh sent me here on a mission. Somehow that mission involves serving David."

The three men skulked down the hill, moving short distances at a time, hiding behind cover, rocks, bushes, and holes in the ground, like a thief in the night. They were thankful for a full moon so they could see where they were going. It appeared all the sentries had dozed off so the men snuck into Saul's camp, right past the sentries. After what seemed like hours they found Saul with Abner near his side. Uriah had never been so frightened, except maybe when he fled his home in Hatusha. Perspiration ran so profusely he imagined it could be heard running down his chest. He was looking everywhere at once to be sure no one woke up. His dagger was ready to kill anyone so foolish as to wake up right now. He wondered whether Abishai and David felt the same fear.

Abishai drew his sword and was about to kill Saul when a wave of fear overcame David. "I changed my mind. We cannot do this. He is anointed by God. We cannot kill him. The wrath of God against us would be more severe than this is worth." David whispered.

"I believe it, but we need to let him know we were here." insisted Abishai.

"Humiliate him and scare him into leaving us alone. Make him as scared of you as I am about being here in this camp tonight." stated Uriah.

They looked around. David found Saul's water jug. Abishai took his spear. Uriah wondered what to take. He looked at a golden drinking cup, a wool king's blanket, and a basket of fig cakes. Uriah picked up the cup and found out it was one of a pair, there were two of them. He thought, "These must be worth more than I have made in my lifetime. Maybe I should take these." They looked valuable. Even in the night they glimmered. Then he began to feel the warning in his heart. "Samuel told me about the lust of the eyes, the lust of the flesh, and the pride of life. I do not want any of these things." He told David, "Let us go, I do not want anything."

They arrived safely back at the top of the hill. Then David realized, "If he wakes up and finds his items missing he will wonder who took them. I want him to know who took them." Then he called out, "Saul, Saul wake up."

Saul stood up and reached for his spear but it wasn't there. "Who is calling me? Is that you David?"

"Yes King it is me. Where is your spear? Where is your water jug? Has Abner been negligent in protecting you?"

"Abner is protecting me well. How did you know about my water jug and spear?"

"I have them here with me. Entered your camp. Found your bed. Took your water jug and your spear. Thought to kill you. God stopped me."

Filled with horror at the thought he was nearly killed he answered, "Son, you are more righteous than me. Tell me what you want and you can have it."

"Great. I am not trying to kill you. I have proven to you twice that I could have killed you but chose not to. I want you to stop trying to take my life."

"Agreed. You have proven that you love me by not killing me. I will not kill you either."

"Tell me where you have taken Michal so I can retrieve her back to me."

"Son, when you left without her, according to our law, you divorced her. If any man leaves his wife in the home of her father, and abandons her, she is divorced. What I did was legal. I cannot tell you where she is."

"I left her at my home. Not your home."

"True, but I rescued her from her from where you abandoned her and took her to my house. You did not come for her yourself. According to our law you divorced her. I gave her to another. Accept it. You will never have her again. But I will keep my word to stop trying to kill you."

"Send some of your men up here to retrieve your lost items. I rescued them from where you abandoned them. Or should I just give them to someone else?"

David was happy Saul agreed to stop trying to kill him, but he was still so angry about Michal he paced the hillside half the night. He returned to his tent until sleep overpowered his anger.

Uriah went to sleep wondering if he should continue to follow David. Is this what Yahweh wants? Will I ever find my mother and sister? Am I a victim of circumstances again?

CHAPTER 20

Uriah had been asleep when his mother woke him. With a fear-filled voice she warned him the Achaeans were attacking. He killed a soldier who had broken through their front door and they escaped out the back door. However, an unseen essence told him to return to Hatusha where he led a defense of the city while his mother and sister continued their flight to Tarsus and safety. Realizing that the Achaeans would probably attack again, the people of Hatusha chose to attack first and invaded the garrison at Ankara.

After Uriah successfully led the attack, the people wanted to make him their governor. Declining, he went in search of his mother and sister. Uriah struggled with trying to determine what the gods were doing to him and why he was always being caught in situations in which he had no control over his choices.

Trying to find his family, Uriah ended up joining David's men. It seemed that King Saul had promised David his daughter in exchange for one hundred Philistine foreskins. Uriah and his men helped David and the king gave him his daughter. Eliam promised to give his daughter Bathsheba to Uriah for his wife.

Jealousy got the best of him. King Saul tried to kill David.

Fleeing for his life he left his new wife, Michal, behind. Saul gave his daughter to another man.

Uriah made several attempts to locate his mother and sister without finding them, sometimes arriving only a few days after they left where he was looking.

Through their wanderings around in the territory of Israel, David acquired two more wives but he did not love them the way he loved Michal.

King Saul, who had been trying to kill David, unknowingly camped in the valley below where David was hiding. David took Uriah the Hittite and Abishai with him into the king's camp. When they found the king, they decided not to kill him but stole his water jug and spear.

Uriah chose to take nothing, remembering the Prophet Samson's words about the pride of life, the lust of the eyes, and the lust of the flesh.

David agreed to allow the king to have them back if he would stop trying to kill him and return his wife to him. The king agreed to stop trying to kill him, but said he would not return his wife.

The next morning David sat down cross legged beside Uriah and Abishai in the cave. He had been pacing the hillside most of the night rehearsing his conversation with King Saul. "What did you make of Saul's promise?"

"Honestly. I cannot believe . . . he might have been . . . it could be another ruse. Or not," said Abishai.

"Well stop muttering and stuttering and tell me whether you think I should believe him."

"Think about it. We humiliated him in the presence of all his men. He gave you an oath in front of them. If he fails to keep the oath he will lose their respect," said Abishai.

"We are continuing to outsmart him and he has to keep changing his plans. Then he says things he does not intend to keep. That is not news," said David.

"But David, Saul's men did not wake up. He must believe that Yahweh caused a deep sleep to fall on his entire army so none of them would wake up. You know he is the superstition of superstition," replied Uriah.

"Yes, he might?" said David. "In fact he already left the valley."

"I believe that when we entered Saul's camp he realized you are a leader of leaders over him. He will stop chasing you now. He may even fear you. But he is definitely committed to not let you have Michal. Not after being humiliated like that," said Uriah.

"Well, do not just stand there! Tell me what I should do," replied David. In all of his pacing he could not think of anything he should do next.

"The king has already been a victim of your surprises for the past year and will continue to be as long as he pursues you. Take your men and begin preparing them to serve in your kingdom. Go somewhere the king will not dare to chase you. Enjoy your wives and forget about Michal. The king's job is to not acquire a harem but to lead and protect his people," said Uriah.

"I thought you would say something like that," David said as he stood up and walked towards the entrance of the cave.

"Then why ask?" Uriah said.

That afternoon David paced around hillside again still angry at Uriah for telling him he should be planning for his kingdom instead of killing men and marrying women. Who is Uriah to tell him anything? David is the man who was chosen to be king. He did not know why. David is the man that Saul has been trying to kill. He did not know the reason for that either. Does Uriah know how it feels to be running for his life from his own father-in-law? No! Uriah's father-in-law loves him.

Many times during the day, David would think about Michal. Then he would remember the advice of his men: forget Michal and get a new wife. Well, now he has two wives. He smiled as he thought that sometimes his men made good sense.

In spite of his anger, David had to admit that even Uriah made sense. He saved his life in Jezreel and again when the Amalekites attacked. David sighed, between dodging the king, fighting off ambushes, and meeting new women, he had not put much effort into planning for his kingdom. But then not much could be done until he became king. He had asked their opinion and Uriah gave it to him. Maybe he should listen to him.

What does a king do? Israel has had one king and he is a failure. Kings in other countries attack their neighbors, steal their wealth and women, and kill their men. At least Saul was not doing that. The problem is he is letting others steal our wealth, enslave our women, and kill our men.

David realized his first priority was to protect his country's resources. Uriah was right again. He needed to begin preparing his kingdom for when he became king. He must defeat all the enemies that have been piecemeal destroying the nation.

He knew Uriah was right. He could not establish peace in the region from the Cave of Adullam. It was time to move. Where could he go? He needed to go somewhere that Saul would not change his mind and pursue him again. Somewhere Saul was afraid to go. Saul would not go near the Philistines. He sent David out to kill them in exchange for Michal.

He had to choose a city. After consulting with Joab, and Eliam, David chose to go to the Philistine town of Gath, the same city where Goliath used to live. No one would think to look for him there. First, he had to convince the king of the Philistines that he was there in peace.

In Gath he could stop running long enough to plan his next moves. The hills at Gath would allow him to see anyone coming for miles. A few scrub trees and some date trees were scattered around, but except for the grape vines, the area was grass and small bushes. The grapes grew well and there was a winepress. It was close to the Israel border and centrally located. He would use Gath as his headquarters and begin to stop the small bands of nomads, and others who were continually attacking and robbing travelers. He was certain that Achish, the ruler of Gath, would approve him staying there after David told him his plan.

That night around the fire David asked," What do you think a good king should do?"

Eliam replied," A king keeps his country from dividing against itself."

"A king protects his country from its enemies," replied Joab.

"A king provides safety and security so his people could live happy, healthy, and prosperous lives," Uriah advised.

"Interesting, a king does the same thing that I did as shepherd," said David.

In a sudden epiphany at hearing those words from his own lips David realized why God chose him to be king. Goose flesh ran down his back and neck as he realized that those years as a shepherd were preparation for leading God's people.

He was like another Moses.

Instead of being a weight on his shoulders the thought of kingship became a joy in his heart. He determined to be the best king Israel ever had. He knew it would not be hard to be better than Saul. But he wanted his name to be remembered down through the ages, as is Moses.

His excitement spilled over as he began to talk about what kind of people he will need. He will need military advisors, economic advisors, agriculture advisors, priests who know Yahweh, political advisors, and anyone else who can help him lead his country. Uriah, Eliam, Joab and his brothers will all be leaders of my army in my kingdom.

David sang," Shout joyfully to the Lord, everyone! Serve Him with gladness, come before Him with singing. Know that He is Lord, He made us, and we did not make ourselves. We are the sheep of His pasture. Enter into His gates with thanksgiving and His presence with praise. Be thankful to Him because His mercy is everlasting and his truth never ends."

David and his advisors stood and formed a circle joining hands as David prayed," God, who am I that you have chosen me to be king of your people? Yet you know me and you chose me, thank you. You alone are God. You chose Israel to be your people, to make your name great on the earth. This is your plan for all mankind, to show yourself to us, so we can know you. You demonstrated your mighty power when you brought us out of Egypt and gave us the land you promised to Abraham and Moses. Re-establish the covenant you made with Abraham and Moses, and make it with me, your servant. Bless the House of David forever. Now Lord, make your word established forever among men."

"I think we finally are beginning to see a new king," said Uriah.

"I cannot believe it," said Abishai.

When they learned that David planned to go to Gath, a few of the men who went to the cave because they owed the king some money thought they would find favor with King Saul. Maybe he would cancel their debts in exchange for information. So they went to Gibeah hoping to see the king. They were planning to tell him that David was going to Gath. But when the king realized they were some of the people who owed him money, he put them to work in the vineyard to pay their debt without granting them an audience with him. A month later they were in the vineyard they were grumbling to themselves and anyone who would listen about how unfair the king is. Annitis, working nearby, happened to hear some of their murmuring so she set her basket on the ground and approached them.

“You men do not seem to be very happy here,” she said.

“You would not be happy either if you knew what we know,” said one of the debtors as he chopped off a large cluster of grapes and placed them in his basket and slapped a spider running down his arm.

“Is that so? Tell me what you know. See if it makes me unhappy. You know that is bad luck?”

“What is?”

“Killing spiders.”

“Oh, I knew that. I also know that the outlaw David, who thinks he will be king someday, has plans to move to Gath. We tried to tell that to the king, but we ended up here.”

“David?” she asked.

"Yes, he is the leader. He has got Eliam, Joab, and Uriah helping him too.""

"Is Uriah a Hittite?"

"How come you ask? You know him?"

"May the gods give us favor. He is my brother."

"Your brother? You are the sister he has been looking for?"

"Yes, and his mother works as a weaver for the king."

"You want us to tell David you are here?"

"Would you, could you?" as excitement began to overflow in her heart.

"We will leave tonight to find David. He knows us."

When the debtors left Annitis, instead of going to David, they decided they could gain favor with Achish by telling him this information about Uriah's mother and sister working for King Saul. Maybe Achish could use it to have some control over David. Maybe he could use it to make peace with King Saul.

Annitis could not wait until she saw her mother and told her what had just happened.

CHAPTER 21

The next morning David assembled all his men. "I have decided move to Gath because the cave is not a place for families. All you who have families prepare to leave tomorrow. Go set up your homes. Single men will maintain a headquarters at the cave for another few weeks for training and recruiting."

David had chosen the cave as a hideout for his band of outlaws.

He never intended it to be a gathering place for so many people. He needed to find a better place for his followers to live.

Uriah was resting under a tree and remembering the day he became betrothed to Bathsheba. He remembered going to Eliam and telling him he had completed his part of the bargain, now he wanted Bathsheba for his wife. Eliam agreed it was time to proclaim the betrothal. Excitement and joy overflowed his soul but his mind still doubted his good fortune.

Uriah began running throughout the camp looking for Bathsheba like a bee looking for nectar. When he found her she was helping a poor woman in ragged clothing find something nice to wear, and something good for her children to eat. He remembered their conversation.

"Bathsheba, I just left your father. He said we could get betrothed. This is what I want and your father gave the approval of approvals, but what do you say?"

"I thought I already answered that question."

Uriah asked her. "Yes, but, is this what you want to do? Are you certain you want to marry me, Uriah, a Hittite?" Uriah remembered how much his mother loved his father and wanted to be certain his wife would love him the same.

"A woman seeks for spirituality in her life as much as men do. God created Eve for Adam. He also created Adam for Eve. I cannot be complete until I am one with the man who loves me. I believe you will love me like that," she said as she placed her hands on his shoulders and slid her hands around his neck until her fingers on both hands interlocked with each other.

Touching her softly on her cheek he said, "I would love you more than you could ever know!"

"I would be honored to have a man as revered as you, yet as kind hearted, and as much in love with Yahweh as you are, for my own husband. That means, yes. My own spirituality depends upon having you as my husband. My plans for my life can only be fulfilled with you." She gave him a broad smile to reassure him of her sincerity.

"You are the best of the best. You are the best thing that ever happened to me. I promise to always love you. I will live my life to please you. When I fulfill my mission to

Yahweh, I will do whatever you ask me to do. But before we are married, David is calling a meeting in the morning. More changes could be occurring. I need to know, are you with me through whatever decisions he announces tomorrow?"

"Wherever you go, I will go. Wherever you lead, I will follow." She took his hand and led him to her father. Uriah could not believe what was happening to him. It was a good thing she was pulling him because he was too ecstatic to walk on his own strength. Were people watching him? He could not see them. Were people talking? He could not hear them. Were people patting him on the back? He could not feel them. Life was a dream. The only person in the dream was Bathsheba. Was that Eliam they were talking to? He could not see him. He heard him say something about arranging the betrothal and the next thing he knew everyone at the cave was shouting congratulations. Despite the meeting in the morning they celebrated with singing and dancing until sunup. Uriah had to wait another year before the wedding ceremony itself.

She said wherever he went she would follow. Now it is time to follow him to Gath. He would go tell her about the move. But before they moved, David wanted to look for his family one more time.

While six hundred men and their families left the cave with new excitement about what was about to happen, Bathsheba traveled with Uriah to Jericho, Jabeth-Gilead, and Kedesh. No one had seen his family. A month later they went to Gath to join David. No one knew what would happen next, but for the families it had to be an improvement over staying in the cave. Achish welcomed them when they arrived in Gath and gave them some land on the edge of the town to live in. Homes or tents could be put up. They could mingle with his people and become friends

About three days later a tent city was built with a meeting place in the center. The single men were given the areas near Gath, on the south side of their area. Men with families were placed on the east and west sides, while women with children who had no one else to protect them camped on the north.

When all the families and men had arrived David called all the men to a meeting. "I am tired of being chased by Saul and ambushed by everyone. Saul will not follow us to Gath. We are safe here because he will not go into Philistine territory. But we still have bands of raiders roving the wilderness and attacking everyone. No one is safe from them. From now on they will not be safe from us."

"If the king will not do his job to protect his people, we will do it for him. I will leave one hundred men here to watch over the women and children while the rest of us patrol the wilderness. When we return, you will rotate so another hundred can stay behind. The first patrol leaves at mid-day."

As she weaved her cloth Ravia was thinking of how she became an employee of the king. The Achaeans attacked her home and killed her husband because her son was foolish and sold his ring to some Assyrians. They fled town to escape but then her foolish son went back to Hatusha. She went to Yozgat and from there on to Tarsus. She found a caravan going to Gibeah but they stopped in Jabeth-Gilead. She was kidnapped by some Ammonites but escaped just before a huge battle was fought there. Eventually she ended up in Gibeah and was working for the king. Annitis told her she met some men who knew how to find Uriah. They said her foolish son was with David and his derelicts. How did he go from being a legend to being a derelict?

Things could not improve much now. She wondered where David was. Uriah would be there too. Was he the Uriah in the legend? She hoped she would see him again soon. If not, Annitis would probably marry one of Uriah's friends, but what life was in her future? Does Uriah even know where they are? Annitis said she talked to some men who were supposed to go find David and tell him where they are. What is taking him so long? That was six months ago. The Ammonite deserter who was supposed to help her never returned to Jericho. Perhaps these men had made a false promise to Annitis too.

As long as they continued to work for Saul there was a chance Uriah would find them. But if Saul found out her son was the Uriah who rode with David, his enemy, maybe he would send her away, or worse. She prayed for the gods to give her favor.

David's first sortie was the Judean wilderness and the Desert of Ziph. He had some unfinished business there. Those people had annoyed him once too often. It was time to end it. David's five hundred men began at the south end and rode northward. They slew any man, woman or child they encountered and kept any animals or valuables. They attacked until it was time for the evening meal, then they would return back to Gath. They gave Achish all the bounty but they kept the livestock for themselves.

This routine became a daily event. Whenever Achish asked where they had been, they replied they had been helping him defend his town. They went out every day for seven days into the Desert of Ziph. David gave orders to take no survivors. Everyone must die. No one from Ziph will ever cause him distress again. When the Desert of Ziph had been purged, David turned to Maon, then to En Gedi. He cleared the entire area from any inhabitant who was a threat to peace in the area.

Men rotated for duties in Gath while David kept his pressure on all of Judah. All nomads, raiders, and any inhabitant surrendered all weapons -- anyone who refused lost not only their weapons but their lives. One thing a king does is make his country safe for his people. David had succeeded in making Judah safe. No one rode to tell Saul where David was or what he was doing. No one was allowed to escape. Meanwhile all the peaceful residents of Judah knew it was David who had fought for their safety, not the king. Peace spread around the region.

Saul remained in Gibeah, happy that the number of attacks on travelers through Judea had been reduced to almost zero, with no clue as to why it was happening. He summoned Abner and rewarded him with a raise for his good work. He told Abner to prepare for him to visit the area in two days. He wanted to personally assure the residents he was doing all he could to protect them. Maybe he could increase the levy since they were safe to produce more.

CHAPTER 22

While Uriah was clearing the wilderness of bandits Bathsheba reminisced on her wedding day. Eliam, her father, had arranged for a priest to be present and a canopy to be built. As the priest walked to his place under the canopy, the attendees became still, ending their conversations and watching Uriah as he joined the priest. Everyone waited for her. She learned later that her grandfather, Ahithophel, had wondered if she would appear. Eliam hoped she would appear. Uriah said he prayed she would appear.

As she approached the priest he said to the guests," Blessed is she who comes in the name of the Lord." Everyone repeated in chorus fashion "Blessed is she who comes in the name of the Lord." Uriah placed a ring on her finger and with a trembling voice said to her, "With this ring you are wed to me." As tears fell from their eyes they drank a cup of wine together. She began circling Uriah. She walked around him once, twice, and stopped with a mischievous look in her eyes and a smile on her face. Then she slowly began the third and last walk around Uriah. When she returned to his side again, they shared another glass of wine. As soon as the glass was empty everyone shouted, "Congratulations!" The thought of that scene made her smile. She was one step closer to achieving her dream.

A seven day celebration of food, music, and dancing followed. After the marriage contract was signed which provided for her in case of Uriah's death, the celebration was over. But the adventure had just begun.

She stayed in town while he went off on adventures. He usually returned in the evening with news about their exploits for that day. Sometimes he would bring her something he had taken from one of the people he had killed. Once it was a scarf, one time a ring, things like that. She knew she had a good husband, and her respect for him grew steadily, but she still wanted to become queen.

One morning, after they had been in Gath for a little more than a year, as Abishai sat outside his tent he heard a loud voice hollering at him. "We do not want any Hebrew dogs living here!"

When he turned and looked he saw two giants coming towards him. Looking around he saw no one was nearby to help. He remembered that Goliath came from Gath. Good idea, David, for choosing this as a place to settle.

"I cannot believe this. I have come here in peace, not looking for any trouble," said Abishai.

"Believe it. We come to give you trouble. Your uncle killed our brother. We are going to kill you."

"I believe you mean you want to join him," Abishai corrected them.

At those words they rushed Abishai with swords.

Abishai drew his sword and began thinking. David killed a giant with only a stone. He had a sword, so maybe he could kill two giants. Asahel was swift as a deer and when he saw from his tent what was happening to Abishai he ran unarmed, into the conflict. Asahel ran in circles around the brothers taunting them and causing them to chase him. Whenever they approached Abishai he ran in between them and taunted the giants. Asahel got too far away once and a giant took a swing at Abishai with a huge sword. He ducked under the blow as the giant's arm swung beyond him. He lunged up with his sword and struck the giant in his rib cage, penetrating his lung. The giant rocked back on his feet, wavered, then charged again. Asahel grabbed the giant's garment from behind and slowed him enough that Abishai escaped, just in time to run his sword into the other giant's abdomen. The men from Gath were screaming and swinging at both men but were not hitting anything. One of them bent over because of the bleeding in his abdomen and Abishai struck ferociously with his sword against the back of the giant's neck, cutting off his head. That left only one giant.

The giant faced Abishai tossing his sword from hand to hand, bleeding from his chest and struggling to breathe. His eyes were beacons of hatred. He cursed as he stalked his prey. If looks could kill, Abishai would already be dead. Asahel's distractions were ignored. Abishai was less than four cubits and this giant was at least six cubits. Abishai's head was a little higher than the giant's waist. If the giant hit him with his sword, he would be severed in half. Around and around a slow circle Abishai lead the giant as he cursed and fumed and bellowed. Death comes when we least expect it. Just as the giant thought he had Abishai in range to kill him and brought up his sword for the swing, the Abishai lunged at the giant and thrust his sword with all his might into the giant's chest again penetrating his heart this time. Abishai quickly retrieved his sword and jumped back out of the way. The giant staggered two steps backward, and then fell face first into the dirt. Abishai and Asahel embraced each other and began laughing loudly. About that time Uriah came up and asked, "What are you guys up to? You are interrupting my prayer time."

"Unfinished business," they laughed.

While they were still laughing there was a loud scream from Uriah's house. It was Bathsheba. Uriah ran as fast as he could, followed by his two friends. When he ran into his house he found Abigail and Ahinoam kneeling down beside Bathsheba. They scolded him and said wait outside.

Outside Uriah heard his wife scream louder than before then he heard a baby crying. A few minutes later Abigail came outside and said, "Congratulations papa. You have a little boy."

"Can I see him yet?"

"Yes and your wife want to see you too."

When he went in he looked at the baby, then at Bathsheba. Tears filled his eyes and ran down his face. "I love you, I love you. I love you." He said as he took her hand in one hand and wiped tears from her cheeks with the other.

"You are a good man Uriah. Yahweh blessed you with a son. We will name him Aksaray, after your father."

"You are the wife of wives." That was all Uriah could say because his throat was too tight and too soar to speak. He nodded his head in agreement and smiled at his son. "Aksaray." He whispered. Then he picked up the baby and cradled him in his arms until he started making noises. Then he quickly gave him back to Bathsheba.

The next morning Achish came to David," For sixteen months you have served me well. You fought off my enemies and brought me plenty of valuable items. But because your men killed two of my men you have to leave Gath. I will give you a town of your own. I have decided to give you and your people the town of Ziklag. You may begin moving today."

"As you wish, but you know my men were attacked. They were defending themselves."

"Exactly, I do not want any more bloodshed here. By the way, about a year ago three scoundrels who said they used to be with you tried to bribe me with some information. I thought they were lying so I did not believe them. They told me Uriah's mother and sister work for King Saul. Funny, they wanted me to give them money for the information."

"Why did you not tell me then?"

"I thought if I told you, you might leave and stop giving me all that bounty."

"Could be that is where they are. It is no wonder Uriah has not been able to find them. Thanks, I will tell him. Who are the men? I would like to reward them appropriately."

"Do not worry. I rewarded them the same as you would have."

Before the move David and his men patrolled the route between Gath and Ziklag for three days and drove off anyone they found within miles of their route. He let Uriah stay with Bathsheba so he could help her recover from the delivery. When they were sure the route was safe David positioned his men in strategic locations for protection. On the fourth day they moved to Ziklag.

Everyone felt a greater sense of security, loyal to the common goal -- enthroning David as king of Judah. No one else shared the town with them. Children were allowed to play outside, something they could not do in Gath; the Philistine children kept making fun of them and wanted to fight them. Women shared stories without fear when gathering water or washing the clothes, preparing the meals, or anything else. No Philistines would harass them.

Joab established security positions at the four corners of the city and a fifty man reserve was always on the ready in case of trouble. This was the happiest the people had been in three years. Ziklag provided safety because Saul did not pursue them and no enemy dared to ambush. No one came bearing bad news. No one wanted revenge. This was a good place to live.

Uriah wondered about his mother and sister. They probably would not recognize him today. His beard was full, his body was tan, and he had gained several pounds. He too looked like a god. He was no longer the lanky bird-like person who met David. His references to the Law of Nature were gradually replaced by seeking the Law of Yahweh. His mother would not even know him he was sure. She certainly would never think he was living with the Philistines, after having killed so many of them. Yahweh works in mysterious ways. What would he do next?

CHAPTER 23

The southern borders of Judah were still plagued with various tribes and people groups who were trying to steal what they could from whomever they could. David, making it his mission to stop them, left the women and a few men at Ziklag and headed south taking Uriah and the other leaders.

The first group he encountered was the Girzites. No one was spared. Uriah ordered his men to make the half moon formation, a formation he had used to defeat the Achaeans in Ankara. This ploy prevented the Girzites from knowing the exact number that Uriah had with him because all they could see wee the men in the front ranks. They underestimated and charged toward the front line. But before they got there, the archers decimated them. Too late to retreat. They went the way of the Ziphites.

Next, they found the Geshurites. As David and his men approached them a man with a long white beard and long white hair, wearing a purple and red robe came to greet him. He bowed low to the ground and said," David, may you be king forever. I, King Talmai, your servant, wish to welcome you to my camp. May I serve you in a manner worthy of your position?"

"Tell me one reason why I should not kill you right here and now!" David demanded.

"I have three virgin daughters who are willing to go with you in exchange for your kind consideration on our behalf."

"We have enough women already and . . ." He began to say as he turned to look at Uriah's scowl. From a nearby tent the three women came and stood where David could see them, stopping him in mid sentence. They were dressed in pink satin blouses with matching bottoms. The blouses, which exposed their navels, had lavender palm trees and decorations of gold and blue fruit along the sleeves. Their bottoms had the same decoration down the legs and hung tightly from their hips. Two of the women wore their black hair braided all the way down to their waists. The other one had black hair pulled forward and straight down her chest. Their perfume smelled like wild flowers in a spring field. When they smiled it felt like a sunrise, their beauty was irresistible, even for someone who came here to kill them. They were so beautiful David stopped talking. In fact, he stopped breathing.

Talmai clapped his hands twice and somewhere someone began playing a zither. The clap caused David to begin breathing again. The women danced rhythmically and smiled as the men watched, mesmerized. The show lasted for over two hours before David asked King Talmai," What is the name of your daughter, the one in the middle, over there, the one with the straight hair?"

"Her name is Maacah. She is the eldest and is the right age to be a good wife for the right man. She could be a good wife for a king. I heard you were the next king. Can I offer you some more fresh water? And your men? Perhaps we could make a treaty and seal it with the marriage between you and my daughter?"

As David sat talking with the king, Uriah came up to him, "David, if you are here to get a wife, get her and let us go. If we are here to protect this border from these people let us do that. You are wasting our time and breaking the law of your god by sitting here. And you know very well that this is the time of times."

David gave him a sidelong glare, angry over the interruption. "How am I breaking Yahweh's laws?"

"Your own law says a king should not multiply wives to himself. All you do is collect more wives and more wives," said Uriah.

"That is why we do not cast our pearls before swine. That law means I can have no more than eighteen wives. I am less than half way there. You see to your Law of Nature with your one wife and let me see to the Law of God for my many wives."

"You can make that law say anything you want it to say! This is still lust of the flesh. Samuel warned about this."

David said, "Be patient a few more minutes, Uriah. Men, what do you want to do, move on or kill these people?" He thought, someday I must kill that man. Then he thought he would allow him to kill himself. He would tell Uriah about his mother and sister and let Uriah try to take them from Saul.

All the men grateful for the entertainment shouted, "Sign a treaty, let us move on."

David rose up, wished his host well and left the camp. Maacah approached David, took his right hand in hers, and bowed low. "I was pleased to have been in your presence and to dance for you. Shall I go with you, now?" She smiled.

David looked at Uriah, and forced himself away. "I may come back for you. Stay here today."

Then he turned to Uriah and said. "Uriah, your mother and sister work for the king. If he finds out you are with me he could harm them. You need to decide what you are going to do. Are you going to stay with me, or go after them?"

"How do you know that?"

"Achish told me,"

"Achish! We left him months ago! What are you just now telling me now for?"

"When we first met you said you were looking for them. I thought if you knew where they were you would leave. I needed you. We do not agree on much but I needed your sword."

"You are partly correct. I will leave to get them. But if they have been hurt, you will answer to me for not telling me sooner."

David and his men rode from there and discovered a band of nomads preparing to ambush them. David told some of his men to circle around behind the ambushers while the rest pretended they did not see them. They would continue on as if nothing was going to happen. When the ambush began those who circled around would attack the ambushers from the rear while the rest of the men counterattacked from the front. When David's men were in the range of the ambushers weapons David's men unexpectedly attacked first, from the front and behind. They tried to run, but there was no place to go. Before a half hour had passed, they were all dead. Gathering up any valuables they could find they returned to Ziklag. The men sang victory songs and praises to Yahweh all the way home.

When they arrived home they were horrified.

All the houses were burned to the ground, the men who had been left behind were all dead, and all the women and children were missing.

Uriah shouted," While you lusted after those women and let that king sweet talk you, my wife and son have been kidnapped!"

Other men began shouting at David and several of them picked up stones to stone him. "Did you bring us all the way here just to let our families be killed?" The men were in a riotous mood. Even his officers and mighty men were shouting at him. David had to act. He would pursue the attackers and free the hostages. He told the men to follow him and six hundred men went with him.

At dusk they found a man near death in a field. After they helped him up and gave him some water he said he was an Egyptian who had been traveling with some Amalekites. They had raided Ziklag and captured all the women and children. He said the Amalekites and the Geshurites had made a deal. The Geshurites were supposed to distract them long enough to allow Ziklag to be attacked by the Amalekites. The Amalekites were to establish an ambush to slow them too. He pleaded for his life by telling them he knew where the Amalekites were going and could help find them.

Uriah suggested bringing the man with them, if they did not find their women, he would be killed. David agreed. Continuing the pursuit they arrived at the Besor Ravine where two hundred of the men said they were too exhausted to continue. David left them with the supplies and told them to stay there. The other four hundred continued across the ravine in search for their families.

When it became too dark to see where they were going they rested for the night. The next day they found the Amalekites where the man had said they would be. David and his men rode in hard. They attacked in four waves of one hundred men. One wave came from the south. After the Amalekites were responding to defend the south another wave attacked from the north. A third wave came in from the east, and the last wave came in from the west. Fighting was fierce. Bows were useless. Spears, swords, and daggers were the weapons for this battle. The Amalekites had never put up this much of a fight before. Uriah remembered the story of how Moses had to keep his arms raised to help the wilderness people in their battle against the Amalekites. He needed a Moses tonight. When it got dark David ordered retreat.

The next morning David and his men attacked again. This time, they all attacked with ferocity from the same direction. This caught the Amalekites off guard because they were defending their entire perimeter expecting an attack from all directions as the day before. Resistance was strong but by mid afternoon they had gained a temporary advantage. Uriah, Abishai, Asahel, Joab, and David fought with all their strength. Uriah kept his swords in their scabbards and used only his dagger. They estimated that over six hundred men were fighting back. Everywhere one was killed, two more seemed to appear. Some men shouted," Are we winning, Uriah?" to which he would shout back," If God is on our side who can be against us? Of course we are winning! Keep fighting?" When evening came on the second day, the Amalekites tried to flee. But

David left no one standing. All the Amalekites were killed while David lost two hundred men in the battle.

The women were rescued and everything that had been stolen was recovered. All the spoil was gathered up. Uriah said that it took a few hours to kill six hundred Philistines, but it took almost two days to kill six hundred Amalekites, who were more skillful and proficient in battle.

The men were even angrier with David. They had lost two hundred of their comrades trying to rescue the women and children when they should never have been kidnapped in the first place if David had kept his mind on his mission.

One hundred men were ready to stone him but chose instead to leave with Uriah when he returned to Gibeah. That would leave David with about half of his original force. Two hundred were killed in the battle with the Amalekites, and one hundred deserted him. He would have to wait for more men to join him before he could do anything else.

When they arrived back at Besor Ravine they set up camp for the night. The men who had survived the fighting wanted all the spoils for themselves. The men who stayed behind to protect their supplies said they also should be entitled to some of the spoils. David intervened to prevent more bloodshed. The spoils were to be divided equally between those who protected the supplies and those who fought the battles.

Uriah tried to reassure Bathsheba that everything would be okay. She was angry to have been kidnapped and angrier that her baby could have been killed. He told her about Ravia and Annitis working for the king and he was going to go find them. He would like her to come too.

In the morning the one hundred men who wanted to stone David left with Uriah and Bathsheba when he left to get his mother and sister. They refused to follow a man so fickle he would allow his town to be destroyed and their women to be kidnapped, while he was dazzled by someone in pretty clothes and pricey perfume.

En route to find Ravia and Annitis, Bathsheba cradling her baby began thinking about her plans to become queen. She asked Uriah, "When we find your family, what then? What are your plans?"

"My plans have always been to find them and return home. They have not changed."

"What about me?"

"You are my wife. You go with me."

"Are you sure you want to go back home? In Hatusha you were a bee-keeper but you will go back to nothing. Here you are a commander in the king's army. Makes more sense to me to stay here. What do you think?"

"What about my mother and sister?"

"They can stay with us. We can stay here together."

"I guess we could give it try. See how it works out," he said.

"I think it will work out fine," she said.

None of David's officers went near him all day. A few wondered whether he was fit to lead. Those who chose to stay with him went back to Ziklag to see whether anything left behind could be salvaged. What were the options? They could not return to Gath. They had nothing left there at Ziklag. Everyone was still angry at David, especially his wives when they learned about what caused their delay in returning from their raids. Where else could they go?

Several of the wives had lost their husbands. What could he do for them?

Abigail approached David and said, “I have a lot of property which used to belong to my husband. I would gladly let you and your men stay there in return for more personal time with you.”

So they went to Maon, near Mount Carmel until they could think of something else. All the enemies in the area had been eliminated, Saul would not know where they were, and it was a good temporary solution.

Abigail was quick to assign living quarters to the few remaining men with families. She assigned the widowed wives their own rooms but not in the same house where David was staying. Ahinoam established work details for the women while David sent the single men to help the shepherds again.

This time, the person who owned the sheep was a benevolent person and would share with them. They were told this was only a temporary arrangement so do not become too comfortable. David thought that if he had not been chosen to be the next king, he could make a nice home here. He decided to stay until the number of his men increased again.

As he traveled to Gibeah Uriah thought he did not see much happening in his life. How could riding around in the desert killing people help anyone? He was happy to have received word about his mother and sister, and was happy to be married to Bathsheba and proud of his son. Then he thought about the men he was with. Not many of these men even talk about Yahweh. Some keep the Sabbath and some pray. Some quote from Moses by memory. Most men acted like there is no God. Strange to believe in a god who seems so insignificant to them. It is good Bathsheba wants to keep his mother and sister with her. That is real religion.

Uriah was learning to pray and learning to lean on Yahweh. It did not seem to matter that the last three years have been spent wandering and fighting. He knew Yahweh was close. He was in his heart. Uriah understood him more each day: He understood that God was love. He understood that only faith brought man close to Yahweh. He understood that the laws were given to help man live a good life, not to restrict him. But he also understood no man or woman could keep those laws all the time. He promised Yahweh his faithfulness to his dying breath. The laws were good and should be obeyed, not as David's men obeyed, but obeyed as Uriah would.

His plan was really very simple. Uriah sent some men into the vineyard and some more to the chief of staff in the palace. It was a little more difficult to convince the chief of staff they had an emergency message for Ravia and had to see her. The men discovered that Ravia and Annitis were not there. Apparently King Saul issued a decree for all foreigners working for him to be replaced with Jewish workers. All of the foreign workers left three months ago and no one knew where they were going.

Uriah shouted so loud he surprised all his men. How could Saul do this to him? How could David do this to him? How could Yahweh do this to him? How could no one know where they went? The men who came with him refused to return to David. Uriah told them he was on a mission and had to return. He had nowhere else to go. He made the men pledge they would not disclose to anyone where David was staying. The truth was they did not know David had planned to move away from Ziklag.

In Hebron Ravia said to Annitis," We cannot tell Uriah where we are because we do not know where he is. He cannot come to us because he does not know where we are. We will live here among the Hittites and try to hear word of him."

"May the gods give us favor," said Annitis. "The men who said they were going to tell him about us must not have told him."

"Like men in general, making promises they do not intend to keep," said Ravia.

"May the gods give us favor, mother?"

CHAPTER 24

Uriah exploded into David's presence accusing him of deliberately withholding the location of his family. His delay caused him to miss his family because Saul had moved them. But as Uriah stormed around the room David was not listening. He was incredulous because he had been told the Philistines were preparing to attack King Saul's army. Uriah's personal concerns were of no consequence to him in this situation. He had killed so many Philistines it would seem they would not want to fight anymore. But the Philistines wanted the Israelite's land and were determined to commit genocide if necessary to get it. In fact, David learned that there was a prophet among them telling them if they attacked one more time they would possess the land. David and his men returned to Ziklag to be in Philistine territory in case Saul asked for his assistance. The Israelites were not going to lose their God given land under his watch! The number of men with him, including those newly recruited at the cave had increased to over one thousand. He would be useful if needed in battle.

His men had been in constant training. It took six months to teach a man how to ride and become proficient with a sword from a horse. It took twice as long to teach him how to shoot a bow while riding. David knew most of his men were ready for battle. Some were more than ready, they were mighty. They lived on the smell of death. Abishai was the best warrior David had ever seen. His brother Joab had a natural gift of leadership: men obeyed him because he expected them to obey. His brother Asahel and the Hittite Uriah were warrior wonders. He could use an army of men like those two. Eliam was not as agile but was more cunning than his opponents and Ahithophel was a wealth of wisdom though too old to fight anymore. He had more than thirty men who could outfight any three hundred Philistine soldiers. Yes, he was at Ziklag in case Saul needed him. He had killed thousands for the king and was ready to kill again. But the king did not send for him.

Saul left Gilead and approached the Philistine army at Mount Gilboah. This was the last thing in the world he wanted to do and it turned out to be the last thing in the world he would do. The Philistines charged with all their might and fought with all their strength forcing Saul's army to retreat. Moving to fall back positions they tried to maintain pressure on the Philistines but it was no use. By mid-day the rout was complete. In panic the Israelite army turned its back on the enemy and ran in every direction. When villagers in nearby towns heard that the army was retreating from the Philistines, they all ran too. Whoever could run the farthest, the fastest, to escape the Philistines was the winner.

Poor Saul! He lost! The Philistines killed Saul's sons Jonathan, Abinadab, and Malchishua. The grief was too great. He lost his sons, he lost his army, he lost his throne, and he lost his pride, so he took his life. Fear chased him, caught him, and paralyzed him. Remorse enslaved him and turned his heart to wax. He had no will to fight. He had no ability to fight. Falling on his own sword was the only way Saul could escape the Philistines.

David and his men stayed at Ziklag, trying to make some type of shelter from the rubble that did not get burned, while training in case Saul sent for him. A week after their return a messenger came from Saul's camp. His clothes were torn, there was dirt on his head, and when he saw David, he fell at his feet and worshipped him.

David asked," Where do you come from, and what are you doing here?"

The man answered," I escaped from Saul's camp. I came to tell you that King Saul is dead. Everyone was fleeing from the battle. It was a terrible rout! Three of Saul's sons were killed also."

"How do you know that Saul and his sons are dead?"

"I happened by chance to pass Mount Gilboa and found Saul leaning on his sword. The chariots and horsemen were approaching him. When he saw me he called to me. When I was near he told me to kill him because he did not want to die at the hands of the Philistines."

"He told you to kill him! What did you do?" anger instantly erupted in David's heart and he clutched the messenger by his shirt.

"I took his sword and slew him as he told me. I took the crown that was on his head, and the bracelet from his arm and brought them here to you."

David ripped open the man's shirt then tore his own clothes and began mourning loudly. All his men joined him. They mourned, and wept, and fasted, and prayed until the evening for Saul and his sons. Uriah could not understand why they should mourn someone who stole his wife and then spent the past several years trying to kill him.

That seemed to be against the law of nature as he remembered. Maybe it was not against the Law of Yahweh.

At sunset David called for the messenger. In anticipation of a reward the messenger promptly obeyed. David asked him, "Did you say you are an Amalekite? The same people who burned down this city you see me in."

"Yes, I am an Amalekite."

"How dare you kill the king anointed by the only God in Heaven?"

"He told me to. He was the king. I had to obey him."

"How dare you come to tell me of your stupidity?"

"I thought you would want to know. So I came."

"Who do you think I am that I should reward a man who not only kills my king, but has the audacity to come to me expecting a reward, an Amalekite at that?"

"You are the new king. I thought you would want to know."

"Uriah what do you think?"

"I think the only good Amalekite is a dead Amalekite." Uriah answered.

David called one of the young men who had just joined him and had never killed anyone before. He told him," You heard Uriah, kill him!" So the young man killed him.

David lamented the death of Saul and his sons. He wept bitterly over the death of his best friend Jonathan, who was closer to him than a brother. He could not sleep that night: he paced the ground and fields around Ziklag. He called his advisors and comrades Ahithophel, Eliam, Joab and his brothers, and Uriah. He called for his mighty men. They sat around a fire discussing their future and the future of the country. The only king Israel ever had had been killed. Was it too early to declare himself king?

David asked his men, "Ahithophel, is there any message in the stars? Uriah, has Yahweh spoken to you? Joab, what is the best military strategy? Eliam, what do the people think."

Joab answered," We are in Philistine territory here in Ziklag. The Philistines just killed our king. We need to return to Judah. The army has probably fled to all parts of Israel. Someone needs to reinstate the army and provide leadership for this country. That someone is you, David. You have been anointed. You have been trained. You are ready. Now is your time."

Ahithophel replied," Truth be known, the stars show turmoil in Israel. New kings will arise in the north and in the south. The two kings will fight for many years. One will win and rule a united Israel. That one is you."

Uriah answered, "This is the silence of silence. Yahweh has told me nothing, but the Law of Nature says you cannot leave the soldiers without a commander or they will not be soldiers for long."

Eliam replied," I believe Joab is correct. The people would want you to settle in Judah. We should gather all our men and their families, and all of our possessions and move to Judah."

David asked," Where in Judah do you recommend?"

"The stars say that perhaps Hebron would be a good place. It's closer to the people and easily defended," Ahithophel advised.

"Hebron suits me fine, there are a lot of my people there," said Uriah.

David approved," Men, you have served me well for years. We now face the biggest battles of our lives. Thank you for your advice. Tell everyone we move to Hebron tomorrow. Send some men to the Cave of Adullam, and send someone else to Abigail in Maon. Tell them to move all our men and their families to Hebron. Tell them to bring all their livestock and all their possessions."

David rode into the fertile valley of Hebron three days later. His followers straggled in over the next several weeks. A week after his arrival, men from all of Judah came to him and anointed him king. David knew that the trials he had gone through for several years were nothing like what waited ahead for him. He sent word throughout the twelve tribes asking for volunteers to join him. To his amazement over three hundred thousand men, some from every tribe, came to Hebron to join the army.

Hebron was the perfect place: a perennial spring supplied all the water they would need and there was fertile ground for crops. The Hittite inhabitants of Hebron had planted vineyards and fruit trees. David saw the apples, plums, figs, grapes, and nut trees and knew this land would support his men. Grain fields could be planted in the gently rolling hillside. Locating a terraced hill rising above any hill in the region, he moved his dwelling to the top. From there he could see for miles in any direction -- he chose the high ground for himself – and told his advisors and followers to rebuild their homes in the region below the hill. This location was great.

Meanwhile, Abner, the commander of Saul's army, disregarding Yahweh's choice, thought that a son of Saul should be the next king so he crowned Ishbosheth. That brought immediate conflict between Ishbosheth and David. After a few years of confrontations and hostilities it all came to an end. At a place called Helkathhazzurim the armies of Joab and Abner prepared to fight each other.

Someone suggested that twelve men from each army fight each other and whoever is left standing wins the battle. His king would rule over Israel. All twenty-four men killed each other in a fierce battle by clutching his opponent by his hair and smashing his sword into his side.

No one won the fight. Abner began running as he did when facing the Philistines, but Joab and Asahel gave pursuit. Abner could not outrun Asahel who ran like a deer, so in desperation he turned around suddenly and killed him by jamming his sword into his abdomen clear to the hilt. Joab continued the chase so Abner ran to the hill of Ammah.

Abner called down to Joab," Why go on killing each other? Are we not brothers? Let us make a truce. If you let me leave this hill I will lead my men across the Jordan and away from you."

Joab answered," It is a good thing you offered a truce. By morning there would be no survivors on that hill. I will let you pass safely."

When the armies regrouped for a battle damage assessment, Abner had lost over three hundred sixty men killed, while Joab had lost nineteen, plus Asahel. Joab and his men took Ishbosheth to Bethlehem for burial in his father's tomb, and then marched all night to arrive at Hebron by daybreak.

One afternoon, about a month after Abner had been defeated, Uriah and Bathsheba were passing near a vineyard when he thought he recognized someone's voice. As he approached, the person was turned to be facing away from him. He called out, "Annitis?"

Annitis thought it was the keeper of the vineyard and answered, “Yes,”

“Annitis. I am Uriah.”

“Uriah!” She did not recognize his appearance but recognized his voice, so she ran to him and embraced his neck so hard he wondered if it would break.

“Where is mother? Is she alright?” he asked.

“She has not been well lately. Let me take you to her,” she said.

“We have been hearing all kinds of stories about you. Are they true?” she asked.

“That depends on whether they are good or bad,” Bathsheba said.

“They are good. He is my dad,” said Aksaray.

“Meet my wife, Bathsheba, and my son Aksaray” He said to Annitis. Then he said, “This is the sister I have been looking for.”

“So nice to meet you,” they both said, hugging each other, kissing each other’s cheek, and joining hands, like old friends.

Annitis took Uriah and Bathsheba to Ravia. Uriah said, “Where have you been? I have been looking everywhere.”

“We thought you would get killed in Hatusha so we waited a couple of weeks then tried to get to Gibeah,” said Ravia.

“Right. But our camels got lame feet and we had to stop in Jabeth-Gilead where we got jobs at the inn,” said Annitis.

“I heard you were at the inn but when I went there you were gone,” said Uriah.

“Yeah, that is correct. We were kidnapped by the Ammonites,” said Ravia.

"But a kind soldier helped us to escape," said Annitis. "I think he liked me."

"But I lead a division of men to Ammon and freed the hostages. You were not there."

"That is because we had already escaped. Our friend was supposed to meet us in Jericho but he never made it," said Ravia.

"I went to Jericho looking for you. I spent three days there."

"We found a caravan going to Egypt so we joined it and stopped in Gibeah," said Annitis.

"We met two men in the vineyard who said you were in Gath. They were supposed to tell you where we were. But you did not come," said Ravia.

"I was not told until over a year later,"

"Then King Saul evicted all foreign workers from the palace so we came here," said Ravia.

"That explains how come you were not in Gibeah when Bathsheba and I went there to get you."

"You two have had quite the adventure, it seems," said Bathsheba.

"Now we want to know how our gentle bee keeper became a leader in King David's army," said Ravia. "Tell us how you two met."

"Yeah, and are the stories about you true?" asked Annitis.

Uriah and Bathsheba told their story, talking long into the night. Since Ravia and Annitis had their own house in Hebron, there was no need for them to move in with Uriah.

David knew he had to secure his borders so he went southeast and entered the land of the Amalekites. "Uriah, what did you say about the Amalekites? Did you say the only good Amalekite is a dead Amalekite?"

"That is the word of words. That is what I said."

"Let us go kill some Amalekites! Since the days of Moses, these people have been a thorn in our flesh. It is time to remove the thorn."

David had organized his forces into three divisions. Two divisions protected the northern border, while one division went with David to face the Amalekites. The soldiers were determined to end the three hundred years of harassment. They faced the Amalekites like two jaws on a vise. Uriah led half of the division from the north while Joab led the other half from the south. David and his command staff remained at the pivot of the vise. Uriah thought this is like grapes being squashed, except we will not get wine from these grapes, only blood. The forces slowly moved closer together, ensuring no survivors. No man, no woman, no child, no beasts, no survivors, none. No one caught in the vise escaped. When it was over, fifty thousand Amalekites were dead. There were no wounded, they were killed. There were no prisoners of war, they were killed.

David observed," That should get the thorn from our side for awhile." He posted two hundred men in each of four outposts south of the Dead Sea to protect the southeast boundary. He grew angrier that Saul had not secured his borders as he should have.

From there he turned westward. After four days he encountered Talmai. "Talmai, we meet again. Last time we met you delayed me while the Amalekites destroyed my city and kidnapped my wives. I just destroyed the Amalekites. Today I am going to kill you."

"Spare my life and I will give you my daughters, my gold, silver, and jewels. My people will clean your camel stables and care for your livestock forever." Talmai, perspiring profusely and crying loudly fell on his stomach, crawled to David's feet like a fat snake that just had its tail cut off and sounding like a mother bear that lost her cub, begged for mercy. He knew his life was on the line.

"Get on your feet and bring your people here," David commanded.

Talmai gave the command and the people who had not escaped into the desert came to appear before David. David gave the signal and his men surrounded Talmai's people.

"Talmai, here is a lesson for you. I do not negotiate, I eliminate. I do not get angry, I get revenge. You made a covenant with my enemy. Give me your daughters."

The daughters stepped forward.

"Not my daughters! Do not kill my daughters. Do anything you want, only spare my daughters," cried Talmai.

"Talmai, you have your wish. But you deceived me. I want you to watch this." He turned to Joab and gave orders, "Kill every man. Spare only Talmai and his three daughters."

Talmai watched in horror as his people were killed. While Talmai cried, shouted, and wailed for mercy, David's men killed his people.

"Talmai, you asked me to spare your daughters. I still have your daughters. They will be safe with me."

Talmai started to say something but David stated, "Be silent little worm," as he stroke his throat with his sword.

Talmai breathed his last breath.

Uriah signaled for Joab to take the women. He dispatched another two hundred men each into four

outposts to protect the south central border. That night after Uriah declined the offer, David gave the two younger sisters to two men who had fought valiantly. He kept Maacah for himself.
Uriah felt he had been used again so David could kill more men to obtain another wife. Let him have them all. Uriah had Bathsheba, she is all he needs.

As they continued south and west they discovered a Girzite encampment. The Girzites had heard from those who escaped that David took no prisoners and would not accept servitude, so they attacked first. The surprise almost gave them a fighting chance. But they were facing an entire division with less four hundred men. The fighting was difficult because they would fire their bows, and then hide in ditches, ravines, behind, or even in trees. Little by little, all the Girzites who joined the attack were killed. When the army searched the camp they found a woman named Haggith under some blankets in one of the tents. She was pregnant. Instead of killing her, they brought her to David.

She had no fancy clothes or perfume. She had plain brown robes and no shoes, her hair was unkempt, and her face was smudged and covered with the tracks of her tears. She bowed low," I know you have killed all my people. My husband and my parents died outside my tent, right over there and she pointed to the spot. I watched them die so I hid. All the people are afraid of you. We had no choice but to attack. I am also a Girzite and I should die with my people. I ask only that you let me have my baby before you kill me."

Uriah told David," No men are left alive to care for this woman. The law of nature says that you either kill her or give her a husband. Yahweh says you should not kill in cold blood."

David told her, "Since I am responsible for your widowhood, I will care for you. You can live with me and be my wife. I will take care of your child." Then he posted another two hundred men to protect the rest of the border.

When David had secured the southern borders of Judah he went to Jabesh-Gilead to thank the men and bless the town for looking after God's anointed. No one opposed him, everyone cheered him. The leader of the town gave a three day celebration in honor of David being anointed King of Judah and securing the southern borders against neighboring enemies. At the end of the celebration the town leader offered his daughter to David for his wife, as a peace agreement between them. The bargain was agreed upon so David took Abital for his wife. David posted a detachment of five hundred men in Jabesh-Gilead, extra security to protect the treaty. Some of the military commanders also found wives for themselves in Jabesh-Gilead. Joab had to provide a special detail just to care for all of the new wives.

As they were returning to Hebron, they passed through the Ziphite desert again. When David discovered some Ziphites still alive he gathered up all the survivors. When they were all present David said to them, "Here is my offer. Each of you and your descendent will serve me and my descendents caring for our livestock as long as one of my descendents is one the throne in Judah. If you refuse, you will all be killed. What is your pleasure?"

The Ziphites agreed to be slaves forever so David let them live. To seal the bargain David ordered the most beautiful virgin be brought to him. They brought him Eglah. "When you think of your position as slaves in my kingdom, remember Eglah who has spared your life. She will be my wife, as a symbol of your dependence on me. When you are hot or cold and sore because of your labors, thank her that I did not kill all of you. Is that understood?"

Everyone understood, so David added Eglah to the other women in his expanding harem and they began their return to Hebron bringing all the Ziphites with them as slaves. David had secured the borders of Judah and obtained four new wives in this campaign. He thought it was time to build his kingdom. Maybe Uriah would agree with him.

PART SEVEN

CHAPTER 25

Lost in his thoughts, Uriah strolled through the garden behind his house, stopping to look at every flower, and then stopping at his bees. Once a bee keeper always a bee keeper, he mused. He continued to think about his situation. Twelve years ago his life changed forever. He became a warrior and joined the army of David. Uriah promoted to division commander, in charge of over one thousand men in the Army of Israel, a leading military tactician, and one of David's thirty mighty men, could not believe it. Who could have predicted that?

Eliam gave him Bathsheba for a wife and they had three children, two boys and a girl. He had found Annitis and Ravia. Praise Yahweh! Bathsheba has been a good mother and a good wife. Sometimes she seems distant – pre-occupied with other thoughts – although she always said everything was fine. David's wives had given him sons and daughters. Peace has filled the country for the six years they lived in Hebron. The borders are still secure despite the occasional clashes between the army of Israel and the army of Judah.

Uriah contemplated his future. Had he accomplished all that he could? With the peace that existed, and the nearness he felt to Yahweh, could he assume he fulfilled the mission Yahweh had given him? Or is there more for him to do? Uriah realized he never felt this unsure before. Instead of being a victim of his environment, he wanted to chart his own future. Maybe it was time to return to Hatusha and bee keeping. Give up his career as a soldier. He thought about telling his ideas to Bathsheba. What she would say? She would say she liked the flower he picked for her.

Bathsheba soaked in her warm bath and let her thoughts drift. Twelve years ago Eliam told her she was going to marry a Hittite. She rebelled at the idea of marrying a heathen, but thought that he might help her become a queen in Israel.

What a dumb idea!

Instead, she had helped care for the homeless in the Cave of Adullam and bandaged battle wounds. She followed her husband to Ziklag where the Amalekites kidnapped her. When she was released she thought about asking for a divorce, especially when Uriah dragged her with him to go find his mother and sister and they were not even there. But then David became king over Judah and they all moved to Hebron. Maybe there was still hope she could become queen. She had three children but even though Uriah was a great husband, she was no closer to becoming queen than she was twelve years ago.

David had taken six wives, seven counting Michal. Maybe he would still be interested in her – if she was available. With peace in the region, there was little chance her husband would be killed, freeing her to marry someone else. Maybe she should just ask Uriah for a divorce. She was not permitted to divorce him, but perhaps he would agree. No he would not; he was a good father, husband, and soldier. No doubt he loved her.

Maybe he was too good to die.

Bathsheba thought, if I die before him, I will never be queen! She thought about telling Uriah about her ideas. She wondered what he would say. Maybe she could convince him to try to become king. What would he say?

David paced on his roof top stopping occasionally to look over the neighboring rooftops, his mind preoccupied, a concern in his heart, and contemplated the future. He looked at the stars and wished he could read them like Ahithophel. Twelve years ago he fled from King Saul. His wife let him out a window and he escaped, leaving her behind. She had cost the lives of six hundred Philistines. How many men had he killed since then? He could not even count them!

And he still did not have Michal.

He still wanted her. He was anointed to be king over Israel and knew that a strong army was necessary. He would need skillful men. Uriah was one of those men, but he was a thorn in the flesh. Now that the borders of Judah had been secured, there was not much fighting. Someday he would have to face the enemy across the Jordan and in the north but today everything was good. His wives all had children, he was wealthy, the people in Judah were happy. He asked himself, what else is a king supposed to do? Maybe I can save the country some money by reducing the size of my army. All the men could be discharged and placed on ready in case they were needed. They could divide into units of twenty-four thousand each and serve one month a year. During the other eleven months they can live at home and have normal lives. Uriah's thousand would be one of them. Maybe he would return to Hatusha. How would Bathsheba like that? He thought about telling Uriah his ideas. What would he say?

The next day, Ahithophel and Eliam came to see David. "Gentlemen, to what do I owe this pleasure?" he asked.

Ahithophel replied," Truth be known, King David, we came to talk with you about Uriah and Bathsheba."

"What about them?"

Eliam answered, rubbing his hands twice down his beard, and then rubbing them together. "As you know, Bathsheba is my daughter and you were present when I offered her to Uriah the Hittite. She was reluctant at first but agreed to the marriage. He even got circumcised so she would have him."

Ahithophel continued," Ever since she was young she wanted nice things. She has been a faithful wife and good mother. Truth be known, Uriah has been as loyal to you as a puppy."

"You mean bulldog. What is it that you want?" asked the king.

"Since they have served your kingdom for so well for so long, we request that you promote Uriah to one of your ministerial positions. He could become your Minister of State to Anatolia since he knows the people, the economy, and the history. It's in the stars." Ahithophel stated.

Eliam agreed saying," There is no one in your kingdom more qualified to be the Minister of State to Anatolia. We ask for a promotion, and separation from the army. He has served you well for twenty years. He deserves a reward. Of course with his reward, Bathsheba would benefit too. He does not know we have approached you in this matter."

"Are you thinking about Uriah or Bathsheba when you make this request?"

"Bathsheba," said Ahithophel.

"Uriah," said Eliam.

"Thank you for your suggestions. I was already thinking along the lines you suggested. I will let you know what I decide," David stated as he escorted them to the door.

When they left he summoned Joab, his commander. He explained to Joab what he had been considering and how Ahithophel and Eliam had just presented a good way for him to send Uriah back to Hatusha while still working for Israel. Joab agreed that during the peaceful times they were experiencing, maybe they could reduce the army to twenty-four thousand, as long as the rest of the men were still on call if needed.

While they were still talking Recab and his brother Baanah charged into the room and declared," Here is the head of Ishbosheth, King of Israel, son of Saul, your enemy."

"How did he die?" Joab asked

"How did you get his head?" David asked.

"We entered his house at mid-day on pretense, stabbed him, and killed him while he was sleeping. Then we cut off his head." they stated.

David exploded with anger. The more they spoke the angrier he became and the more anger he felt the louder he spoke. "When someone came to me in Ziklag and said to me Saul was dead, do you know what I did? I killed him. Now two wicked men, you two, have killed an innocent man, and dare to tell me as if it is good news. Then you bring the head of the man as evidence of your wickedness into my presence, how much more will I do to you!"

He paced around the room for a few minutes. Then he said to Joab, “Strip these men of their clothes and tie them to a donkey. Parade them around all of Hebron so everyone can see their shame. Then cut off their hands and feet and hang their bodies upside down in the garbage pile until the flies and maggots have eaten all but their bones. Put a sign over their heads that tell the people what will happen to wicked men in my kingdom.”

Joab bowed,” Yes, your majesty.” and took the men out to do as David had commanded.

Just as Joab left the room a large delegation of over one hundred men, representing the tribes of Israel wanted to see him. What now? David thought as he summoned the men into his presence. One of the men acted as spokesperson, “We have come from Saul’s kingdom. As you probably know Ishbosheth is dead and we have no king. Many years ago God chose you to be our king. We think it is time that you accept the throne of Israel and rule over a united kingdom. It is time to put our differences behind us and unite as brothers. Saul was king over a united kingdom, and we want you to rule over a united kingdom.”

David said he would accept the throne on one condition -- if they would bring him Michal. Everyone agreed. The coronation would not occur until Michal was back with David. Even though he had many wives, Michal is the one he loved the most. David would have the bride he wanted so badly. He paid for her with two hundred Philistine foreskins. Perhaps his anger would be abated.

Four days later Abner returned Michal, Paltiel, and her sons to the king.

"This is your reward for stealing my wife," David said to Paltiel. David made Paltiel watch as five archers fired one arrow each into the hearts of his five sons. "None of your sons will ever think they can usurp their way past my sons to become the next king."

Turning to Joab, David ordered," Tie this mongrel outside the city until he is dead. He is to receive no food or water. Keep him bound day and night. I want him to die thinking about the bad decision he made when he married my wife. Take Michal to my palace."

Michal watched when the soldiers buried Paltiel. She danced and sang on his grave. "I said to you I would dance on your grave, you heathen!"

David could not believe that he had Michal again. She was not just another person in his harem. She was the wife he loved. He gave her a private room near his and assigned twelve servants to care for her. He dressed her in the finest clothes in his kingdom and put a crown on her head. Everywhere David went, Michal went. He even set up a throne near his so she could be present as he conducted kingdom business throughout the day. No two people had ever been so in love. Samson had his Delilah, Isaac had his Rebecca, Jacob had his Rachel, but David had his Michal. No one could compare to that. Everything in her eyes, her face, her countenance, her smile, indicated Michal felt the same. This was a marriage made in heaven before time began that would last until after time ended. Being with Michal was more important to David than running the kingdom. He let the kingdom run itself for a week so he could be with her.

CHAPTER 26

The splendor of the coronation exceeded expectations. Each tribe presented its own dancers, performers, soldiers, and musicians, each tribe trying to outdo the others. David and his wives and children all rode in beautiful carriages pulled by white horses decorated in the patterns and color of royalty. Men from cities all over the world came to pay their respects to the king. The dancing and feasting lasted for twelve days, with each tribe of Israel hosting one day of the celebration. Performers from as far away as Greece, India, and Ethiopia came to take part in the festivities. Parthians, Medes, Elamites, and inhabitants of Egypt, Libya, and even Rome joined the celebration. On the final day of the celebration Uriah and David's mighty men led a procession of one thousand chariots, one thousand horsemen, and one thousand foot soldiers through the main street of Jerusalem, ten mighty men in front of each thousand, led by one hundred skilled musicians playing music for the king, as all the people cheered and sang. Nearly everyone in Jerusalem praised Yahweh for their new king. This was a wonderful time to be a citizen of Israel.

David, after considerable meditation, loss of sleep, and pacing the roof top of his home, decided to offer Uriah the position as Minister of State for Anatolia. He asked him to come to his chambers the day after the coronation so he could tell him. While Uriah was with David, visitors from Tyre barged into the room. What now? David thought as he was invaded by these unscheduled guests. Before the king could say anything, the delegation said to him that two hundred galleys, and five merchant ships from the Sea People, sometimes called Achaeans, had placed a siege on their harbor. A great deal of commerce was conducted in and through Tyre. It would be to the king's advantage if he could help. The king of Tyre estimated the enemy to be about eleven thousand men, assuming the vessels were fully manned. They were helpless if the Achaeans attacked. Would King David send some of his army to help defend them?

Uriah realized that if they did not help, the Achaeans would be on the northwestern border of Israel. Before the king could say anything Uriah told David he would be happy to fight his old enemy. Caught off guard, yet realizing the potential threat to his security David asked how long it would take him to get ready. Uriah said he could leave that afternoon.

David dispatched ten thousand men to Tyre under the command of Abishai and Uriah, each leading five thousand men, with ten of David's mighty warriors in charge of a thousand each. Five days later the men were encamped outside of Tyre. Israel had no navy so they could not sail out to them and engage them at sea. They had to wait for them to come ashore. Uriah suggested that the citizens of Tyre take a few belongings and move north to Zarephath until after the Achaeans were driven off.

All the citizens of Tyre did as they were instructed, moving north along the coastal road, until out of sight of the ships. Meanwhile, Israel's army moved into concealed positions just inside of town and waited. The next day all the Achaeans -- except for a few men on the ships' crews -- launched a full scale military assault intending to capture Tyre. They did not expect much of a fight.

Unknown to them Abishai and Uriah had their men in place.

Usually Abishai liked to divide his army and attack from two places at the same time. This time he decided to attack from one direction with Uriah leading the charge. He did not want to divide his army when facing a larger army.

Waiting until all the vessels had landed on shore Uriah's men launched a devastating volley of arrows into the center of the Achaeans. Uriah led a three thousand man charge in a six deep line formation attacking the same area that had been showered with arrows. Right on their tails was another two thousand whose job was to produce a gap in the Achaeans. Abishai's army would attack the left half with four thousand men while one thousand secured the landing boats and prevented escape. When the left and center were defeated, Abishai and Uriah turned their men like a swinging gate to attack the right.

Uriah was a killing machine, missing the battle field, he felt at home again. He moved skillfully, artfully, naturally. Warfare was not a job to him, nor was it an art. It was a life! He could fool his enemy with his feints in one direction and assaults in another. His men were at his side. They were having as much fun as he. Achaeans were dying everywhere. Men encrusted in blood and missing limbs littered the battlefield. Within minutes of their death the corpses were covered with insects; within hours the birds and dogs reduced them to a few bones.

Uriah's leading force succeeded in making a large hole separating the Achaeans from each other. The second wave fought their way through and widened the gap. Abishai led the rest of his men into the gap, and then they turned to fight outward against the left side of the Achaeans formation. The battle on the beach became a brawl: spear to spear, sword to sword, dagger to dagger, and death to death.

Afraid that if anyone on the merchant ships realized what was happening, they would try to sail away, Abishai told Uriah to stop the ships from leaving. Five hundred of Uriah's men began rowing swiftly and silently back toward the ships. The darkness would prevent anyone on board from seeing them. Once on board the ships they fought with daggers. Men scurried from deck to deck clearing all the ships from any Achaeans left behind. By the next morning Abishai and his men had secured the ships, saved the town, and celebrated their victory. Three thousand Achaeans surrendered, sacrificing their manhood for life, and were made slaves. Uriah and Abishai killed five thousand and wounded three thousand so badly they would never fight again.

The joyful citizens of Tyre returned home in praise of King Hiram of Tyre, Abishai and Uriah. Uriah suggested that King Hiram keep the ships for commerce, using the prisoners and wounded as slaves on the ships. They could transport animals, men, and supplies. He would pay taxes on any merchandise he transported across Israel in either direction. In exchange for the taxes Hiram would receive the five merchant vessels and all the galleys. As payment for their help Hiram would trade with Israel and King

David as long as one of David's descendants was on the throne of Israel. Abishai said Uriah was brilliant. Hiram said Uriah he was brilliant and they all laughed. Uriah asked Abishai," How do you kill an Achaean?" Abishai answered," I believe you cut off his head." And they all laughed. They put the treaty in writing and everyone signed it.

When King David heard about the deal he was amazed. "Not only did you secure our northwest border but you also raised enough money to rebuild a united Israel. Uriah, before you went to Tyre I was talking to you about an idea I had." He led Uriah into his private meeting room, used only for visiting heads of state.

"We have had our disagreements, "said David.

"That is a truth of truth."

"Anyway, I want to move the kingdom to Jerusalem. I want to make that city my home. My dream is that city will always be known as the City of David. We all want to be known in history. I want to be remembered for Jerusalem."

"I feel the presence of an unseen essence. What you said must have been a message from Yahweh."

"The Jebusites control the city. None have found a way for an army to enter. I want you to take a few of your men, not many, but as many as you need, and scout the city. Find a way to get in."

"Not a problem of problems."

"If you can get me into the city here is what I will offer you. You will be promoted to Minister of State to Anatolia to help in commerce and defense between our peoples. You would get a raise in salary commensurate with your position. I would give you a private home on the same street I live on, with the other ministers to other friendly territories as your neighbors. Your sons would be guaranteed positions within my government. What do you say?"

"This is the offer of offers. What is the catch?"

"As Minister you have to spend every other month in Anatolia representing me and my kingdom. In between months you would be here representing them to me."

"I could take my mother home and be paid for living with her?"

"Yes, that is my offer."

"I accept."

"Remember this offer is contingent upon you locating a way to enter Jerusalem."

"I remember." Uriah remembered studying about the battle between Hattusillis III and Ramses II over control of Syria. The Hittites were able to break in on one side of the camp, while the other side knew nothing of what was happening. In the end a peace was formed when King Hattusillis III gave his daughter to the son of Ramses II. That was before the Sea People destroyed the peace. Uriah hoped he could find a way to surprise the Jebusites in the same way. He would attack at one end of town while the other end was unaware of what was happening. He must find a weakness in their defenses.

Uriah searched the Hinom Valley to the Southwest of Jerusalem. He hated the sight and the stench of the children being thrown on the garbage and dung pile to be burned as sacrifices to the Ammonite god Moloch. He wondered where the mothers of those babies were. What was that god doing for them? Then he worked his way around to the Kidron Valley on the east. The Kidron Valley separated Jerusalem from the Mount of Olives. He worked his way north and then back through the Kidron Valley to avoid Hinom Valley. On his second pass through the Kidron Valley he discovered Gihon Springs and a small cave leading into the hillside, apparently in the direction of, and possibly passing under, Jerusalem. The entrance was behind a large boulder and was not visible except from behind the boulder. He discovered it while answering a call of nature.

Uriah entered the cave and followed the stream of water feeding into the spring. After about three furlongs he discovered a shaft of light entering the cave from above. As he thought about the spring he remembered that Yahweh is the fountain of all being and power. He could lead Joab through this passage to victory. After all, Yahweh is all seeing, and can even see into the depths of the earth, in the secret places of men. He departed the cave and meandered into Jerusalem posing as a man going to the market. To his surprise, at the Pool of Siloam he found where the shaft of light leading down into the cave originated. It was also forty cubits to the floor of the cave but it was undefended. The Jebusites ignored it. This shaft apparently used as a well during the rainy season was only two cubits across. He must return to tell David this discovery. He must also tell him the pool is located on the south end of the city.

But as he turned around two Jebusite guards had the spears pointed at him.

“Who are you? Why are you here?” asked one of the guards.

“What have I done that you point your spears at me?” asked Uriah.

“We ask the questions. You answer,” said the other guard as he pointed his spear at Uriah’s midsection.

“I am a Hittite. I am here on business,” said Uriah.

"What kind of business? What is your name?" the guards asked.

"I am here as a merchant looking for merchandise to sell. What does my name matter?"

"Where is this merchandise you are buying?"

"I have bought none yet. I wanted to see everything first, buy later."

"Your name?"

"I said I am a Hittite. My name does not matter. I saw other Hittites in town as I looked at the different merchants."

"Those people we know, they live here. Who are you?"

"What if I was someone thinking about moving here. What if I was a relative of someone?"

"I am tired of these questions. Come with us." The guard who seemed to have the most rank poked him with his spear and motioned with his head to start walking. They forced him into a building in the center of the city. It looked like the command center for the guards.

"Who is this?" asked the guard captain.

"Someone who will not tell us who he is except that he is a Hittite. He could be a spy."

"Very good," tie him up, blindfold him and make him sit over there on the floor until he is ready to tell us who he is and why he is here."

"Yes sir." They answered.

"Wait, I was thirsty and saw the well. Thought there was water but there was none. Turned around and you stopped me. I do not know this town. I did nothing wrong," said Uriah.

"Tie him up. Keep him here overnight for being a nuisance to us. Check the visitor sign in at the city gate. See if you can find a Hittite. Check it against him. Find the other Hittite visitors. Match their names to the list. You will find out who he is. Tomorrow if he correctly tells us his name, let him go," said the captain. "If not, kill him. The Hittites in Hebron may be foolishly planning an attack. He could be a spy."

Uriah was led into a small room. Blood stains on the wall and floor indicated what happened here. After allowing Uriah to see the blood, the guards blindfolded him and tied his wrists with his back to the wall. One of the guards got a whip and struck Uriah across his chest with one strike.

"Tomorrow you tell us your name and why you are here, or get more of this," said the guard.

"You do not have to do that just for me," said Uriah.

Uriah could not sleep. His throat was dry. His chest burned where he was struck. He tried to think of how to escape but he was tied securely by leather straps. He believed that the Hittite gods were impotent in situations like this but Yahweh would somehow deliver him.

About three in the morning Uriah heard a noise in the front room where he had entered the building. It sounded like someone falling on the floor. Then he smelled the fragrance of lilacs in the spring and thought he was hallucinating. But when he felt his wrists being cut free he knew it was real. He removed his blindfolds and standing in front of him was the woman from Jezreel who wanted to be his wife so many years ago.

"How . . .?" Uriah began.

"Quiet. We go now," she said.

Taking his hand she led him past a guard lying on the floor. He appeared to be dead. They went out the door and behind the building, down an alley that Uriah had missed before. Soon they were at a small opening in the wall, wide enough for one person to go through at a time. They went through and down a narrow path to the Hinom Valley.

"I saw them capture you. You remember me right? From Jezreel," she said.

"Yes I remember you. How come you did this? Where is your husband?"

"My first husband was killed in battle fighting for David. My second husband was killed in battle fighting against David. You know how to stay alive. I go with you."

"What are you doing in Jerusalem?"

"It was the only city not fighting someone. I am a maid to the army commander. When he finds me gone he will look for me. If he finds me with you we are dead."

"He will not find you. I will take you with me. Maybe you can find another husband among my men."

"Fine. When do we attack the Jebusites?"

"King David, there is a way into the city. I found a way to sneak into the city and no one will even know we are there." proclaimed Uriah.

"If anyone could, I knew you could." said David.

"I found the way in but was captured. They thought I was Hittite spy from Hebron. I told them nothing."

"How did you escape?"

"The woman from Jezreel who wanted to marry me saw me get captured. She killed a guard, cut me loose, and showed me a secret entrance that the Jebusite soldiers use. Can she work for you in the palace?"

"Perhaps, after we capture Jerusalem. How do we get into the city?"

"We sneak into the city the same way I snuck into Ankara many years ago. We go through the tzinor, up to the Pool of Siloam and into their bellies."

The next day Joab took twenty thousand men with him and marched to Jerusalem. They stopped three furlongs from the northern edge of the city in sight of the Jebusites. They reacted by positioning several thousand men along the northern approach to the city.

During the dead of night Joab and Uriah leaving the rest of the army, took fifty men with them and entered the cave at the Gihon Spring. They waded the distance to where the shaft leads to the pool moving slowly so no one slipped or made unnecessary sounds. They had assigned one man to enter the city during daylight hang a rope securely down the shaft after nightfall, then walk away as if not knowing anything about it. When they tested to be sure it was secure, the men began climbing the rope one person at a time. Meanwhile one hundred of the men who remained outside the city with the army had built fires to give the impression the army still threatened them, with a possible morning attack. Another hundred approached the secret gate in the wall. The rest of the men, over nine thousand, were approaching the city from the south. The sentries focused on the camp fires to the north and did not see the army approaching.

When the fifty men were inside the city, they gave the signal to the men at the opening in the wall, and began looking for any security guards that might be posted. They located a few men on the south side of the city and killed them quietly with their bows. In accordance with Uriah's plan no one on the north side of the city knew what was happening. The fifty men inside methodically moved from east to west along the south side of the city, moving outward from the Pool of Siloam killing any Jebusite soldier they could find. The hundred men came through the opening and helped secure the south side of the city. As Joab's men gained control of the south side of the city they began working their way northward. They set fire to the command center as a signal to the Israelite army causing the Jebusite soldiers to be distracted by the fire.

Quietly Joab's men moved northward through the rest of the city. They were more than half way through the city when a security guard thought he heard something. As he lay in concealment he saw men like shadows moving quickly from building to building without a sound. In panic and fear, thinking the death angel had arrived as in Egypt, he sounded a warning with his trumpet. Upon hearing the warning, the Israelite army charged into the city.

The surprised Jebusites who deployed into the street to engage the enemy to the south were shot with bows or decapitated by swords. Joab's men were killing as ferociously as a hungry dog eats fresh meat. Their swords were insatiable. Groans, screams, cries of anguish and pain came from everywhere. Uriah located the commander of the army and ordered him to surrender. He chose to fight so Uriah killed him with his dagger. With the death of their commander the rest of the Jebusites believed their gods had abandoned them and fled from the city. When the sun came up, Joab and his men divided the city into sectors, searched to ensure no enemy was still in hiding, and sent a messenger to King David to tell him of their victory. The prisoners, locked up like sheep in a sheepfold, were offered the choice of working for the king caring for the horses or facing a firing squad. Most made the correct choice. Thanks to Uriah the Hittite, Jerusalem had become the City of David! The first thing he was going to do is prohibit the massacre of innocent babies. Moloch will have to accept that. He dispatched his men to clear out anyone not burning their trash and to stand guard to prohibit the slaughter of babies.

CHAPTER 27

David, dispatching ten thousand additional men, ordered everyone to begin preparing for the move to Jerusalem. Yahweh had promised this land to Abraham. But after a famine in Canaan Joseph's family ended up in Egypt. Four hundred years of slavery later, Moses brought them out of Egypt into this Promised Land. A long period of theocracy ended when Saul became king, but he never established his kingdom. David wouldn't make the same mistake. Yahweh defeated Jerusalem with a shepherd and a bee-keeper.

David invited guests from friendly cities or nations to Jerusalem for a week of celebration greater than his coronation. Musicians, dancers, singers, jesters, and all types of entertainers were invited. This would be day to remember long into the history of the world.

Not everyone was happy about the victory.

The Philistines realized that from Jerusalem David would be able to establish Israel as the world's greatest empire, equal with Egypt or the Hittites a few hundred years ago. With sea ports all along the great sea, and located in the center of the trade route from Africa to Asia, from Syria to Egypt, David could create an economic and military system to rule the world. But, if they captured Jerusalem, the Philistines would rule the world. This had to be the time to destroy the Israelites forever. If any survive, they would be exiled to the frozen north, somewhere north of the Black Sea.

They had been fighting for centuries. It was time to eliminate the enemy invader once and for all. If a wolf is let into the sheep pen, it will eat the sheep. The wolf -- David -- has eaten enough Philistine sheep! They could have killed him years ago when he lived in Gath or Ziklag, but regarded him as a nuisance, an outlaw, not a potential king. They had not seen this coming, but they must put an end to it!

During the spring equinox -- when the Philistines knew the Israelites would be celebrating the Feast of Passover -- they departed from Gath through the Elah Valley with plans to use the Rephaim Valley to attack Jerusalem, but they could not hide their large army. When David learned of the situation he immediately summoned Joab and his division commanders to his throne room.

"Why do the Philistines think they can attack us and win?" David asked.

Joab answered, "The kings of earth like to set themselves up to plot against whoever is in power."

"It is folly of folly. They think they are stronger than Yahweh's anointed." answered Uriah.

"I believe they may think they can weaken us enough that we can be defeated by another enemy who they feel they can defeat." Abishai stated.

"No, they know now is the time to fight us, before we are able to establish ourselves as a nation. And if we defeat them now, they are defeated forever. But truth be known, if we are defeated we are defeated forever. I think they know that," advised Ahithophel in his slow but serious diction.

"Joab, I want you to break them with a rod of iron. We must defeat them so badly they will never fight us again." ordered David. Then after a second to think about it he changed his mind," I will lead this battle myself. We will be wise in our planning, strong in our fighting, and brave in our winning. When it is over, I promise you an inheritance in this land."

"Based upon the route they are taking, they are heading straight towards us. If we mount a defense, they would expect it to be between them and Jerusalem. Their strongest force will be in the lead." advised Joab.

"One of the first principles of warfare is to deceive your enemy," Uriah commented. "We could move our men to Adullam and wait for their army. Then as they approached Jerusalem we would march beside them but unseen. When they see no one in front of them they will think we do not know they are coming. We avoid their strongest force, then attack the weaker force in the rear, when we have the best opportunity, and they least expect it. "

"Great idea!" agreed David. "Let us work out the details."

Just as planned, David and his men arrived at Adullam unseen. Scouts reported the Philistines encamped over the hill and about eight furlongs away, seeming to not suspect anything, preparing camp for the evening, and using their strong drink carelessly, acting like an unsuspecting mouse about to be eaten by a snake. The next morning David's men were up early and ready to march, ready to fight, ready to win. As the Philistines began to move, the Israelites moved with them. After two hours, the route of travel was obvious. They were following the North Rephaim River. The river was only knee deep because it was summer. In the spring and fall it is over a man's head.

The thick trees along the river forced the army to march down the river to maintain command and control. The Philistines were taking their time moving through this terrain so it was easy to keep pace with them. David ordered his men to find a place to ambush them on their right flank. Archers, spearmen, sword men, and Uriah with his dagger were ready.
They waited from concealed positions.

While they were waiting for the Philistines to continue their advance, King David said, "I am thirsty. I wish someone would go to the well at Bethlehem and bring me some water from the well near the gate."

Uriah heard the king and told Abishai. Uriah reminded Abishai of the time they snuck into Saul's camp and stole his water and spear. They should be able to do the same to the Philistines. So, Abishai, Uriah, and Eliam secretly left the army of Israel on the field. They overpowered three Philistine soldiers and took their outer garments. With this disguise they were able to enter and pass through the Philistine line, which was between the Israelite army and Bethlehem, and preparing for a major assault on Jerusalem. The three men drew water from the well and carried it back to David. But when King David saw what they did he could not drink the water.

As he poured the water on the ground he said, "Should I drink the blood of men who went at the risk of their lives to do this. God forbid that I would drink this. I could not do such evil to mighty men who risk their lives for me."

About mid-day the Philistine army began to move. Uriah ordered the attack. The main force of about ten thousand Philistine chariots continued churning through the mud down the river, turning it a muddy brown. When the main force had passed the second group of about ten thousand men without chariots entered their sight. The archers notched their arrows and waited for the order. Suddenly, like a swarm of Uriah's bees hundreds of arrows were in the air seeking out their targets. A second volley and a third killed a third of the second unit. With a mighty roar David lead his men into the river. Ferocious is not the word to describe the fighting. The men were told the Philistines were coming to commit genocide, steal their wives, and drive them from the land given to Abraham. Men fought with fury. Spearmen, swordsmen, bowmen all competed to see who could kill the most. Most of them had thirty or more kills. Uriah entered the fray with his dagger and fought like the anointed warrior he was. The muddy river quickly became the bloody river as heads, arms, eyes, ears and other body parts flowed everywhere as men and animals breathed their last breath, and saw their last horror of battle.

When the ten thousand from the lead unit heard the commotion they tried to turn around and counter-attack. Horses trampled on other horses. Chariots got stuck or tipped over resulting in the biggest chariot jam in history. Men in the rear trampled the men in the front. No one could launch their arrows or join the fight. Far from the main battle and stuck in a quagmire they became targets for Israel's archers who mowed them down by the rank. Horses, men, and chariots piled so high in the river they formed a dam and stopped the flow of the water until it became waist deep. The charioteers who survived retreated over the hills and far away from the battle, leaving their chariots, horses, and weapons behind. They retreated all the way to Gath. The larger force in the rear had been unable to get to the battle area due to congestion, so those who survived retreated back to Gath with the others.

"Do not think we won the war yet. They will try again. We must be better prepared. Next time we must win decisively! We let too many escape," David said to Joab.

David sent one-fourth of his men to Adullam with Abishai as a scouting and diversionary unit, as well as a barrier between Gath and Jerusalem if the Philistines retreat along the river. He sent the main force to Hebron with Uriah. The rest stayed in Jerusalem with him.

When the Philistines began a second attack a scout from Adullam notified the men in Hebron. Uriah marched his army from Hebron to an area south of Jerusalem called the Bechaim Wood. They entered the woods, hid under the trees, and waited for the Philistines. While they waited a thunderstorm passed overhead. Torrential rain soaked their heads and ran down their beards to their necks and torso. Lightning crashed, branches broke off the trees, while thunder echoed the drums of death. The army was more afraid of the storm than the Philistines. Uriah made them stay in position. Everything they wore or carried was drenched. When the rain stopped the cool breeze caused men to shiver with cold and there was no way to get warm. Most wanted to abandon their positions but Uriah ordered them stand firm and think of the victory. The Philistines would not expect them to be here. Meanwhile, David took the men who had been in Jerusalem and placed them west of the river opposite the wood.

The Philistines believed the god Pan lived in the woods so they would not enter them. When they passed the

Bechaim Wood it was at mid-day. The breeze was just picking up causing the leaves in the trees to rustle while the rain had silenced the leaves on the ground, muffling any noise the Israelite soldiers would make. The Philistines stopped just north of the woods for a final rest and equipment check before the attack on Jerusalem. They began eating their lunch and preparing their weapons for battle.

Uriah and his men charged out of the woods: arrows flew into the center of the army, spears destroyed the flanks and swords killed everything else. The Philistines, surprised and terrorized, believing Pan had become angry with them, tried to retreat across the river again but ran into David with his men, who killed hundreds in seconds. Fearful, the Philistines retreated in panic and ran in desperation. Uriah and his men gave pursuit.

Just when the Philistines thought they were safe they ran into the force from Adullam led by Abishai. Philistines began killing anything that moved, including each other. Thousands were slain in the carnage. Uriah and his men caught up and joined in the fight. He and his dagger killed over one hundred, while all the other mighty men nearly equaled his feat. The few who escaped were chased until darkness prevented any more killing.

Two days later David stationed one thousand men in Gath to subdue and collect taxes from the Philistines. Another one thousand went to the rest of the Philistine towns to destroy their weapons. David dissolved the Philistine army. Everyone old enough to fight had to choose servitude or death.

The war with the Philistines was over! To eliminate the potential of a strong Philistine army arising again in a few years, a thousand single women were loaded aboard merchant ships and sold as slaves to the Carthaginians. Five hundred women with children were deported to Crete.

David gathered the senior officers of his army together in the Rephaim Valley to reward them for their victory. Each of them received a home near David's palace and a plot of land in the Valley for an inheritance. "We have enemies across the Dead Sea and in the north of Dan that we must fight. When we win these battles we can turn our attention to our people. We can stay home with our families, raise our children, take care of widows and orphans, and live in peace with our God.

I need you to stay with me. Perhaps in two summers these battles will be over and we can rest from our fighting." David said to Joab he would like him to train another forty-eight thousand men for battle and begin the next campaign before someone else tries to attack him. The officers agreed. He told Uriah he could begin his new duties as Minister of State as soon as he was ready.

CHAPTER 28

David marched back into Jerusalem leading a celebration of rejoicing at his victory over the Philistines. The procession included 50,000 archers and 50,000 spearmen marching in step while one hundred musicians offered praise. Uriah and Abishai took the hero's position while five thousand chariots followed them, and 5,000 horsemen riding behind, their horses decorated for the occasion. The drums beat out the cadence, while the trumpets announced the arrival of the army. Men cheered and women cried as the procession marched by.

Cymbals sounded and the high sounding cymbals resounded. The harpist played, singers sang, and dancers danced. Acrobats tumbled, jugglers juggled, and men walked on stilts carrying bright banners. Anyone who could sing or play anything, or perform any type of trick was in the procession. Someone brought in elephants, some brought zebras, while others brought peacocks and pelicans. The psaltery, stringed instruments, and organs played the melody of praise to Yahweh, Most High God. Scribes read from the law as everyone praised Yahweh that the Philistines were defeated. People joined the throng from every village within a two day's walk from Jerusalem. David rejoiced more than anyone. He jumped, pranced, skipped, hopped, leaped, and tumbled in his dance before the Lord.

He knew if he did not praise Yahweh, the rocks would cry out, and he did not want to be outdone by a rock!

The festivities lasted all night and into the morning before everyone had worn themselves out with their celebration. When David went to his chambers to prepare for bed, Michal came in to join him. David could see by her angry eyebrows and pursed lips that she was upset. No cheery welcome. No attempt to help him undress. No glass of warm wine. No congratulations for his victory. Only a cold glare confronted him.

"Why do you come into the king's room with such a scowl, dear wife? Any man who approached like that would be considered to be an enemy," David remarked.

"Why do you think, dear king, that you can act like a mere barbarian and expose yourself before all your subjects in public?" Michal asked, her voice rising with every word.

"What is the matter with you? Yahweh gave us a victory over the Philistines. You know yourself that your father could not defeat them and many before him for centuries could not defeat them! Yes I rejoice in the victory!"

"Leave my father out of this. I am not talking about him! I am talking about you! I am talking about my maidservants seeing my husband exposed to the world. How do you expect to appear before your people again after appearing before them like that? How am I going to talk to my servants again after that?"

"I am talking about your father. He is the reason for all of this. I killed six hundred Philistines just to get your father to agree to let me marry you because he was afraid to attack them himself! Then he gave you to Paltiel. I should have killed your father those many times I had a chance."

"Yes. You killed six hundred men to marry me. Then you disgrace me like this?"

"Maybe I should have let your father fight his own battles."

"I am not talking about my father, I am talking about you! When are you going to stop acting on your emotions and start acting like a king?"

"No one talks to me like that. I may expose myself even more than this! I may parade in the street nude tomorrow and bring your handmaidens naked with me if that is how I choose to worship."

"You cannot do that. You are the king!"

"No one tells me what I cannot do. When I feel the Spirit of the Lord move in my heart, I will move as he tells me to. I may jump, or dance, or shout, or tumble. I may even crawl on my belly like a snake. It may be emotion, it may be theatrics, but it is true worship. That is something you need to learn."

"It looked like debauchery to me."

"I want you out of your room and moved into the harem within the hour. If you leave the palace I will have you killed. You will be the least in the harem and you may never come to this room again."

"What about my maidservants?"

"After today you have no servants. You are the servant to my harem. Get out!"

"You cannot do that to me. I am the queen!"

"There is no such thing as Queen of Israel. You were my wife, and you will always be my wife so no other man can have you. After today, I do not want you anymore. Get out!"

"What about those six hundred men you killed? Is that all in vain? What about their widows, widowed for nothing?"

"You should have thought about them before you came here tonight."

"How could I think about them? I was too embarrassed watching you!"

"So you dared to exalt yourself to a position where you thought you could rebuke the king. Did you forget what happened to Lucifer when he exalted himself over Yahweh?" He walked to the door of his room and shouted, "Guards!"

When they arrived he repeated to them the orders he just gave Michal. Then he said, "Just for good measure, put her on bread and water for three days also. Maybe then she will remember who is king."

The guards asked him if he wanted someone else to move into Michal's chambers and he instructed them to leave the room empty, but send him the Jezreelite.

Bathsheba gave Uriah some honey cakes -- oat cakes covered with honey and figs mixed together – then snuggled next to him and asked, "Have you ever wanted another wife, like some of the men? You know, two or three, or more?"

"When you have the best, why bother with the rest?" he asked as he finished his cakes.

"You are my honey," she said as she hugged his neck.

"You are my honey cakes," he cooed.

They both laughed as she elbowed him in the side. She decided to wait until later to tell him what she had been thinking.

CHAPTER 29

David, enjoying the peace he had established, and wanting to continue to strengthen his country, summoned Uriah and Joab to his throne room. "Uriah, I have made you our Minister of State to Anatolia. I want you to go to there for three months instead of one, while the new men are being trained. Establish any type of trade or economic policy that would benefit both countries. As you know you Hittites were in our land even before Moses. Your empire extended to the River of Egypt and many of your people became Israelite citizens. Many even fight for me in my army.

Do what you can to build better bridges between your people and my people. Take this ring to seal any agreements. You may take your family and as many men as you need." Uriah's reputation among the men was getting too colossal. Not only was he a great warrior, he was a great man. His morals were always impeccable and his love of Yahweh was being sung about in the ranks. It was time to make him disappear for a while. It was a perfect time while new men were being trained and no major battles were being fought anywhere.

Joab replied, "I will begin the training tomorrow. While Uriah is away I would like to give all my men a 30 day leave by companies, so my active force could heal and rest. By the time they are healed and rested we will have another two divisions."

"Good idea," replied David. "We still have a lot of fighting ahead of us. I want everyone trained and ready for battle."

"This is a dream of dreams," replied Uriah. "I have been killing enemies of Israel for twenty years. Now I get to go home."

Although Uriah could not see for certain what Yahweh had planned he mused that must be the way God works. He works in ways we do not see and do not understand. We need to trust Him and obey Him. When God makes his plans for us he does not ask our permission, he expects our obedience. It may not make sense to us but it makes sense to him. He resolved to continue obeying.

Ravia and Annitis lived with Uriah because they did not have any other man to support them. When he arrived home that day he stated," David has made me Minister of State to Anatolia. He wants me to go on a three month visit and take anyone with me. Who wants to go?"

"May the gods give us favor!" screamed Annitis. She had often said she thought the Israelite men were bold, handsome and intelligent, but they were all so strange because they worshipped only one god, a male god at that. She could not wait to get home where she could worship Cybele, the Mother Goddess again.

"Praise the God of Israel," Ravia rejoiced as tears filled her eyes. Maybe in her old age she would be allowed to go home where she could die and be buried with her own people. She did not want to be in Israel. She had no purpose here, yet had no way to go home. At last, she could go home in time to die.

"For what reason would I want to go to Anatolia?" Bathsheba wanted to know. "I have plenty of things here to keep me busy while you are gone. Besides, all that political stuff gets confusing to me."

"You once promised to go anywhere with me. But you can stay here if you wish. This is a dream for me. It is a chance of a lifetime. I will bring you something from my hometown. Would you like that?"

"Yes that would be nice. Bring some of their fine woolens so I can make some new clothes. You could even bring some of their silver utensils, how about some jewelry: something no one else has. Bring me something fitting for a queen."

"Maybe for now there are things there we do not have here. We have things here they do not have there. That is why I am going, to establish trade where things like that can be bought right here in Jerusalem. I will find something nice for you. If I do well enough, maybe I can get out of the army and be a career diplomat."

"That would be great." She said while thinking her dream would never come true.

The day before he left Uriah talked with Bathsheba. "I want you to know how much I love you. I am devoted to you. I am happy to be your husband."

Bathsheba said, "Thank you for the nice house near the palace and for always providing for me and our children." Putting her arms around his neck she said, "I am proud of you and of the respect you have among the people in Jerusalem."

She thought that now she was closer to achieving her dream than any time in her life. If she left Jerusalem she could possibly lose it. She might try to arrange an accidental meeting with the king. She had heard that David had just taken another woman for a wife. She was formerly the wife of one of his officers who had been wounded in the battle with the Philistines, and eventually died from his wounds. David married her to provide for her in the absence of her husband. Bathsheba could see no reason why she might not be the next wife.

That night Uriah prayed as usual. "Dear Lord, thank you for choosing me to be your servant. I was a bee keeper in a town that most people ignore and have never heard of. But you have made me a mighty warrior. You have led me through many battles and I am still alive. Although I still do not know what your plan is, I will continue to follow you. You have given me a beautiful wife and children. My family has a home to live in, food to eat, and nice clothing to wear. You have made me Minister of State for your chosen people to my people. Thank you for these blessings. I praise you. I praise your might, your wisdom, your sovereignty over the nations. As I leave tomorrow for my new duties I pray a blessing upon my king, David, and on my wife Bathsheba. Bless them in the city and in the field. Bless the fruit of their bodies. Bless them when they come in and when they go out. Lead David in victory over his enemies. Make Bathsheba a woman of women. Let all the people of the earth call you Lord. Prosper your people to make them leaders in the world. They will be the head and not the tail. Many nations will buy from them instead of them having to go out to buy from others. Bless them all the days of their lives. May the works of my hands and the words of my mouth be pleasing to you and to the Anatolians and may you establish prosperity in both nations. Fulfill your plans for my mother and sister and bless them beyond their dreams. Amen."

Uriah had a military escort from Jerusalem to Joppa. He heard Annitis tell Ravia that the last time they had a military escort they were prisoners. The military escort left them as they boarded the ship and he continued with Ravia, Annitis and three advisors, Chaim, Joshua, and Tavia. Their ship stopped for one day in Salamis, then sailed on to Mersin. They disembarked in Mersin, and arranged to join a caravan to Ankara. They would travel by horse the rest of the way to the city of Hatusha.

When they arrived in Hatusha, everyone welcomed them with cheers of "Uriah! Uriah! Uriah!" They declared a holiday. Children danced around the sculpture of Uriah while men gave speeches and women tried to touch him. The women questioned Ravia and Annitis while the men joined Uriah and his advisors. Tokat announced that when the Anatolians heard that so many ships of the Sea People had been destroyed in Tyre, they formed a small army and recaptured Troy. The Sea People had been driven from Anatolia. Troy and Ankara were thriving cities once again under control of Anatolians.

Uriah announced he had been appointed as Minister of State to Anatolia and he wanted three things. First, he needed a home built for his mother and sister. Second, he needed some men to work for him as his assistants in Anatolia while he was back in Jerusalem. Third, he needed some fine woolens, some silver utensils, and some Anatolian jewelry to take home to his wife.

During his visit he went to every major city in Anatolia including Smyrna, Thyatira, Pergamum, Troy, Ankara, Derbe, Tarsus, and many others to make treaties for the exchange of their goods. He established trade agreements for iron, horses, purple linens, jewelry, spices, fruit, fabric, leather, chariots, and armor, and even some barrels of Anatolian ale. He sternly warned them against betraying him the way that Egypt betrayed the Hittite Empire. He took his advisors to Troy, Tarsus, and Thyatira and appointed one to be the minister of trade with Jerusalem in each of those cities. They each had nice homes to work from and were given the authority to modify current agreements and initiate new ones if they were mutually beneficial.

Ravia and Annitis rejoiced in their new homes. They begged Uriah to stay with them instead of returning to Jerusalem but he insisted he had a job to do. The town wanted him to be the leader of Hatusha, but after he convinced them he was leaving, they chose Tokat. Tokat, whose first wife passed away, asked Uriah if he could marry Annitis. Uriah agreed. “Praise Cybele” remarked Annitis. “The gods have finally given me favor!”

One Sabbath day while Uriah was still in Anatolia, Bathsheba left her house and went to the synagogue. But she did not go there to offer sacrifices or pray. She waited outside, hoping for a chance to see the king. She knew he went to the synagogue every Sabbath and she knew she had a good chance to see him. Not knowing whether he would talk to her, she waited, trying to be inconspicuous, in her long brown leather skirt that reached her ankles and a light brown woolen blouse. She covered her head with a brown shawl with orchids embroidered around the edges. She did not want anyone to see her, except the king.

As David was leaving the temple area Bathsheba pretended to accidently lower the shawl from her face to her shoulders. David looked in her direction and she thought he recognized her. As he walked up to her, her heart seemed to dance out of rhythm as he asked, "Bathsheba? What are you doing here?"

"I was hoping to get a chance to talk to you."

"Really, to what do I owe this privilege?" He remembered the first time they met at the cave. She is still as lovely as she was then. Love still runs after he like puppies.

"As you know, my husband Uriah is in Anatolia. I have not heard from him and was wondering whether you have heard any news?" In her mind she was really saying, "You know I am alone. Is there any reason we cannot talk?"

"So far I have not heard anything. He may have sent a message to one of my officers that I have not received yet. Come to the palace around lunch time tomorrow and I will try to find out something for you?"

"I will see you tomorrow. Should I bring anything?"

"Just yourself, it is my treat." He remembered he made the comment when he first met her that he would like to have been the person she married. But he was still in mourning over losing Michal then. It is strange how things work out.

"Okay, until tomorrow then." She walked away delighting in her invitation to the palace. Uriah still has not been killed in combat and probably never will be. She had to take the initiative to achieve her dream. Let's see what happens tomorrow.

Uriah sat on the bank of the Halys River and reminisced that this was the place where it all began for him. This is where his life had changed; where he had run in haste to escape the Sea People but returned to fight them. He remembered he had been told that a man does not try to figure things out for himself, but relies on God for help and direction. He will direct that man's path to accomplish everything he has planned for him. I wonder what else Yahweh has planned? Have I fulfilled His plans for me or is there more to do? Is he orchestrating all my daily events so I do what he wants me to do? As he mused he fell asleep and began to dream.

A large hollow rock was in front of him. The rock was a big as a house. He found the way into the rock through a small underground tunnel. Somehow a window appeared in the rock from which he could see out but no one could see in. Throngs of soldiers ran toward him. They shot arrows, threw spears, and attacked with swords but Uriah held his dagger up toward the window and no weapon touched him. Instead of him being harmed, hundreds of soldiers died. He could not understand why he wasn't touched by the enemy.

Then a brilliant white light filled the rock and he dreamed he heard an angel. "Uriah, the rock you are inside of is the Word of Yahweh. His Word has protected you for many years because you have proven yourself faithful to him. Not a weapon formed against you has prospered. Yahweh gifted you to be a warrior. You will remain inside this rock until your work on earth is done. Many more will die, but you will be protected. When your work is done you will come out of the rock and Yahweh will take you to be where he is. Go to King David as you have determined in your heart, and continue to serve him. Yahweh has heard your prayers and they will be answered. Listen to me -- in famine Yahweh will redeem you from starvation, and in war from the power of the sword. You are in league with the stones of the field and the beasts of the earth are at peace with you. You will dwell in your home in peace and your legacy will be known throughout the entire earth."

That was the first time Uriah knew for certain that serving David was a part of his purpose in life. He could not wait to tell Bathsheba his dream. He would depart for Troy tomorrow and take a ship back to Joppa. He had good news for the king about the trade agreements, and he had his gifts for Bathsheba. He thought he would give the king a comb of Anatolian honey. Then he thought he would probably prefer some Anatolian money. Actually, through his negotiations, the king would receive both honey and money.

PART EIGHT

CHAPTER 30

Bands of robbers frequented the route between Anatolia and Israel. It was not safe to travel that route alone and it was especially not safe for a caravan to travel that route without an armed escort. Uriah arranged for small fortresses to be built in Damascus, Antioch, and Tarsus. These fortresses would house enough military to escort the trade caravans safely to the next town. Once in Tarsus, each caravan had to provide its own security. One escort would take them from Jerusalem to Damascus, the next from Damascus to Antioch, and the last would take them from Antioch to Tarsus. The same strategy applied southbound caravans, except in reverse.

No caravan would be allowed to move until the escort was in place.

The escorts loved the duty because as long as no one bothered them it was easy. Just ride along and talk to people, spreading lies and listening to rumors. At the end of the trail the caravan leader would give a small reward. Sometimes they would give bread or cheese, or nice new cloaks. What the guards preferred was the skins of wine or a few gold pieces.

When Uriah arrived back at the king's palace and gave his report the king was exuberant. "Uriah, your efforts will fill our coffers with bounty and provide safety for our northern boundary as well as the sea coast. How would you like a promotion and a raise?" Uriah could not resist the offer. "There are some problems to the east that I need you to take care of for me. Joab will go with you."

"You mean the Edomites and Moabites?" asked Uriah.

"You got it right."

"I can take our new divisions and in one summer can secure our borders."

"I knew I could count on you."

"There is something you should know. I believe that when we defeat the enemies of Israel and the borders are secure, my duties will be done. I would like to retire then."

"You defeat the Edomites and Moabites you can retire. You and your wife can have several happy years together. In the meantime, I plan to give you a bigger and nicer home, closer to my palace, so everyone can see how the king rewards good service. My ambassador who also serves as a division commander deserves a fine home to live in, right? As your king I should be doing the best I can to provide for you."

"This is an offer of offers. Let me have a week to rest and I will be ready to serve you one more year." replied Uriah.

Uriah wondered what Bathsheba was thinking. When he told her he was getting a bigger house closer to the king her eyes lit up but when he mentioned he could retire after defeating the last few remaining enemies, maybe within a year, the sparkle in her eyes went out. Uriah expected her to be happy about his upcoming retirement. He tried to explain to her that when he retired he could spend all his time with her. They would be wealthy from the trade arrangements he had made and the pension the king would provide for him. She replied that it would be good as long as they did not have to move from Jerusalem. When he assured her they would not move she smiled again, but was it a façade? She was not that impressed with the gifts he brought her either, even though he brought the best in Anatolia.

He had not sought after other wives even though there were many who wanted the job. He believed in Yahweh and the sanctity of marriage -- many times he had been tempted to take things that were not his or ask for more money or booty from battle -- but he had not been tempted by other women. All his devotion had been to Bathsheba. He treated her as a precious jewel and never spoke harsh words to her. He never gave her any reason to be unhappy. He wondered what was bothering her. When he asked, she always said there was nothing wrong. If he did not know better it appeared she had lost interest in him and become interested in another man. But in their culture, she could be stoned for that. Still, he wondered what was bothering her. Since Bathsheba would not talk to him, he thought he would talk with Eliam to learn what he might know.

David studied his enemies and considered who he should attack first. He wanted to secure the West bank of the Jordan River. The Ammonites occupied the north and the Moabites occupied the area west of Jerusalem. In the southeast the Edomites were still a threat. The Ammonites had been peaceful for years so they were not a problem. But he did not want to take his newly trained men into battle with the Moabites and Edomites right away. He told Joab to secure the interior all the way to Damascus to provide safety for the new trade with Anatolia. Rid the entire area of bands of thieves or threats to the kingdom. That will provide some on the job training for his new men and prepare them for the next war. He would try to renew a peace treaty with the Ammonites.

Joab wanted to be sure the old enemy, the Philistines, did not cause trouble so he suggested they attack there first. David led the army as they fought against Methegammah where they slaughtered them: every male who had reached puberty was killed and the women were left to care for themselves. After the victory over the Philistines, David led his army north to Damascus. When the Syrians attempted to rescue Hadadezer king of Zobah in Syria, David's army killed twenty-two thousand Syrians. He took their gold shields, silver, and brass vessels and brought them back to Jerusalem to offer to Yahweh. On his return from Zobah he slew another eighteen thousand Syrians near the town of Hazor. From then on the Syrians were servants to Israel.

David placed a garrison of his soldiers in Damascus and continued north. He marched his army as far north as the Euphrates River. Everywhere he went his army destroyed small bands of criminals, or rebels who were trying to raise an army to fight against the king. He secured the country from the Euphrates to Kadesh-barnea, from the Jordan River to the Mediterranean Sea. The army was allowed to garrison in Jerusalem for the winter and prepare for the major battles to come. He let it slip that he would go south around the Dead Sea to attack the Moabites sometime after Passover. That information would not remain a secret for long, and that is what he was counting on.

Spring warmed the air and brought new life, new hope, and new adventures. The soldiers had been training for battle for the past three months. They practiced their formations, archery and swordsmanship. They sharpened swords, polished their shields, and repaired broken equipment. Captains of tens, fifties and hundreds learned commands and how to use them to move their men. David trained his men to be the best army in the known world. Kings of nearby regions as far away as across the Euphrates and even Cyprus sent envoys of peace to King David. After his rift with Michal he had begun taking more wives. He married a daughter of the king of Cyprus and other lesser provinces to seal the peace. By the end of the campaign King David had established long-lasting peace with all nations within a thirty day journey from Jerusalem, except Edom and Moab. They were next on his list.

David paced to and fro on his rooftop as he thought his kingdom and of how Yahweh had led them through many years of combat. He decided to summon his military leaders and advisors to discuss the situation. David asked, “How prepared are we for the next battles?”

Nathan the prophet stated,” The Lord in heaven will tell you that the people of Edom have sinned many times, so he will use you to punish them. They chased Israel with swords and were ready to strike them down without pity. They were always angry, it could not be stopped so he will send fire to destroy and burn up Bozrah’s forts. Also, the people of Moab have sinned again and again so Yahweh will use you to punish them too. They burned the bones of Edom’s kings to ashes so Yahweh will send Moab crashing down with a loud noise. Yahweh will cut off Moab’s ruler and kill all of its officials.”

Joab replied," No enemy in the region could stand against Israel."

Uriah stated," We have the army of armies. Even the army Egypt would not be much more than a training exercise for us. Although, I have heard that the Assyrians are becoming stronger. We should strengthen our northern borders as a precaution next summer. Then the following summer, we could launch a campaign deep into Assyrian territory. You know, attack them while they are still too weak to attack us."

"Yes, but before I send my army into Assyria, we will secure our own borders. I want the world to know that Yahweh, the God of War, has blessed us and has brought us from one victory to another. What can I do to show the entire world that Yahweh led us to these victories?"

"Truth be known, some nations build statues to remember the men God used to defeat their enemies. We could erect a statue of you in the center of Jerusalem." advised Ahithophel.

"No, I do not want a statue of me. I am already in the history books."

"I am grateful you do not want a statue. We could do what they did in Troy and build a temple to honor our God." replied Uriah. "But the temple should depict him as a god who loves his people, not as a god of war. He is the one who deserves honor. Did you hear what Nathan said?"

"Nathan, what do you think about me building a temple for Yahweh? It would be a place we could honor him. Should we honor him as a God of War or a God of Love?" asked David.

"God has shown me through his spirit that because you have the blood of many men on your hands, as long as you still think of Yahweh as the God of War, you may not build this temple for Yahweh, but your son will build it. He will realize that in heaven there is only one God, his name is Yahweh, his name is love."

David stated," Now you have it. Through our treaty with Hiram, King of Tyre, and all our other trade agreements we can begin collecting building materials for the temple. Cedars, gold, silver, fine linen, and many other resources can be collected and stockpiled." He was angry that Nathan had agreed with that foreigner Uriah instead of him. God had always shown himself strong as a god of war. Where has he ever shown love? Uriah was getting to be more of a nuisance because he seemed to always have the right answers.

David began thinking of all the important things he had to do, plan for the temple, prepare for the coming battles and provide security for Jerusalem during Passover. All that while placing army garrisons in Arad, Gezer, and Tirzah to protect Jerusalem from any possible enemy in the future. He assigned duties to each person present to oversee different phases of the preparations. Uriah was chosen to provide security in Jerusalem for the Passover. Maybe he could keep an eye on him if he stayed in Jerusalem.

While in Jerusalem, Uriah had time to meet with Eliam. He explained to him how Bathsheba had reacted when he told her he was retiring in another year. Eliam replied that no man can know the mind or heart of any woman. Perhaps she was concerned over what she would be doing after he retired. She would not be the wife and an ambassador and division commander. She would be nobody again. Maybe Uriah should allow her to seek new interests to occupy her after they retired. She will be fine when the time comes to actually retire. Uriah turned his dagger over and over in his hand and thought about what Eliam had said. He concluded that Eliam was correct.

Fortunately for Uriah most of the people coming for Passover would set up tents in the Kidron Valley and would be no real threat to the city. He selected one hundred of his best men and stationed them at strategic gates, gathering places, and points of interest to foreigners. During Passover, Israelites would come from all over the country, and in some families, they came from neighboring countries where they had moved to.

Passover was one of the pilgrimage feasts, requiring men from every tribe to gather in Jerusalem to celebrate the Passover meal. Naturally they brought their families with them. This would be the first Passover in Jerusalem, everything had to go well.

The city was bursting and bustling with the people purchasing ingredients for their meal, and utensils and cloth that they could not get at home. The streets were so crowded Uriah thought he once saw honey melt from a hive faster than these people were moving.

Some were not moving. They were bartering for the best price, arguing over spoiled meat, rotten vegetables, or inaccurate scales. Of course they were not rotten, or spoiled, or inaccurate, but to get a better price they had to argue anyway.

The usual method for distributing products was that all the local merchants, farmers, herdsmen, and wood cutters would take all their merchandise to the palace for storage. The king required twenty percent of all products be given to the palace as taxes. If the person wanted to donate more than that, the palace would pay for the excess donation. Then it would be distributed to those who needed it. This system was begun in the Cave of Adullam to ensure everyone had enough food. When David became king he instituted that system into his government.

On the three pilgrimage feasts: Passover, Pentecost, and Feast of Tabernacles, people were allowed to bring their goods to the town and try to exchange them or sell them for profit. This was because the temple magazines and storage rooms could not contain enough food for everyone who came to Jerusalem for the feasts.

Uriah saw that the distribution system, the bartering, and the flow of the traffic of pilgrims functioned effectively. He prayed to Yahweh thanking him for his help and for bringing all these people here to celebrate him. He wondered how Bathsheba was dealing with all the people.

CHAPTER 31

Jerusalem erupted into a cacophony of noise: men, women, and children shouting, laughing, playing, crying, and arguing, cows mooing, sheep bleating, chickens clucking, dogs barking, camels spitting, mules braying, and horses neighing. Bathsheba thanked God this lasted only a week! Thank God she lived in a large home with secure gates to keep the people out. She could not wait for the celebration to end and peace to return.

Then she remembered that these were the people who would be her subjects when she became queen. Not "if she became queen". Her mind was made up, it would happen! She had enjoyed her weekly lunches with David at the palace while Uriah was away. They were no more than lunches where they talked about the social condition of Jerusalem and nothing of a personal nature. So far her new strategy was working. The old strategy of waiting for Uriah to be killed had not worked. Her new strategy was to make the king want her. She opened her door--time to get acquainted she thought as she stepped into the crowd.

Bathsheba began to have a great time stopping at produce stands and talking with people. She found carrots, celery, garlic, onions, almonds, dried apricots, prunes, asparagus, olives, horseradish, lamb, chicken, wine, and all kinds of spices. It took most of the day but she met many people. One man came from Dor with his fish, another from Hebron with fruit, and one man came all the way from Tarsus with his sheep to sell at the market. Each person had a unique story of how they felt free and secure now that King David had defeated all the enemies and eliminated the bands of robbers. They told her it used to be a frightening trip to Jerusalem and some even stayed home, but now they traveled freely without fear. Everyone also talked about the king's mighty men and his warrior Uriah the Hittite. When she told them she was Uriah's wife they sold her the goods for half price to show their gratitude.

She hugged many children and talked with many women who traveled with their husbands. She met a young family with two small children who could not locate a place to stay because every room was full, and they did not have a tent to put up. They had slept under the stars for three nights. She found them begging for bread at the bakery. Bathsheba invited them to her home for the next seven days while they celebrated the Passover. Jorab and Miriam lived near Capernaum in Galilee. He had been a fisherman for a few years and was just beginning to make a profit. She sold eggs and hand woven rugs to help with expenses. Jorab's father had an extra room built in his house and that is where they lived. They had been married for seven years and did not yet have a home of their own. They lost hope of ever having one. It took all the resources they had to get to Jerusalem.

Late that night when Uriah came home he was thinking he would have Bathsheba all to himself for a few days until the crowd cleared out. He was surprised to find visitors. Bathsheba told him about their guests and how she welcomed them into their home. He welcomed them and asked them to make themselves at home, which they already had done. She showed him all the things she had bought while shopping. Uriah said," You do not even like to shop. How did you manage to get all this by yourself?"

"I like to shop now. Look at all the good stuff I found: food, fun, fabric, and friends. I think it is a great way to meet people. You should try it!"

"Thanks of thanks, but I will pass on that." Uriah exclaimed. "I have enough to do just keeping the peace."

"I said to Miriam they could stay with us until after the Passover. You do not care do you?" asked Bathsheba. "Maybe she can teach me how to weave a rug."

"You are truly amazing me. Every day I learn a little more about you. I think it is great we are sharing our home with others. You are learning to shop. Now you want to make rugs. Maybe I will teach you how to care for bees someday."

"You are amazing if you think I am going to play with bees for the fun of it." She replied. Jorab and Miriam laughed and nodded their heads with her.

"I will purchase a rug from you. When we are in the field it is good to have a mat to sleep on. In fact, I will take two," Uriah said to Miriam.

Uriah prayed for his wife, for his king, and for his guests. He asked God's blessings on those he loved and thanked Yahweh for leading him. Then he wished everyone a good night and went to his bed.

The next day when Uriah came home the aroma of cooked food filled his home. Bathsheba and Miriam had prepared the Passover meal: broth from chicken with added garlic, almonds, dried apricots, onions, olive oil, red wine, prunes, and other spices; roasted lamb, braised with the broth; cooked asparagus laced with horseradish, roasted carrots with garlic, and almond pudding. Uriah, amazed, broke into tears. He said, "No one is as blessed as me. I have a good home, a good wife, live in a good country, and have a good God."

As they sat down to eat the Passover meal with their guests Uriah prayed," I will praise the Lord with all my heart, soul, mind and strength. His works are wonderful, honorable, glorious, and they endure forever. He has given us meat from his bounty and grain from his fields. He has shown us his power. He has sent redemption to his people when he brought them out of Egypt and made them his own. His praise endures forever."

After the meal was served, Uriah read the scriptures where they explained the ten plagues that God sent to Pharaoh before he finally agreed to let the Israelites leave on the night of Passover. He ended the meal by singing a hymn in honor of Yahweh, "Sing a joyful song to the Lord, serve him alone with gladness and know that he is good. We are his people and not our own. We are like the sheep of his pastures. We praise him, honor him, exalt him, and worship him. His love and mercy and kindness are everlasting to all generations." They all lifted their goblets, drank their wine, and shouted, "Hallelujah!"

While they were eating Uriah explained that Yahweh had delivered the Israelite slaves out of Egypt on the eve of this feast. From that day on to this day the Israelites celebrated this meal every year. It was a time to give thanks, to remember their blessings, and to celebrate freedom.

Bathsheba said, "Uriah you sound like one of us."

Jorab confessed, “Uriah, from your reputation I thought you would be a brutal, heartless killer. But I have never known a man who loved Yahweh so much. Someone who was so generous with his food and home, and so much in love with his wife. I plan to tell everyone I know what you are really like. We are blessed to have you leading our men.”

Uriah explained,” I am just trying to obey my God. This year is even more poignant because the king has eliminated all threats to peace on the east side of the Jordan River. Now the Israelites can enjoy their God-given land in peace. It was time to shout, to clap, to sing, to dance, to worship, and to pray.”

Bathsheba stared at her man, admiration on her face and a smile on her lips.

Uriah was pleased when he caught her looking at him.

Uriah’s heart was so full of love and thanksgiving he thought it was going to burst. He had never known so much joy. All he could say was,” The love of the Lord endures forever. The word of the Lord endures forever. The joy of the Lord endures forever.”

He went to his private chambers. A room he entered when he wanted to be alone to think, to pray, and to worship. He sat at a small table drinking a glass of spiced wine. He knew he was sent to help the king. But he still wondered how much of an impact he was having on God’s plan. It seems all he has done is lead men to kill other men. He believed it would not be long before he would know what Yahweh’s plan is. He was looking forward to that day. His thoughts were interrupted by a knock on the door.

Uriah stared at Ahithophel as if he did not know him. He could not believe what he had just heard! Ahithophel had told him that he heard about his most recent discussion with King David. He thought it was the right time to tell Uriah his interpretation of the stars and how he believed that he or one of his descendents was going to be on the throne of Israel someday. That was strange all by itself, but Ahithophel tried to persuade Uriah to join him in a plot to overthrow the king, and place Ahithophel on the throne. He would appoint Uriah as his prime minister and let him run the country. That way when he died, which certainly was only a few years away, Uriah would become king and Bathsheba would be queen.

"The king and I argued about offering sacrifices as instructed by Moses." Uriah said with a little frustration in his voice. "It was really nothing."

"Nothing? Truth be known, everyone in the palace knew you had a disagreement before you even left the building. How could that be nothing?"

"I tried to convince the king that he should offer sacrifices of animals like his subjects do. He said to me Yahweh does not want his sacrifices, only his songs."

"What did you say?"

"I said to him to show me in scripture where God told us to sing to him and I would show him where we are to sacrifice our animals for forgiveness of sins."

"He said he did not need forgiveness because he did not sin. He was God's own chosen king. He said me to keep killing my animals and he would just keep on singing!"

"Where did he get that from?"

"The same place that says it is okay to risk the lives of other men to get a wife."

"What do you plan to do now?"

"We just celebrated Passover. You know the significance of that celebration. God will have his way when he is ready." Uriah replied. "God will be the judge, not me."

"Yes, I know. But I believe he is ready now. That is why I came to you tonight."

Uriah asked him," Do you really believe I would betray my king? I believe Yahweh sent me here to serve him, do you think I would betray him?"

"It is not a question of betrayal. It is a question of fulfillment."

"Fulfillment of what? Not my commitment as a husband. Not my commitment as an officer in the army. Not my fulfillment of my duties to my God!" Uriah slammed his fist into his other hand with every exclamation.

"Look, Uriah. The stars clearly show that I or someone close to me will be on the throne of Israel. Something significant will happen soon. What can be more significant than getting a new king? Who can replace David? One of his sons! Not hardly! But you and I can. Bathsheba will become a queen. You would be king."

"What would she want to be queen for? How come would I want to run the country? What makes you think that I would be interested? What makes you think the people of Israel would let a Hittite be their king?" Uriah could not sit down, he had to pace as he asked these questions. As he paced he rolled his dagger over and over in his hand. He did not plan to use it, but needed something for his hands to do as he paced.

"I told her about this revelation before she even knew you. I think she still believes she will be the one, just as I believe I will be the one."

"Then what did she marry me for! I cannot help her become queen any more than I can help you become a king."

"Uriah, you are wrong. If you join me, I could become the king now and in a few years when I am gone, you will be king and she will be queen."

"No. This is not why Yahweh brought me here. I know I must serve the king. Somehow that is my mission!"

"You have served the king. You have served Yahweh. You have served them for many years. Now it is time to serve yourself! Man do not you see it. It is as plain as anything can be in this world!"

"Ahithophel, this I know, every good and perfect gift comes from God. They are not earned by intrigue and secret plots or starry revelations."

"Yes, I know that. Everyone knows that. But, you can help him speed up the giving. Side with me and watch Yahweh do wonders in your life. I am not getting younger. We need to act soon."

"He has already done wonders in my life. Do you remember what happened to Abraham when he tried to speed up God? Did not Job learn that no one can control God?" He made the heavens and the earth and everything in them. He can promote me in his way and his time. Who am I to try to help God?"

"No one else will ever know about our plan. They will all believe it was Yahweh's will all the time."

"Come now, let's really reason this together. Do you believe That God cannot see what we do in secret? Do you not believe that what is done in secret will not be shouted from the rooftops? Can we hide our secret intentions in our heart without God knowing it?"

"You are a foreigner, how do you think you can tell me about Yahweh? Truth be known, I was serving him while you were still swatting bees!" Ahithophel's voice began to sound like he was frustrated.

"That may be true. I have learned from you and others that man conceals his sinful works. Evil things are done secretly, honorable things are done openly. If this was honorable, we would have had a meeting of the entire council. I say this as loving as I can, to the grandfather of my wife, let Yahweh have his will. I will accept whatever happens if it comes from him, openly, in the light, where everyone can see."

"My son, times are changing. At one time we did not have a king, now we do. At one time the twelve tribes did not control their territory, now they do. At one time Israel did not possess Jerusalem, now we do. At one time we had no peace in the land, now we do."

"You are correct, Ahithophel, times do change. But before the mountains were made, before the highest part of the world was made, before the earth fell into sin, God existed. He still exists today. He is not like the stars. He does not change with the times or the seasons. He is from everlasting to everlasting. He is the same yesterday as he is today and will be tomorrow. We are dying creatures. I will die, you will die. He never dies. I must serve him and not myself, not you, not even my wife! I want to be known as the man who loved Yahweh so much he could only do God's will and not his own!"

Uriah stabbed his dagger into the top of the table and it vibrated back and forth. Then he walked up and hugged Ahithophel. "Father, Yahweh has his plans. He will carry them out. We do not need to rush him. We need to wait for him and comply. You know I love Bathsheba, I also love you, but I cannot betray Yahweh, David, or myself to gain an advantage that may not even be mine for the taking. This is an example of the pride of life trying to raise its ugly head. I am sorry but you have come to the wrong person."

"I am sorry too, Uriah. The stars are not wrong. Your wife will be the queen someday, with or without you. I was only trying to help you."

"Have a blessed Passover."

"You have a blessed Passover too, Uriah." The men hugged and Ahithophel left.

Soon after he left Bathsheba came to him and asked, "What did my grandfather have to talk about that was so urgent he had to come tonight?"

Uriah replied, "He just wanted to talk politics, that's all."

"Politics?"

"Politics."

Immediately after Ahithophel left there was another knock on the door. A messenger stood there and asked to speak to Uriah. When Uriah came to the door, the man said, "I have news from Annitis in Hatusha. Your mother, Ravia, has passed away. There is no need to go home since she will have been buried by now."

"No!" said Uriah. He went to the nearest chair and sat down placing his hands over his face. He sobbed loudly as Bathsheba stood beside him with her hands on his shoulders. When he stopped sobbing Bathsheba helped him to his bed so he could try to sleep. Tonight he needed to mourn because tomorrow was another day. David had another idea he wanted to talk about tomorrow.

CHAPTER 32

King David addressed his closest military advisors in a private meeting. He announced that in the past others had tried to secure the borders of Israel, but this year he would finish the job because Yahweh will lead them. They won battle after battle from the time he was a refugee in the Cave of Adullam until today. Yes, a few thousand men died along the way but it was worth the cost. This summer Israel will become one of the mightiest military powers in the world. Israel was stronger than the Philistines, the Egyptians, the Phoenicians, and the Assyrians, establishing trade with all their neighbors all the way from Cairo to Troy.

There were only two enemies left to defeat: the Edomites and the Moabites. David said he was a better leader than Moses, a better general than Joshua, and more important to the history of Israel than Abraham. Yahweh had made a covenant with Abraham but he made a new covenant with David. Nathan had prophesied that Edom and Moab were to be destroyed. This would be the year.

Uriah asked," I understand why you would want to defeat all the people we have fought over the years. They were all your enemies. But is it true that both the Edomites and the Moabites are your relatives?"

"That is true. They are distant relatives, very distant. But they have no place in my kingdom. We will defeat them and subjugate them. However, we will not annex their territory into my kingdom. They are not worthy." replied the king.

Uriah asked, "What makes them so unworthy?"

"It all began with Abraham. Yahweh told him to lcave his home in Ur and move to an unknown place. He stopped in Haran for several years then continued on to Canaan, possibly here to Jerusalem," began David.

Joab joined the story, "When Abraham traveled he took his nephew Lot with him. When the flocks became too large Lot left his uncle and settled in Sodom."

Eliam jumped in," Lot had two daughters who lived with him and his wife. He was a righteous man and had no business living in that wicked city."

David continued the story," Because the city was so wicked Yahweh destroyed it with fire and brimstone. Yahweh sent some angels to lead Lot to safety . . ."

"He sent him angels?" Uriah asked.

"Yes angels. Anyway his wife looked back at the destruction – in an instant she turned to stone."

"That is true. A stone pillar. Anyway, instead of trying to find his uncle again, Lot hid in a cave with his two daughters." Joab interjected.

"The law of nature says that is no place to raise two daughters!" Uriah exclaimed.

"That is what they thought too," said David. "So they both encouraged Lot to drink until he got drunk, and enticed him to get them both pregnant."

"He is not as smart as the ninth part of a sparrow!" exclaimed Uriah.

Joab stated," Do you want to hear the story or tell the story? The eldest daughter had a son she named Moab. He became the father of the Moabites. The younger daughter had a son named Benammi and he became the father of the Ammonites."

David explained, "So they are relatives because Lot was the nephew of Abraham who was the grandfather of Jacob, who was the father of Israel. I am also related to the Moabites because a Moabite woman named Ruth married a man named Boaz. Boaz had a son named Obed. Obed had a son named Jesse, who is my father."

"So your great-great grandmother was a Moabite. And now you want to go to war with her people?" asked Uriah.

"It is not a question of wanting to go to war. We have to stop their raiding parties from coming in and stealing the crops and cattle of the Israelites living near them. They asked for a war. Now they are going to get one!" David said.

"Maybe they are just hungry. We are going to kill them because they are hungry?" asked Uriah.

"Yes, and you will lead the first attack!" shouted David. "Joab, see to it!"

"As you wish, king" Joab stated.

"One thing I did not tell you. When Moses was leading the people out of Egypt, the Moabites hired the prophet Balaam to curse Moses," said King David.

"Fine, I will fight your family's battle for you. What about the Edomites, how are they related?" asked Uriah.

Eliam could see David did not want to say anything at the moment so he quickly began answering the question. "Abraham had a son named Isaac who had a son named

Jacob. But his mother Rebecca had twin boys: Jacob and Esau. Rebecca loved Jacob but Isaac favored Esau."

Joab continued, "One day Esau came in from the fields very hungry so Jacob tricked him into selling his birthright to Jacob for a bowl of lentil soup."

"That was the hunger of hunger," noted Uriah.

"That is not all Jacob did, he also pretended to be Esau and received Esau's blessing from Isaac, because Isaac was too blind to tell the difference." Eliam began again.

"But Rebecca sent him to Haran to his own people to escape Esau's fury. Somehow Yahweh chose Jacob to have twelve sons who became the heads of the twelve tribes of Israel. Esau married two Canaanite women. One of them was a Hittite, Uriah. The other was a Hivite." Joab stated.

"A Hittite!" Uriah exclaimed turning to look at David.

"Esau took his family and settled at Mt Seir, Esau is Edom, and his descendents are Edomites." David was able to talk normally again.

"So that makes Esau the uncle of the twelve tribes, and his descendents are your cousins." said Uriah. "We are not only fighting your cousins, we are fighting my cousins too."

"There is more to the story," said David. "When Moses was leading the twelve tribes from Egypt he requested permission from our so called cousins to go through their land. They refused. He even offered to pay them. They still refused. They threatened to attack them with swords. Moses had to lead the people around Edom to get to the Promised Land."

"They were probably still upset over Jacob stealing the birthright with a bowl of soup and receiving Esau's blessing." Uriah stated.

"I do not care how they felt. They refused a simple request. Now it is time for them to pay. By the way, you lead the attack on Moab first, then Edom."

A week later David assembled the army: forty-eight thousand men, two regiments, trained, equipped, and ready for war. In Hebron everyone checked his weapons, his armor, and his supplies. Everyone understood the plan. They lined up according to divisions with Uriah's division in the lead. Fifty divisions formed up in a column of divisions seemed like an endless line of men. When they began to march they looked like some giant swarm of insects, or slow moving lava covering the land. Everything in front of it got out of the way. The commanders of each division and Joab, the commander of the army, rode in chariots in front of their men. David was sure the Moabites would be strengthening their defenses, but that was good. When the battle is over, there will be fewer of them. He had let it be known he was attacking from the south, around the Dead Sea, and hoped the Moabites would be in defensive positions somewhere between the Edom and Moab borders. But he was coming in from the north. He would pass through Beth-hoglah in the territory of Benjamin, and then move south to Didon in the territory of Reuben.

David was certain that Uriah knew the plan well. When they arrived at the Arnon River the forty-eight divisions would form into four wedge formations with twelve divisions in each wedge, Uriah's division would be the point on the wedge and would go in first. So be it. Each wedge would follow the other at first, then alternatively flank left and right to expand the forward edge of the battle area. The army would move fast, fight hard, take no prisoners, and destroy the Moabites.

The Moabites had petitioned their neighbors for help. Egypt sent ten thousand men and the small villages and nomadic tribesmen gathered to form an additional five thousand. The ten thousand who were the elite of the army were positioned somewhere just north of Zared Brook facing to the south. Five thousand men were left at the capital city of Kir-hareseth to protect the women and children. Egypt's forces were on horses and were held back. Presumably if the Moabite army received too much pressure it would retreat to the first fallback position. Then the Egyptian horsemen would charge in and drive out the Israelites. David thought it was a good plan, except he had a plan of plans.

Uriah led his men south along the Arnon River until he accidentally discovered the Egyptian garrison at Ir-Moab with five thousand horsemen who were supposed to help the Moabites fight against the Israelites. Caught off guard and not expecting the Israelites, the battle lasted about two hours until the Egyptians surrendered. After the battle Uriah turned to the southwest toward the capital city. At Kir-hareseth the Moabites did not have a chance. They tried to defend their city but within ten minutes twelve divisions had killed all the soldiers.

Joab left one division behind to secure the civilians while the rest of the Israelite army continued moving south. Joab changed the plan of battle when they left the capital city. He sent ten divisions, ten thousand men, east of the mountains, along the western edge of the Eastern Desert. Five divisions went to the eastern shore of the Dead Sea and moved south while the rest of the army moved through the hill country between the Dead Sea and the Eastern Dessert.

As Uriah's men came over one of the ridges they stumbled into the rear of all the men in the final fall-back position. They were expecting him from the south. He ordered his archers into ranks and began a hail of arrows onto their positions. Surprised, they panicked and ran in every direction. Some surrendered, some killed their own men in panic, and some tried to run to the next position to warn them. But the Israelites were too quick. They gathered up all the confused and frightened men, and killed all those trying to escape. When they began to interrogate their prisoners it did not take long to learn about another five thousand Egyptians and where the elite soldiers were positioned.

Joab ordered Abishai to take five divisions while Eliam took another five divisions and they were to find the Egyptians and convince them they should go home. They located them just where they were reported to be. Joab decided to greet them in the morning.

Meanwhile Uriah was still advancing and discovered the next fall back position and about five thousand men. Uriah drew his dagger from his belt and told all his men to use swords or daggers. Kill the enemy quickly and silently. From out of nowhere the Moabites were swarmed with soldiers they never saw or heard coming. Within minutes the fall back position had fallen. Many were killed but most surrendered without even a fight. Uriah did not know how many such positions the Moabites had, but he knew they had not really had a fight yet.

In the morning the Egyptians were surprised to learn they had lost their horses during the night. Then Joab appeared to them in a clearing and told them they were surrounded. If they resisted, they would all be killed. If they surrendered, they would all live. Either way, they lost their horses. They chose to surrender and walked, escorted by Israelites, and unarmed, back to Kir-hareseth.

At mid-day Joab found the king of Moab at one of the fall back positions. He sent a messenger to King David who straight away came to meet with him.

"King Eglon, your nation is defeated. I have captured Kir-hareseth and the Egyptian soldiers you were expecting to help you. I have also killed ten thousand of your own men, and captured many more as prisoners. My men surround you and there is no way to escape. You are outnumbered and will surely die in battle. Let us talk about a peace treaty" King David said to the king of Moab.

"I do not have any daughters you may have for a wife." the king began.

"His reputation precedes him" laughed Uriah.

"I do not want a wife. In fact maybe I will make you take one of mine. I want tribute. Give me what I want and you may live."

"What is it that you want?"

"I thought you would never ask. First, no more raids into Israel. Second, you will send me one hundred cattle and one hundred sheep each month. Third, I will station a garrison in Didon, near your borders to ensure compliance. Forth, tell all the Egyptian forces in your territory to go home."

"I can stop the raids, and I can send the Egyptian home. I can allow your garrison. But I do not know how I can feed my own people if I give you so many animals."

"What can you give us?" David asked, remembering what Uriah had said about them being hungry.

"I will send you fifty animals: sheep, cattle, or oxen every month."

"If you teach your soldiers how to farm, you should have no problems meeting your quota. By the way, I know your best soldiers are still waiting for us to cross the Zared Brook. You might want to tell them they have just become farmers."

King David assembled his men on the southern shore of the Dead Sea. He had one enemy left, the Edomites. This is the beginning of a new world for them. He ordered Joab to assemble the army in the same formation with Uriah's division in the lead.

David believed that today was a day of destiny.

He had already doubled the size of the kingdom of Saul, established lucrative trade with all the neighboring cities, and today he will defeat the last of his enemies. This was a great time to be the King of Israel.

The king of Edom dreamed of a fierce battle between him and King David. In the dream he saw certain destruction unless he acted to protect his men. The king assembled his army, seventy thousand men, including mercenaries he hired from neighbors, and prepared them to meet David's army. The entire army lay in wait in the hills north of Bozrah, the capital city.

The Edomites were organized into seven units of ten thousand men each. Seven was believed to have a magic to it that would enhance their success in battle. The road from Tamar in the north of Edom to Ezion-geber in the south of Edom passed through a narrow valley that extended from the southern shore of the Dead Sea to the northern tip of the Gulf of Aqaba where Ezion-geber was located. Hills on both sides of the road were high and steep in places. Bozrah was located in a small valley just east of the road about half way between these two cities. The Edomites placed four units on the road to block it, placed one unit on each side of the road into the hills, and kept one unit in reserves south of the main force. The plan was to engage the Israelite army on the road, then attack from both sides, catching them in a trap. The seventh unit would assist if the battle started going in favor of the Israelites.

King David assembled his generals in his tent. He wanted this to be the last battle to gain peace for all of Israel. He refused to lose. He began his operations order with the usual information. When he came to the plan of execution he began asking for advice. " We have several options. We could proceed along the road and fight whatever gets in our way until we reach the gulf. We could proceed along the Zared Brook until we are east of Bozrah then turn south and attack from the east. We could send a token size force down the road while the main forces proceed along the hills on either side of the valley. We could build a garrison at Tamar and station men there to patrol the border with Edom and avoid a fight completely. What are your opinions?"

Joab suggested," Let's attack Bozrah from the east, the Edomites will not be expecting us from that direction and it will be easy for us to use the advantage of surprise to gain a quick and complete victory."

"You are right," agreed King David.

Eliam objected," That will take too long and wear out our men. I say go down the road and fight whoever gets in our way. It will be safer, quicker, and less exhausting."

"You too are right," agreed the king.

Abishai said," I believe they will have ambushers in the hills. We need to at least send part of our forces into the hills to drive out the ambushers. Then we can proceed more safely down the road."

"You too are right," agreed David.

"You are all right said Uriah. This is the battle of battles. We need to do all three. We need to send some of our men into Bozrah and attack from the east. From there they can go cross country to Ezion-geber. Another part of our forces will patrol along both sides of the hills and when the ambushers are routed, rejoin the main force on the road and continue to Ezion-geber. The rest of the forces will go straight down the road and fight whoever gets in the way. At Ezion-geber they will join the force coming from Bozrah. Then we all go back to Tamar where we establish a garrison to protect our borders."

King David agreed," I hate to admit it, but you are the most right. Joab you take one third of our men and go down the Zared Brook and attack from the east."

"Yes, king David."

"Abishai and Eliam, take one third of our forces and go through the hills, Eliam on the east and Abishai on the west, rout any Edomites there and join Uriah on the main road."

"Yes, King David."

"Uriah, I want you to take the remaining third of our men and travel down the road fighting whoever gets in your way."

"Yes, King David but I request that the thirty mighty warriors join me. I want to wait three days after Eliam and Abishai depart before I move out. They will be travelling slowly through the hills. I can catch up with them in no time."

From there the king completed the rest of the operations order and the leaders divided the teams according to the plan.

The next morning Joab departed with his men and began their march along the Zared Brook. They were ready for anything. With arrows notched, swords drawn, and javelins at the ready they advanced on their appointed route. By the end of the first day they had passed the hills and were near a large valley. The next day they moved quickly towards Bozrah but stopped about two hours walk from the town. Joab was correct, no one was expecting him. The next day he led his men into the town killing the few men who resisted. He stayed there two days to see who came to resist him, but no one knew he was there. Edomites were all on the highway expecting a huge battle. Joab turned to the southwest and led his men cross country to Ezion-geber.

Eliam and Abishai led their men through the treacherous hill country. They left the same day as Joab but travel was much more difficult with rocks, briars and shrub bushes to contend with. The first day they had no resistance. The next day Abishai was surprised when his force was attacked with arrows from the Edomites in the hills. A few hours later Eliam's force had the same experience. Hearing the battles in the hills, the commander on the road believed the Israelites were coming and sent half of his men into the hills to join the battle.

About the same time Eliam and Abishai met the enemy, Uriah left with his men, going straight down the road. Travel was easy so his men made good time. About mid-day on the third day Uriah encountered the Edomites still on the road, their forces reduced by half because they were sent into the hills. Uriah led the thirty mighty men and the rest of his men into the battle.

When the two armies met it was like to oceans clashing together on the same shore. Where the white foam was supposed to be, there was crimson red with blood from the dead. The mighty men attacked so fast and with so much force they were like locust going through corn.

Men bleeding from large, gaping wounds filled the air with fountains of blood. The earth soaked it in like a dry sponge. Sometimes the army followed the mighty men. Sometimes they fought side by side with them. At other times they were in front of them. Edomites were better fighters than expected, every man determined to repel the Israelites.

Uriah pressed his men forward, his subordinate commanders directed the men in their battle formations, and men fought on using swords and javelins were used in close in fighting. No time or space to use arrows. No time or space to think: only time to kill.

Uriah drew his dagger and charged into one man and then another. As soon as he saw someone, the person was dead. He was a killing machine turning, jabbing, dodging, slicing, kicking, slashing, maiming, and killing. No one was quick enough or strong enough to stop him. His anointing was more powerful than anything they had and no weapon used against him could prosper.

The Edomite commander on the road ordered reinforcements. The unit in reserves joined the battle. Realizing what was happening, the men sent into the hills tried to get back to the road. But they were exposed to the Israelite men in the hills. As the sun beat down Eliam and Abishai pressed hard, driving the Edomites who were still alive out of the hills and into the road. By dusk the road became an all out killing field as Eliam and Abishai's men joined the battle. Men fought for their own life forgetting why they were even there. As it got darker they could not even tell who they were killing. No commander ordered retreat. Kill or be killed was all anyone had on his mind.

The moon was new, the night was dark, and the air was full of groans of dying men, wounded men begging to be killed, helpless men crying, hoping to be found, and vultures trying to land on the dead. During the night the Israelite army began achieving victory. At dawn the Edomites, exhausted and defeated, threw their weapons down and begged for mercy.

King David left Tamar one day after Uriah. When he arrived at the battle scene the men were still resting and caring for the wounded. Amazed at the number of casualties in his army, he ordered all the Edomite prisoners to be brought into his presence. They were made to lie on the ground side by side. King David cut a rope ten cubits long. He placed the rope along the men on the ground. Then he ordered that everyone within the range of the rope be killed. Every two lengths of rope the men were killed. In the third length, the men were allowed to live.

The next day King David led Uriah, Eliam, and Abishai down the road to Ezion-geber. They entered the town without opposition. David said to Abishai to get the rope and do the same to every resident in the town as he did with the Edomite soldiers. As the sun set two-thirds of the men in Ezion-geber were dead.

Meanwhile Joab was surprised by a large force of Egyptians who just happened to be in the area. When they saw Joab and realized he was an Israelite in Edom, they attacked. As the day wore on Joab killed all the Egyptians and kept their horses so some of his men were able to ride. After defeating the Egyptians, he continued to meet brief resistance in the hills but arrived at Ezion-geber the next morning.

The Edomite army had been defeated. King David gave the order to go to every town in Edom and using his rope to measure, kill two-thirds of the Edomites. No one was allowed to take any booty or a wife. They were to be killed and warned what would happen if they ever joined with an enemy of Israel. On the way back to Israel King David left a division at Tamar to patrol the border

King David had expanded his kingdom from Wadi el-Ariah to Ezion-geber in the south, the Eastern Dessert in the east, the Mediterranean Sea in the west all the way to Tyre except a small tract of land between Gaza and Joppa, and to Tiphsah on the Euphrates River in the north. All his enemies within Israel and among neighboring states had been killed. For the first time in history, Israel was the most powerful nation in the world. Uriah said," Look what Yahweh has done! If it had not been that Yahweh was on our side when men rose up against us, then they would have overrun us as waters cover the land. Blessed be Yahweh, creator of heaven and earth, who is our help. Praise his name forever!"

PART NINE

CHAPTER 33

Uriah strolled through his garden holding hands with Bathsheba. He was thinking about retirement and spending the rest of his life enjoying his wife, children, and grandchildren. He would teach them how to care for bees, how to shoot a bow and arrow, and how to worship Yahweh. Maybe he would take Bathsheba to Tyre and board a merchant ship. Then he would sail to the end of the Great Sea. Maybe they would return, maybe not.

Bathsheba was also thinking. She admired her husband for his heroism, faithfulness, and respect he had in the entire country. She thought that in a way she was already a queen. The women in the king's harem do not go outside, no one knows who they are, and the people do not love them. She is treated as a queen in her home, and in the market.

They treat her as a queen because they knew what her husband had done.

He was a good man. She thought, perhaps this is the type of queen I am destined to be. It is not what I thought it would be, but it is not bad. She looked up at him and smiled. For the first time since they were married, Uriah saw admiration on his wife's face that he read as her saying I love you. His heart grew so big it almost forced him to tears. He knew he was where God wanted him. She wrapped her arms around his arm and placed her head on his shoulder as they stood there in the moonlight. She cooed, "You are a good man Uriah the Hittite. I am glad I married you. I will be your's forever."

That night Uriah had another dream. He was inside the rock again, but this dream was different. While he was inside the rock it began to expand. It grew larger and larger until it burst apart into many pebbles. The rock was gone and he was alone. When the enemy attacked he held up his dagger but this time they did not stop.

He sat up with a shout, looked around, and went back to sleep. When he went back to sleep he heard an angel say, "You have completed your work for Yahweh -- you have been a faithful servant and you will enter the joy of the Lord." Uriah wondered what those words meant.

The next day a messenger told King David that King Nahash, the Ammonite, was dead and his son Hanun had become king. Wanting to re-establish the treaty he had with the Ammonites David sent a delegation to Hanun to negotiate a peace treaty with him. Upon their arrival Hanun's advisors told him they were spies sent to report the best way to defeat them. Because of his advisors, Hanun ordered his men to shave off half of the beard of each man in the delegation, and then cut off their clothing in the rear from the waist down, and send them away. When David found out he told the men to remain in Jericho until their beards grew back. He called for Nathan for advice.

Nathan said to David," The people of Ammon have sinned again and again so you must punish them. They have humiliated you, your men, and Yahweh. Yahweh says they want war and you are to give it to them. You are to destroy Ammon's god Molech, burn up their forts, and conquer the people."

King David called for Joab and all his military advisors including Uriah. When he explained what had happened, and what Nathan had said to him, they all wanted to pay their respect to the Ammonites. David led them to Rabath-ammom to confront King Hanun.

As King David drew closer Rabath-ammon he realized he had enemies on two fronts. He found mercenaries on his left and Ammonites on his right. He told Abishai to lead the attack against the Syrian mercenaries, while Joab with Uriah and the mighty men would lead the attack against the Ammonites.

David called his men together and said, "If the Syrians are too strong, Joab will help him. If the Ammonites are too strong, Abishai will help him. Fight courageously for our people and for the cities of Yahweh. Let the Lord do what is good in his sight today."

Abishai's men fought hard and routed the Syrians chasing them away from the battle. They fled all the way home, destroying seven thousand chariots and killing forty thousand foot soldiers. King David secured a peace treaty from the Syrians that they would not fight against Israel or join with anyone who is fighting against Israel.

When the Ammonites realized what was happening they withdrew into the city of Medeba and closed the gates. King David said, "The Ammonites hide like cowards behind their walls. They do not realize that walls do not protect men, men protect the walls. We will wait for them.

Abishai set a siege on the city and kill them all. I am returning to Jerusalem until the fighting is over."

That night Abishai was talking with Uriah and asked him," Do you ever get frightened before a battle?"

"Why? Yahweh sent me on a mission. He is my salvation and has given me my strength and abilities." Uriah answered.

"You ever believe this could be your last battle?"

"No. When my enemies come against me they stumble and fall. I do not care if even a host of men come against me, I will not be afraid."

"I cannot believe it. Where do you find such courage? I know we will prevail in battle as an army, but I also know we might be killed as individuals. Does that ever cross your mind?"

"What crosses my mind is all I desire is to dwell in the house of the Lord forever. He has shown me he will hide me in his rock and I will be victorious over my enemies. I have nothing to fear."

"What do you think will happen here at Medeba?"

"I know if we wait upon the Lord, keep up our courage, then he will strengthen our hearts. We will win here because the Lord wants us to win. Whether you or I live or die will be in his hands." Uriah talked with so much conviction in his heart that Abishai believed him.

"I guess you are right. Let' us go to sleep so we can prepare for the siege in the morning."

King David grew restless in his palace in Jerusalem thinking about the siege so he did what he always does when he cannot sleep. He had thought about sending for one of his wives, but instead he went for a walk on his roof. He was thinking about the war and walking around when he happened to look towards where Uriah lived. To his surprise Bathsheba had lit some candles, taken off her clothes and was bathing in her courtyard. He watched her for a moment then sent for a servant.

He ordered the servant," Go three houses down the street to the home of Bathsheba. Tell her the king wants to see her tonight."

Bathsheba entered the King's chambers and asked," You sent for me? Is something wrong with my husband?"

"No nothing is wrong with your husband, and yes I did send for you."

"What is it you want?"

"I saw you bathing and I realized something that I should have realized sooner. You have been finding excuses to be with me for years. I never realized it because you are married to Uriah. But it is true is it not?"

Bathsheba felt ashamed, and began to blush. "Yes I was doing that. I had hoped you would notice me and like me. I thought if anything happened to Uriah you might want me. But things have changed now."

"What do you mean, things have changed?"

"I know what a good man Uriah is and now I just want to be a good wife. He is supposed to retire as soon as he returns from Ammon. I want to retire with him."

"You need to know the king is not some puppet on string who will dance when you say dance and stop dancing when you say stop. You played the flute for me for years, now you must dance for me. Do you understand?"

"Yes, I do. Please call for one of your wives. Let me go home."

"Not a chance."

Bathsheba had dreamed for years of this situation and now that it was here, she wished it was not happening. Uriah was always faithful, and while he is in battle she is here with the king. While he had been fighting for the king she had secretly hoped he would die for the king. Now she just wanted him to live so they could have many years together. She felt remorse and shame. It became worse when before she left the king said to her," I will see you again tomorrow night. Come right after the sun sets if you want to see your husband alive again."

In the harem Michal said to Abigail, "Have you noticed that the king has not requested anyone for over two weeks?"

"The king has not been here, has he? I thought he was in Ammon."

"Where is Ammon?" asked Ahinoam.

"I think it is near Moab," answered Abital.

"I do not even know where Moab is." replied Ahinoam.

"I bet you do not even know where Jerusalem is." jested Haggith.

"Of course I do, we live in Jerusalem. Right?" replied Ahinoam.

Michal said, "Getting back to the king…"

"I would like to get back to the king," said Abital. All the women laughed and agreed with her.

"But why are not any of you getting back with the king? I know he is in the palace. Who has he been sleeping with if not you?" asked Michal.

"Maybe he is ill. I will take him some warm spiced wine tonight and tell you how it went." offered Abigail.

"It is your funeral." They all stated in unison, and then they all giggled.

That night Bathsheba came as she had every night for the past two weeks. Every night she begged the king to not treat her that way. Every night he refused. Abigail came quietly into the king's chambers. As she approached she thought she heard talking so she came close enough to see who it was then remained silent. She thought the voice of the woman was Bathsheba's but it could not be because she was Uriah's wife. After a few minutes she was certain it was Bathsheba. She left the king's chambers and took the wine back to the harem.

In the harem she drank the wine herself so she could get to sleep. The next morning when the others asked her what happened she said to them she had been afraid to go without being requested into the king's chambers: it would be best if they all stayed away. But Abigail thought Michal suspected something.

Finding a time when the others were not present, Michal pressed Abigail for what she had seen. When Abigail informed her the king was with Bathsheba, Michal's temper erupted first at Abigail because she did not believe her, then at the king when she realized Abigail was telling the truth. "I need to let Nathan know what is happening!" Michal said. "Maybe someone else will be anointed king. It serves him right for what he did to me."

"You are right. It serves him right. When you sow the wind, you reap a whirlwind."

CHAPTER 34

One night when Bathsheba came to the king she asked him," I am pregnant. How am I going to explain my pregnancy while my husband is in Ammon? You know what the law says. I am supposed to be stoned to death. How could you do this to me?"

"Do not worry. Do not say anything to anyone. I will take care of everything."

"How can you take care of it? You are the cause of it!" Bathsheba cried.

"Like this," smiled the king. He quickly wrote orders for Joab to send Uriah home at once. He called for a servant and ordered him to not stop until he delivered these orders. Then he said to Bathsheba, "When Uriah gets home be good to him. When the baby is born, tell him it is his, it came a little early."

Uriah came to the throne room in the palace and spoke to the king. "I hope you called me here about my retirement from the army. I would like to get busy being your ambassador to Anatolia again."

King David recognized his opening and said," Yes, I would like to give you larger salary and a bonus. I would start by sending you to Athens tomorrow for a vacation with your wife. Maybe you could stay there for a year at my expense. How does that sound, Uriah?"

"It sounds great!" Uriah agreed.

"I want you to go home and talk this over with your wife, Bathsheba, I believe, and then let me know in the morning what you have decided."

The next day at dinner time the king called for Uriah. "Well, Uriah, what does your wife think of your retirement plan?"

"I did not tell her yet."

"What? Why not?"

"You know the soldier's creed, king. I cannot go home to my wife while my men are sleeping in the grass laying siege on an enemy."

"Oh, yes, the creed, I almost forgot about the creed. Tell me about the creed again." The king poured Uriah a large cup of wine as they began talking. They talked military strategy, politics, and economics until Uriah was quite drunk. Uriah told the king that he had defeated Troy by going under the gate at night through the water supply. The king said that was a good plan and he would write out instructions for Joab to try that strategy. King David advised him that since Uriah had been with him they had more than doubled the territory King Saul controlled. The trade agreements Uriah made had tripled the revenue to the country. After many hours, the king sent him home.

The next morning the king called for Uriah. "Did you go home last night? I heard someone saw you sleeping on the ground in front of the palace." King David asked Uriah.

"Yes I slept on the ground. My men are sleeping on the ground and so did I."

"So you have not even been home these two days in Jerusalem?"

"No I have not. You know the creed."

"I see. If I gave you a choice of retiring today and going home to your wife, or going back to your men until the battle is won, and then retiring, what would you choose?"

"I cannot abandon my men in the middle of a battle. Let me retire when the fighting will be over."

"Very well, take these new orders to Joab and tell him I want to know when they are completed."

Michal disguised herself and snuck out of the palace to find Nathan the prophet near the temple. She said to him she had something important for him to know. Then she informed him about Abigail going to the king and discovering Bathsheba. Nathan looked very distressed and said he would talk to the king.

Joab read the new orders. They said," Place Uriah in the heat of the battle, where the fighting is the fiercest, then withdraw his support." Strange orders but not the first time Uriah went into the heat of the battle. Joab told Uriah to take his men and begin a frontal assault on the main gate of Medeba. He believed the forces there were getting worn out and they might be able to break through.

The next morning at sun-up Uriah aligned his men on the center of the main gate, Abishai aligned his men to Uriah's left while Joab held the rest of the men in their positions around the city. Abishai was ordered that when the fighting became fiercest to take all of his men and five hundred of Uriah's men, and begin a slow retreat.

After Uriah had begun to achieve a little headway, Abishai was to charge in with all his speed and help push through the gate. Abishai thought those were the strangest orders he ever heard.

Uriah, agreeing with Abishai, thought these were strange orders, with not much chance of working. Besides, this is not what he and the king had discussed a couple of days earlier. He thought he was going to attack the water supply, not the main gate. But he had been the point man on previous occasions and had been victorious. He began his assault by telling his archers to shower the area outside the gate with arrows when the Ammonites come out. Hold off any arrows until the gates open and men start coming out. Then he advanced with his two thousand men. As they approached within range of the Ammonite archers on the wall the arrows came down like hail. But Uriah had trained his men to put their shields over their heads and kneel down on one knee and wait for the arrows to stop. When they were close together, they acted as a tortoise shell and kept the arrows from doing any damage. Under this tortoise of shields hundreds of arrows fell but none hit anyone.

Hanun estimated there were about two thousand Israelite soldiers facing him. Furious that none of the archers were hitting anything but shields he decided to engage them in the open. He chose five thousand of his best warriors and lined them up at the gate. Outside the gate they were to form ranks with five hundred men in a line. He ordered them to advance swiftly, strike fiercely, and kill savagely.

As soon as the gate was opened and men were seen Uriah gave the order for the archers to fire. This time it hailed arrows from Israelite archers and these began finding their targets. Hundreds of men were killed just going through the gate. Uriah ordered javelins in place and as the first ranks of Ammonites reached the Israelite soldiers they were impaled. Then the soldiers drew their swords as hand to hand combat ensued. Men on both sides began dying.

Outnumbered, the Israelite army began a slow retrograde action. Abishai saw this as a good time to withdraw all of his army. Five of Uriah's centurions had been ordered that when Abishai falls back they are to join him in preparation for a counter attack. Three fourths of the Israelite army had withdrawn, leaving Uriah and five hundred men to fight against Hanun. Seeing the retreat as a chance for victory, Hanun sent another five thousand men into the battle. Abishai, realizing that Uriah could not withstand an army that large gave orders for his men to counter-attack and go help Uriah. Joab saw what was happening and gave the order to retreat to a designated fallback position. Abishai could not believe the order but he obeyed. He led his five hundred men into a retrograde action.

Uriah, bleeding from several wounds and his strength declining saw the fresh men being sent into battle by Hanun and thought to surrender. Most of his army had been killed. He wondered why he was not reinforced by Abishai and Eliam. But could fifteen hundred win against five thousand? He kept remembering the words, "When the enemy comes in like a flood, Yahweh would rise up a wall against him." The archers were gone. The javelins were gone. The swordsmen were disappearing. His team formed into a circular formation. The Ammonites were so thick most were not even engaged in the battle. Uriah asked Yahweh to send Abishai and Eliam to help. Before long, they and a few surviving men were surrounded. He slashed skulls, severed heads and arms, and smashed his dagger into one heart after another. The enemy was everywhere. Where was his wall?

He remembered his dream about the bees. Except he realized they were not bees, they were men. They came from everywhere. He used his sword in his left hand and his dagger in his right hand to fight them off. The more he killed the more they came. He was bleeding everywhere. Men were dying everywhere. Then he remembered his dream about the rock. It grew large and then exploded. The angel told him he was no longer protected by Yahweh because his work on earth was over. That's what happened to the wall! He had killed so many he had no place to stand. He stood on dead men to kill other men. His mind was racing as he realized Joab had abandoned him, but why?

He always feared being led someplace he did not have control over and then being abandoned.

Uriah had no time to fear now. He had been loyal to the end. He tried to use the sword to kill an attacker but realized he had no arm with which to use the sword. He jabbed his dagger into someone while someone behind him hit him on the top of his head. He fell on his knees. A sword entered his side. He cried out with all his strength, "I have been delivered to the ungodly by the ungodly!" An Ammonite archer shot an arrow from the top of the wall and struck Uriah in his heart. The next thing Uriah knew everything was black.

The messenger approached King David with trepidation. He knew that in the past if the messenger brought bad news, the king had him killed. "What news do you bring?" asked the king.

"In the battle with the Ammonites we lost over fifteen hundred men. Joab thought we could draw them out of the city walls, and then attack them before they could get back into the city. Instead of us driving them back, they killed our men. We killed two thousand of them," the messenger reported. To protect himself he blamed Joab then ended with good news.

"So we still have not defeated the Ammonites?" asked the king.

"No we have not. But the worst news, Uriah the Hittite was killed in the battle. But he killed over three hundred men before he fell," again the messenger ended with good news.

"Not Uriah? He risked his life to go with me into Saul's camp. He risked his life to bring me water from Bethlehem. Now he is dead trying to protect my honor."

"I'm sorry to bring you bad news, your majesty."

"No. You did good messenger. Return to Medeba. We suffered a strategic loss. Tell Joab to continue the siege. The Ammonites lost a lot of men. Perhaps they will surrender soon. Also, on your way, tell Uriah's widow to come to see me so I can tell her what happened to her husband. Help yourself to some of the fresh bread from the bakery."

Bathsheba came to the palace and approached the king, his advisor Ahithophel was also present," You sent for me, my king?"

"Yes, I did. In the battle with the Ammonites your husband fought like an anointed warrior. He killed several hundred men single handedly. But despite his valiant efforts, Uriah did not survive. He did not even have to go. I offered him a chance to retire without returning to battle. He said he could not retire while his men were still in a battle. He was a good man."

"No! No! What am I going to do now? "she asked as she broke into tears.

"If you like, you can live here at the palace until you finish mourning. We can plan for your future after that."

Bathsheba could not believe what was happening. For years she had thought her husband would die in battle and the king would make her his wife. But she did not want to be part of a conspiracy to make it happen. This is what she had always wanted, it was within her grasp. But she did not want it to happen this way. She knew she had to make a decision.

"Let me have a month to mourn alone, and then I will come and live with you in the palace," she said to him.

When she left Ahithophel advised him he was not under any obligation to take care of a widow of one of his officers, but if he did it would endear him to the people as a humanitarian as well as a military leader. It would please him also. News of Uriah's death spread quickly.

Nathan heard and he knew it was time to confront the king.

CHAPTER 35

Bathsheba deeply grieved over her husband. She thought about his smile and silly comments. Each new thought brought on another bout of deep violent sobbing. She felt like her heart was being ripped out. He always wanted her to sit and talk but she was always busy doing something important like making bread or cleaning the house. She wished she could talk with him now.

Why had she been so selfish? She did not deserve him but he never saw any wrong in her. He loved the kids. One time when their oldest son was jumping from one large rock to another along the river he slipped and fell in. Uriah jumped in to save him even though the water was less than two cubits deep. The thought made her laugh. The laugh made her cry. The cry made her hurt so badly she took deep gulps of air trying to ease the pain, stop the tears, and choke down the cries. Sometimes she could go for a minute or two, then see his face in her memory, and it would start all over again.

She thought of the time they walked through their garden in the cool evening. He picked a white lily and put it in her hair. Then he said to her, "No flower could ever be as lovely as you." She thought of how she made him get circumcised before they were married. She started laughing, crying, and hurting all over again. She remembered when they were alone he called her Honey Cakes. Oh it hurts! Why does it hurt so much?

Over and over she said out loud," I love you Uriah the Hittite!" She cried until she fell asleep but would wake up crying again. "I am sorry for the way I treated you. You were so good to me, and I was so bad to you. My father was right, you were a good man! It was I who did not deserve you."

One of the grandchildren asked her where he had gone and before she could answer another bout of crying began. Why did he have to die just when she wanted him to live? Why did he have to die in his last battle? Why did he even go into battle? Why?

She especially missed him at night. She missed how he spoke to her, held her, caressed her, and cuddled her. She missed his breathing beside her, the smell of his presence, and his prayers for her. Night went on forever without him. Sleep was evasive without him. Her bed was cold without him. Life had no meaning without him.

The king welcomed his unexpected guest, "Nathan, you must have good news from Yahweh to be coming to see me."

"Yes I do have news for you but first let me tell you a couple of stories. May I?"

"Of course, go ahead."

"Well the first story is about two men. Both men received a special anointing from Yahweh for special purposes. They accepted the anointing as a special blessing.

The first man knew he needed the anointing and was eager to get under God's graces. He knew he was very undeserving of the anointing but accepted it as God's will. He changed his life style from worshipping other gods to worshipping the one and only true God. God blessed him with happiness, prosperity, and respect. The second man knew he was ready for the anointing. He knew it was for him because had enough faith to receive it. In his case, the anointing made his head bigger than his heart. He saw God in an incorrect light, but after receiving the anointing, he only believed stronger in his incorrect thinking. He too received blessing of prosperity, happiness and respect. Both men had been blessed. Both men accepted their blessing. Neither man thought they deserved the blessing. The first man loved God more as a result of the blessing, and changed his entire life to live for God. The second man refused to change his life, thinking that he was already correct and no change was necessary."

"That is an interesting story, Nathan. Do I know either of these men?"

"Actually you know them both. But before I tell you who they are let me tell you another story of two men."

"Okay, then you will tell me what message God has for me."

"There were two men in the city, the first man was poor, and the second man was rich. The rich man had many flocks and herds but the poor man had nothing except a ewe lamb which he brought up and nourished. It drank from his cup, ate his food, and rested in his bosom. A traveler came to the rich man but he did not want to spare any of the flocks from his large herds to feed the traveler so he took the poor man's ewe lamb and dressed it to feed to the traveler."

"As the Lord lives the man that did this shall surely die, and restore the lamb fourfold," the king shouted in great anger.

"King David, in both stories Uriah the Hittite is the first man and you are the second man. Yahweh blessed both of you. Uriah changed his entire life to serve Yahweh, to serve you, and to love his wife. You saw Yahweh as a god of war and never changed your opinion. You took what you wanted from whom you wanted. You took Uriah's wife, made her pregnant, and had him killed by your own enemies."

"How did you know she was pregnant?"

"King David, what is done in the king's bedroom is shouted from the housetops. Everyone knows! It is the talk in the market."

"What have I done?" the king asked sinking into a chair, his sin fully realized, a sense of shame coming over him, like the sinner he knew he was.

"This is the message of the Lord I have come to tell you. I will rise up evil against you from out of your household. I will take your wives before your eyes and give them to your sons and neighbors. These things will be done in public because what you did you did in secret."

David fell down on his knees and lamented, "I have sinned against the Lord. He sent me good men, many wives, prosperity, and gave me a kingdom. I used all of them to please myself. You are right Nathan. I am those men in your stories."

"Because you have confessed your sin, you will not die. However, the child that will be born to Bathsheba will die."

David cried to Yahweh," Have mercy on me Yahweh. Blot out my sins. Wash me clean from my iniquity. I have done evil in your sight. Purge me, hide my sins from you. Now I know you are more than just a god of war. Create in me a clean, pure, and new heart. Renew a right spirit in me. Restore to me the joy of your salvation."

"You have brought peace to your nation, but evil into your home. God has forgiven you, but you must face the consequences of your actions," said Nathan.

David said, "Now I know that Yahweh is not a god of war but a God of love, mercy, and grace. Uriah was right all the time."

David sent for Bathsheba. When she arrived he told her everything that Nathan had said to him. "You will lose this baby. The fault is not yours, but mine. I lusted after you from the first time I saw you, I just wanted to find a good time and place. Now I know there is no good time or place for sin. I asked Yahweh to forgive me, will you forgive me?"

"No, the fault is not yours. As a little girl I always wanted to be a queen, the wife of a king. I wanted you to notice me. I only married Uriah as a way to get to know you. I chased after you until you found me. I need your forgiveness for causing you to sin. I forgive you if you forgive me."

"I forgive you too, but we must also confess to Yahweh. Let us start over with new hearts and live for Yahweh, just as Uriah always wanted. I want you for my wife. We can have more children. I will place you as first among my wives, I guess that makes you a queen. How do you feel about that?"

"I was so prideful. I did not want to end up like my sisters and be somebody that nobody remembers. Now I will be remembered for the evil I have done. I would be happy to live the rest of my life as my husband did, serving the Lord with all my mind, heart, and soul."

They joined hands, knelt down on their knees, and prayed together as tears watered their cheeks and fell to the ground in little pools. "Hear our prayer oh God. From the depth of our souls and out of our sorrow for sin we cry to you, to seek your face, to receive your grace. We have done evil in your sight. Forgive us, have mercy on us, and lead us in your ways for the rest of our days."

King David went to Medeba to lead the siege. He ordered Joab to form a division of one thousand men and report to him as soon as possible. He advised Joab, "Make a tortoise of shields in the same manner as Uriah ordered his men to use them and then approach the gate to the city. The walls and the gate are made of wood. Equip ten men with jars of pitch and ten men with torches. The men with the pitch and torches would be protected by the tortoise of shields. When they reach the gate they are to set it on fire.

Joab prepared the rest of the army for assault through the gate once it was burned. In case the Ammonites tried to attack before the division could reach the gate, archers were ready to rain fire and brimstone down on the attackers. Then King David did something he had never done. He rallied all the men and said to them they had lost a great leader. He led as men began to chant "Uriah, Uriah, Uriah!" in a rhythmic cadence and the men responded with fire in their eyes as they shouted as loud as they could "Uriah, Uriah, Uriah!" With each step they took they shouted. "Uriah."

Joab's men reached the gate without injuries, and set the wood on fire while archers on the walls fired arrows at them in vain because all the arrows bounced off the shields.

Before the gates were even fully consumed the soldiers broke their way into the city and with every blow of sword or dagger, or every shot with a bow the men shouted," Uriah, Uriah! Remember Uriah the Hittite!"

Within hours King David was standing in front of King Hanun. "You killed my generals, my ambassadors, and my friends. You insulted Israel by desecrating my messengers. For that I kill you." Then he plunged his sword into him so hard that it came out his back.

King David ordered his men to kill everyone. Take no prisoners. Joab reminded him that most of the Ammonites were descendents of Reuben and had intermarried over the years. By killing all the Ammonites, they could be killing Reubenites too. David ordered, "Kill them all. The land across the Jordan River was promised to us, if he settled here that was a bad decision." From Medeba they went to Rabath-ammon and destroyed that town as a warning to the rest of the Ammonites. David set up four military garrisons throughout Ammon and demanded tribute.

David attacked the Syrians who helped the Ammonites and killed five thousand men. He set up two more garrisons in Syria and demanded tribute from everyone living there. Through his last campaign at every battle his men chanted "Uriah" in rhythmic cadence. King David noted "Uriah would have loved to see this day. We have defeated every enemy in every direction, the borders are secure, and the people are safe. We have control of all the land Yahweh promised to Moses."

CHAPTER 36

When Uriah could see again he was not on the battle field at Medeba. Instead of the stench of blood and rotting flesh he smelled the aroma of a spring bouquet. All the colors were pastels and the air was perfumed with music praising Yahweh. He wondered if he was dreaming. He looked and saw his arm and thought the last time he was conscious of it, it was missing. Everything was so peaceful he did not move for several minutes.

"God has given you favor," came a voice from behind him. He turned and saw an angel smiling at him. "Yahweh has called you home to receive your reward."

"Reward?"

"Yes reward. You were a good and faithful servant, now you get to enter the joy of the Lord," replied the angel.

Before he could take another step he was surrounded by angels and people he had known. They were all happy. So much love filled the air, which must be what is causing the aroma of spring flowers. They were all welcoming him and leading him somewhere. As he followed them he entered what looked like a temple but it was the most beautiful temple he had ever seen. It was covered with precious metals and stones and was so brilliant no candles were needed. As he entered the temple he could not prevent himself from kneeling down to the floor in praise and worship of Yahweh. He was so ecstatic he did not want to get up again.

"You have passed over from time into eternity. You gave up your mortal life for an immortal life." Uriah could hear a voice speaking to him but could only see the brilliance of the temple. He remained kneeling and listened to the voice. "One life affects many lives but you were chosen to affect many nations. You were not of my chosen people, yet I chose you. You were faithful to me, to your wife, and to your king. Despite their evil intensions towards you, you never stopped praying for them and for their children. I tell you that a fervent prayer such as yours, from a righteous man, such as you, produces great benefits as you will see."

An angel approached him and while he was still kneeling placed the crown of life on his head and stated," Yahweh could intercede in the affairs of men and make everyone serve him like little mindless, heartless creatures, like snakes. But his nature is love and he wants men to serve him because they love him. He would intervene by using his servants to persuade other men to follow him. Today was a day to reward one man who had been faithful. You have passed the tests of the lust of the flesh, the pride of life, and the lust of the eyes. You have left friends and home and family to serve him. You have left your heritage, your culture, and your people to serve a God you knew through his messengers, the prophets and scribes."

Another angel said, "Because you were faithful to Yahweh throughout your life you have received this crown."

"But, I do not know what I did. How was I faithful? What was my mission?" Uriah asked.

The voice from the one he could not see started speaking again "Throughout your life you struggled with someone else always seeming to control your life. You argued about the existence of gods. You struggled with knowing your purpose in life. Your mission was to help King David rid his land of intruders, free Jerusalem and usher in an era of peace where my word could be spread throughout the land. You did all those things. You did that and more. When you felt out of control, God was in control. When you did not believe in God, He still believed in you. Now you have found Him."

"I am still not sure what I did." replied Uriah.

The angel replied," Every day you prayed for your wife, for your king, and for the Israelite people, even though you are not Israelite. Remember a fervent prayer of a righteous man accomplishes great things."

Another angel continued," You were faithful to your men, your king, your wife, and to Yahweh until your death. Because of your prayers, this is what will happen. David will marry Bathsheba and they will have four sons, named Shimea, Shobah, Solomon, and Nathan. Solomon will become the next king and will be the wisest man who ever lived. He will have children who will have children until from his family will be born a virgin named Mary. Nathan will have children who will have children until they give birth to a righteous man named Joseph."

"But what does that all mean?" asked Uriah.

"Let me teach you what you were not prepared to learn before. Some things I am withholding from my people while I test their faith. One secret is that I am sending a Messiah to my people, the Israelites."

"Yes, we are all waiting for the Messiah," replied Uriah.

"The Messiah will be borne by a woman who will be overshadowed by the Holy Spirit and she will give birth to a son. That woman is Mary. She will marry Joseph. They will raise him up in my law, but he will be my own son."

The first angel asked," Remember the man and woman from Galilee that you fed on Passover? Their fishing business will become successful and they will pass it on to children who pass it on to children until they give birth to brothers named Peter and Andrew. They will become two of the Messiah's disciples and tell the world about him. You never know who you are helping when you help someone."

"When the Messiah is born he will not be accepted by his people. So sheep from other pastures like you Uriah will be able to receive my salvation. Men will go out to tell others about him. The Antioch – Tarsus – Thyatira – Troy caravan route you established will become a major road men will use to spread the news about the Messiah. Letters will be written to towns in those areas that will give instructions to my people for thousands of years. Istanbul will become a major city in my kingdom. All this would not have been possible except for the trade routes and treaties you established."

"I did not realize I did so much." replied Uriah.

"This is what you did: because of your righteous prayers Bathsheba will be the ancestor of both the mother and the father on earth of the Messiah. Jerusalem is safe and secure in the hands of my people and will always be known as The City of David. Anatolia is ready to become the key route in spreading my good news to other sheep in other pastures. All because you were obedient, prayed, and lived a righteous life."

"I did the best I could to please you."

"You are counted as righteous because of your faith and obedience, not because of your goodness. That is the point. The best that anyone can be is not good enough."

"Beyond all question the mystery of godliness is great!" remarked Uriah.

"Yes, it is great, but it is also easy. Men make it harder than it really is."

"How come you are showing me all this?" asked Uriah.

"I am showing you this because in heaven God hears every prayer. You simply do not when or how it will be answered."

Uriah stood and raised his hands and joined the angels in a song of praise.

"There is one more thing you need to know" explained a voice very familiar to Uriah. When he turned to see where the voice came from, he saw Ravia smiling at him. "Bathsheba will be made the Queen Mother of Israel, just as Ahithophel said, while Solomon is king, until her death."

"What will happen to Annitis?" he asked.

"Tokat and Annitis will move to Derbe where they will have children who will have children. One of those descendents will be a man named Timothy, who will become a great messenger for the Messiah," someone said.

Uriah thought he recognized that voice but he could not believe it. He turned to the voice and said, "Dad!"

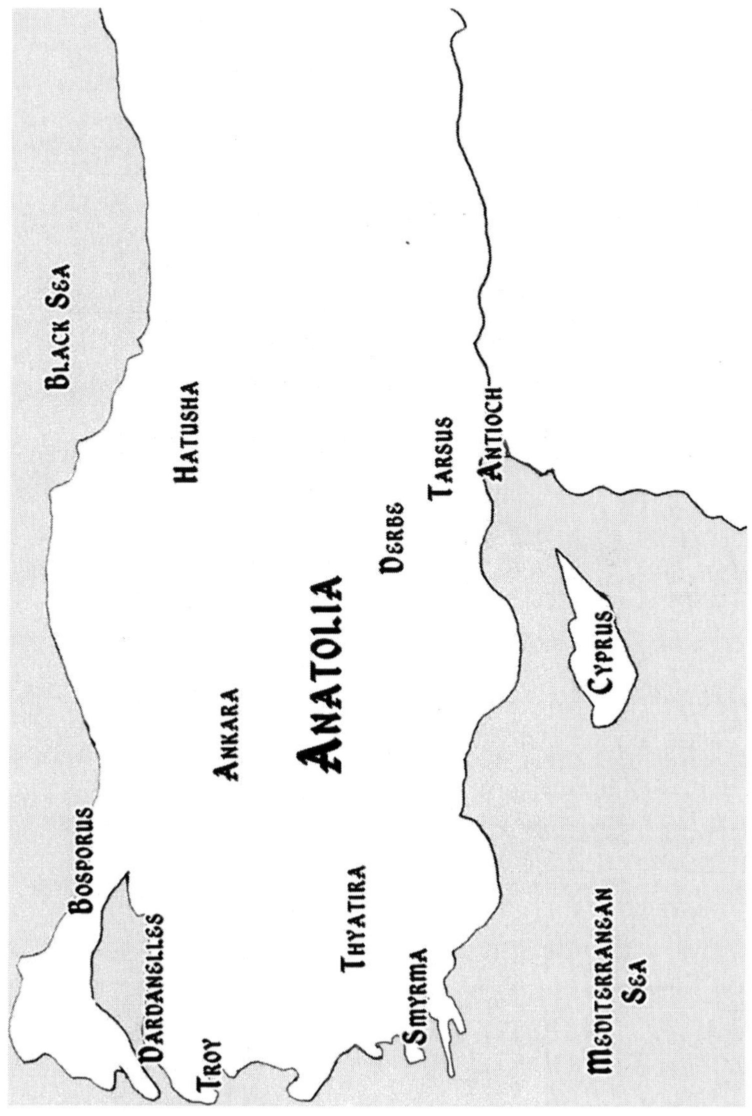
Black Sea
Hatusha
Ankara
Anatolia
Bosporus
Dardanelles
Troy
Thyatira
Smyrma
Derbe
Tarsus
Antioch
Cyprus
Mediterranean
Sea

Tyre
Tarsus
Damascus
Jezreel
ISRAEL
Gibeah
Ammon
Jerusalem
Medeba
Dead Sea
Reuben
Hebron
Moab
Gaza
En Gedi
Kir-hareseth
Ziklag
Edom
Bozrah

GLOSSARY

Hittite -- A person who lives in or comes from the town of Hatusha

Achaeans -- Sea People from the mainland of Greece who settled in Anatolia

Anatolia -- What is referred to today as Turkey